“T[illegible] killer two said.

“That’s because we always work clean and don’t run our mouth. We drop in a city, take care of our business, then disappear,” killer one said.

“This is the first time I was paid all the money up front. We could just bail with the cash.”

“Just like a no good nigga,” killer one said. “Always trying to pull a fast one. Do you know who we’re fucking with? If I pulled some shit like that, we’d be dead before the month was out. This nigga has graveyards across the nation.”

They turned onto a tree-lined, residential street in a middle class neighborhood.

“We’re here,” killer one said. “I’ma go make the block one time, to make sure everything is cool.”

“You see those old folks walking?” killer two asked.

“Yeah, I see them. That’s good. Hopefully they can give the police a description of our car.”

“Pull over. We’ll walk to the house from here,” killer two said.

“I’m gonna position myself behind those bushes on the side of the garage,” killer one said. “After you make the alarm go off on that pretty Mercedes, position yourself on the other side of the house.”

Killer two acknowledged the instructions without speaking. Seconds later the car alarm was blaring. A minute or so after that, a sleepy Tracy McDonald came out of the front door with a pistol in his hand, looking around.

“Bitch-ass cats, jumping on a nigga’s shit,” he said to himself. His pistol was relaxed at his side.

“Nah, homey. It’s not a cat,” said killer one as he stepped up behind Tracy.

“What the fuck?” Tracy was caught off guard. He tried to swing the pistol up, but killer one grabbed his wrist like a vice.

“We’re more like thieves in the night,” killer two said.

“Drop the pistol, before I smoke you,” killer one said calmly.

• • • • • •

DOWN FOR THE CITY

DOWN FOR THE CITY

DEREK C. WATSON SR.

KEITHWALKERBOOKS, INC
This is a UMS production

KEITHWALKERBOOKS

Publishing Company
KeithWalkerBooks, Inc.
P.O. Box 331585
Fort Worth, TX 76163

For information write
KeithWalkerBooks, Inc.
P.O. Box 331585
Fort Worth, TX 76163

ISBN-13 DIGIT: 978-0-9967505-2-3
ISBN-10 DIGIT: 0996750525
Library of Congress Control Number: 2016943501
Manufactured in the United States of America

Second Edition

Visit us at www.keithwalkerbooks.com

This book is dedicated to Derek C. Watson Jr.
I love you, son.

ACKNOWLEDGMENTS

First and foremost, I would like to thank my Lord and Savior Jesus Christ. Without His presence, none of this would have been possible. I would like to thank my little brother Harold Watson Jr. You've been solid throughout my incarceration. I would like to thank my son, Derek C. Watson Jr. for just staying out the way. I'd like to thank my son's mother, Damitra Gage. You did a good job raising our son, virtually on your own. I would like to thank Keith Thomas Walker. It's all Love and Respect for the KWB family. Y'all gave me a lifeline. I would also like to thank Ingrid Watson, Alan Watson and my Aunt Mary Swist. I love y'all. I love you, Mama, Mrs. Easter Mae Watson. You've always been the glue that holds our family together. Lastly, I want to give a shout out to Austin, Texas. I definitely got mad love for my city!

PROLOGUE

Carl Fredrick was a senior at L.B.J. High School, located in Austin, TX. At eighteen he had everything going his way. He was a two-sport star; quarterback of their highly touted football team and shooting guard of their nationally ranked basketball team. His most coveted accolade was when he was named an Academic All-American. He was on every college's radar. He had been receiving scholarship offers from major universities (and a few not-so-major ones) since he was a junior.

It would be easy for a kid from the inner-city like Carl to get big-headed. But his camp kept him well-grounded. That camp consisted of his mother, father and his algebra teacher Ms. Ransom. They reminded him constantly how easy it would be for him to lose everything that he worked so hard for. All it took was one bad decision. His mother Jo Ann called it humble pie. The inner-city was full of negativity in 1998. The crack game was at its height, and so was gang-banging. Jo Ann felt the only way to handle her son was with bluntness.

For a young man Carl's age, he was very charismatic. He could cut on the charm in a heartbeat and turn any situation in his favor. He inherited his good looks from his father. He stood six foot, four inches tall and weighed 215 pounds. His muscles were chiseled. He had a silky smooth, coal black complexion that was complimented with a Colgate smile that melted young women's hearts. He had piercing, dark brown eyes that mirrored those of his mother. He sported a tapered fade with deep waves and made sure to keep his hair cut once a week. To top it off, Carl always stayed dapper. Dress code to the floor.

He was sitting in his third period algebra class when an office aid walked in and whispered something to Ms. Ransom. She called Carl to her desk to let him know that he'd been summoned to the principal's office. He couldn't remember being late to any of his classes, and he rarely got in any trouble. The moment he stepped into the principal's office, he knew something was terribly wrong, and it didn't have anything to do with school. His mother was there being consoled by the principal and a school counselor. Carl rushed to his mother's side and wrapped her in a tight embrace. Jo Ann sobbed even harder and was having trouble breathing.

"What happened?" a worried Carl asked the principal. He had never seen his mom in this state of hysteria.

"Your father was killed in a car wreck this morning," the principal said somberly.

Tears trickled down Carl's face as he kissed the top of his mother's head, trying to comfort her. "It's gonna be alright," he whispered. He idolized his father, and he knew his mother did too.

••••••

The days leading up to the funeral were hectic. Arrangements had to be made. Family and friends were constantly stopping by to offer their condolences and bring dinner dishes. For the most part, Jo Ann was holding up well, and her son was glad to see that.

When all of their guests left one evening, Carl and his mom sat together, thankful for the tranquility. Jo Ann wanted to have a little heart-to-heart with her son, and she thought that was a good time. She went to the kitchen and poured herself a glass of red wine. She returned and sat on the couch across from him. She tucked her feet under her bottom and sipped on her wine as she watched him for a few moments. She loved how he was handling the death of his father. She knew he was being strong for her.

"It's just you and me now, baby," Jo Ann said, speaking softly. "We're gonna have to scale back for a minute on our spending. I know your father had you spoiled rotten, but he's gone, and our cash flow will be slow until I can find a job."

"I understand." Carl's expression was deadpan. "It seems like the only thing everyone's talking about is the fact that you and dad didn't have insurance. On the cool, it seems like some of them are happy about our hardship," he revealed.

"I don't give a damn what they say or think," Jo Ann said as she sat her drink on the table. "My only concern is you and me. Nothing else." She shook her head, thinking about her husband. "Your father always lived for the day. He thought he was invincible." Tears began to stream down her face. "He paid this house off three years ago, and that's a plus. We don't have to worry about a roof over our heads. Do you know his friend Bennie Mays?"

"You know I know Bennie."

"He told the funeral home to send him the bill for the burial, and he gave me a little money to hold us over."

"That's nice and all, but where do we go from here? Dad only left us $7,500 to go with whatever Bennie gave you."

"You knew about your dad's stash spot?" asked a surprised Jo Ann.

"I'm the one who always counted his money and hid it for him," Carl said, smiling at his mother. "So what's the plan?"

"I'm still sorting things out. After we bury your father, I'll start looking for a job."

"Job? Get outta here," Carl said, feigning shock. "*Job* and *Jo Ann* don't sound right in the same sentence," he laughed.

Jo Ann shot off the couch and hit her son in the face with a throw pillow. "That money is not going to last forever, and if I don't get a job, who's gonna put food on the table?"

She gave him a hard look before walking out of the room.

••••••

Carl had lived a pretty comfortable life up until the death of his father. One thing his dad, Marvin, never did was shelter his son from reality. Marvin wanted Carl to know how the real world worked. He wanted him to be able to handle himself, if he was ever put in an uncomfortable situation. His son would never be a lame.

A million things had been going through Carl's mind after his father's death. The main thing he worried about was the welfare of his mother. He knew she meant well by trying to get a job, but he didn't know of any skills she possessed. His Fredrick pride wouldn't allow her to work a menial job. His dad treated her like a queen, and Carl felt it was his duty to continue that treatment. Desperate times called for desperate measures, and he made up his mind to try his hand at the very accessible drug trade. It's not like he would be a novice. He had friends at school who sold drugs, and damn near everyone on his father's side of the family was in the game one way or another.

Carl ran the idea by his best friend Paul Atkins, to see what he thought about it. He was game. Carl asked him to talk to his cousin Red Andre, who was a major hustler in the city. He wanted to know if Andre could help them out by showing them the ropes. Carl didn't want to ask any of his family members, because he knew they would tell his mom. Paul spoke to his cousin about Carl's situation, and Andre agreed to help.

At the time, Red Andre was stacking some serious bread. He had crack houses scattered all over east and northeast Austin. He put Carl and Paul in one of the houses and gave Carl a good quantity deal for his money.

As the saying goes, the rest was history.

• • • • • •

A month after Marvin's death, Jo Ann stayed true to her word and was diligently looking for employment. She had a few interviews lined-up, so she needed to buy a couple of new outfits and get her hair and nails done. But when she went to her husband's stash spot, the money was gone. Only two people knew where the money was, so Jo Ann was hotter than fish grease.

When Carl walked through the door later that evening, Jo Ann got straight to the point.

"Where's that money? And I don't have no time for games!" she said, with her hands perched on her hips, giving him some serious neck action.

"I got it," Carl said. His response was too nonchalant for his mother's taste.

"*You got it*?!" she screamed, working that neck some more. "That money ain't for you to be walking around here spending it as you damn-well please! That money is strictly for bills and to hold us over until I get one of these jobs that I got lined up. So take your ass in your room and get that money!"

Carl left and returned with a bag he kept the money in. He gave it to his mom. When Jo Ann looked inside and saw all of the bills, she frantically asked him, "What is this?"

"Fifteen thousand."

That was twice as much as her husband left them. She dropped the bag and started fighting her son. She got in a couple of licks to his face before he grabbed her wrist.

"Let me find out you trying to sell dope," she threatened. "I'ma kill yo black ass!" Jo Ann screamed, trying to catch her breath.

"Get what you need out the bag, and put the rest in the bank."

Jo Ann was terrified at what she saw in her son's eyes. In a month's time, Carl went from being her only child, her lil' man, and turned into someone she didn't recognize.

"You can't do this to me, baby," she pleaded. "You'll be off to college in a couple of months. You don't have to risk everything you worked so hard for. I can hold us down, baby."

"What about when I go off to college?" Carl shouted. "I'm supposed to leave you here to fend for yourself? You know I can't do that."

"Don't act like you're doing this for me! You're doing it for your own selfish reasons! We're in a bind, but it ain't nothing a little hard work can't fix! What about college? It will be over my dead body, before I let you mess off that education," Jo Ann said, inching closer to her son. She wanted to get one more lick in and try to knock some sense into him.

"I'm going to H.T."

"Huston-Tillitson?" Jo Ann knew that was an H.B.C, located in Austin.

"Yeah," Carl said. "H.T."

Jo Ann wore a defeated look as she walked into the den and slumped down on the couch. Carl was stubborn, just like his father. Once their minds were made up, you couldn't tell them shit! Jo Ann was going to try one more tactic, in a last ditch effort to save her son.

"I see your mind's already made up," she said. "So is mine. Before I let you throw your life away on the streets, I'll call the law on your black ass! If you think I'm playing, try me!" she said, with her poker face on.

Carl just shook his head and walked out of the house, leaving her sitting on the couch with a broken heart.

CHAPTER ONE

Fifteen years later

Carl and his best friend Paul cruised in an Audi A8, en route to their club. They were hosting a concert later that night. Carl rapped to the lyrics of C-Murder's "Down for my Niggas" as he drove. The music blasted from the surround-sound stereo system. Paul reached over and turned the volume down. He had something to run by his partner before they made it to the club. Once they got there, things would get hectic while trying to prepare for the concert.

"Why is you fucking with this radio?" Carl said, staring across the seat at his best friend. "Nigga that's C-Murder! I'm trying to get in my zone, before we get to the club."

"I need to run something by you," Paul said seriously.

"What's up?"

"We've been knowing each other damn-near all our lives, and we've come a long way in this game..."

"I'm trying to get in my zone, and here you come with this soap opera-ass shit," snapped Carl.

"This ain't no soap opera shit," Paul snapped back. "I'm trying to talk to you about our livelihood and about our families who count on us for everything. If something happens to us, have you ever stopped to think what would happen to them?"

"You don't think that shit weighs on my mind, nigga?"

"Fuck weighing it on your mind. We need to start planning the end, nigga, before these white folks plan it for us. Niggas is out in these streets snitching left and right. I'm not taking another fall."

"Nigga, you act like you took that fall by yourself."

"I didn't see you up in no motherfucking penitentiary," Paul said.

"Your wife got your half of the profits from the club and the restaurant," Carl reminded him. "And I maintained all of your properties. We don't even have to talk about how you lived on the inside."

"All that shit was beautiful, and don't think I didn't appreciate it. But at the end of the day, I was cooped up in that funky-ass five-by-nine, and everybody else was out here doing their thing. I'm not going back. Simple as that."

Paul reached over and turned the music back up.

When they reached the club and got out of the car, Carl said, "I respect the way you came at me. You're right; the game is souring more and more every day. We'll talk about it tomorrow."

He patted his friend on the back as they headed for the club's private entrance.

●●●●●●

Federal Briefing
NW Business Complex, Austin TX

"Hello. How is everyone doing this morning?" asked Deputy Director Alexander.

"Fine," the agents answered in unison.

"My name is Lawrence Alexander, and I'm the lead investigator that will be overseeing this probe. I do apologize for having everyone out so early. And I also want to apologize to those of you who were pulled from other assignments. The reason some of you are here now is because you worked on the Carl Fredrick and Paul Atkins case before, and I need some agents who are familiar with the targets. Kind of makes things go smoother.

"Those of you who came in from other assignments were highly recommended by your supervisors. Recently there were new developments that made the bureau want to re-open this probe. For a lot of you, it will be your first time hearing about the two men at the center of this investigation. Hopefully you'll take detailed notes. There will be a series of briefings over the next couple of weeks, and it's vital to the operation that none of the information gets misconstrued. I want precision. As for today, I just want everyone to get familiar with the subjects. When I'm through, I'll field your questions.

"Now, this is a very complex investigation. Mr. Fredrick is far from your average drug dealer. His is a very intelligent man with two bachelor's degrees; one in business and the other in finance. He's thirty-three years old, and he's building an empire through illegal activities. If we don't collar him on this probe, we may never get him. He'll be *untouchable*," he said with emphasis. "We've tried phone taps, visual surveillance, electronic surveillance and everything else. You have a question, agent...?"

"Agent Collins, in from the southern district."

"You're one of the agents in from Houston, huh?"

"Yes, sir," said the smiling officer. "Have you tried to infiltrate his inner circle?"

"From our surveillance and our informant, there is no inner circle. Just him and his best friend, Paul Atkins."

"Impossible. You can't distribute large amounts of coke without a clique. And if this Fredrick guy is as smart as you say he is, he's not doing the footwork himself."

"I guess you didn't hear me when I told everyone that this would be a very complex operation," Alexander bristled. It was obvious he didn't like Agent Collins' cockiness. "So if you don't mind, I'd like to finish this briefing and then answer all the questions at the end."

"Yes, sir."

Alexander took a sip of water before he resumed the briefing. "We have a couple of upper echelon pushers that got arrested. In exchange for leniency, they've offered valuable information. They've informed us that the cartels have flooded this region with tons of cocaine. One of the guys we busted brought up Carl Fredrick's name.

"Now, let me backtrack for a second here. One of the complexities of this case is the wealth of Fredrick and his partner. They own an upscale restaurant downtown and a club. They also own a plethora of residential properties throughout the city. For that sole reason, we can't go after them on tax evasion, like we do with most traffickers. They keep their books squeaky clean and aligned with their businesses.

"After my assistant hands out everyone's assignments and a listing of Atkins' and Fredrick's businesses, this briefing will conclude. At that time, I'll field any questions you may have."

One of the agents spoke up. "My name is Charles Hamilton. If this guy is so air-tight, how do we plan to build a case?"

"We have a team of strategists working on a plan as we speak," Alexander said. "The only information I can offer at this time is that we'll have a light detail watching him; a couple of agents at his club and restaurant. Public places. We don't want anyone to go near his home in Manor. He had it built in an isolated region, and he'd spot us coming a mile away."

Another agent had something to say. "My name is Asha Richards. What did we know about Fredrick before your informant threw his name out there?"

"I know everything about him. This is the second time he's been the focus of a federal investigation," Alexander explained.

Agent Richards smiled at her supervisor. "What I'm getting at is, are we on a witch hunt here? Someone who just got busted has every reason to throw someone else under the bus."

"Little lady–"

"Agent Richards, sir," she said, cutting him off.

"Agent Richards, you better have some good boots, because this investigation is going to get knee deep full of shit, and Fredrick is going to be right in the middle of it," he said, admiring the young lady who stood her ground.

Deputy Alexander looked around the room and saw that there were no more questions. "This briefing is over," he announced. "When the strategists lay out their plan for us, you will all be called back in. Until then, you're free to go."

After the agents filed out, Calvin Scottsdale, Alexander's longtime assistant, said, "Lawrence, could I have a word with you?"

"What is it? I'm busy this morning, and you should be also." Alexander didn't break a stride on the way to his office.

"Do you think we'll be able to secure an indictment on Fredrick or Atkins?" his assistant asked.

Deputy Alexander stopped in his tracks and spun on him. "How in the hell would I know at this juncture, Scottsdale?"

Alexander continued to his office and spoke to his secretary. “Gloria, get in touch with the strategists, and let them know that I’d like to meet with them this morning. I need to give them some insight on a few things.”

“Yes, sir. I’ll get right on it.”

CHAPTER TWO

"What would you two gentlemen be having this afternoon?" asked the waitress and proprietor of the restaurant.

"We've been coming to your restaurant for years now, Ms. Sally, and we always order the same thing. You mean to tell me you don't know what that is?" asked a cheesing Carl Fredrick.

"Let me guess," Sally said putting a finger to her chin. "A pork chop plate for you Carl, and a grilled catfish plate, cooked in lemon sauce, for you, Paul." Sally smiled back at her two favorite customers.

"You're on your stick," Paul replied. He picked up his phone vibrating on the table. "What's up?"

"What it do, big homey? What you got planned for the day?" asked one of Paul and Carl's most loyal soldiers.

"Chillin'. Me and Carl up at Sally's getting our eat on."

"Order me a shrimp basket. I'll be there in five minutes."

"That's a bet," Paul said and ended the call.

"Who was that?" Carl asked.

"Lil Chris."

"I haven't seen that nigga in weeks."

"He'll be up here in a few. That concert was off the chain last night."

"Yes indeed. 2 Chainz had the women up in there poppin' that ass. And them niggas was up in there poppin' bottles," said a smiling Carl. "How much did we bring in?"

"I deposited thirty-two thousand at the bank. That's after we paid the staff and extra security forty-six hundred."

"That's lovely. What about the club?"

"About ten thousand for the week. I took some of that money and paid some of our bills."

"Things are lining up for us, Paul. I've been thinking about what you brought to my attention last night. You were on point. It's time to go all the way legit."

"Here's your order, boys," Sally said, bringing their meal. "Can I get y'all anything else?"

"I need to order a shrimp basket for Lil Chris," Paul told her.

"Okay. Is that it?"

"Yes, ma'am."

"I'll bring your check in a bit. Enjoy."

"Back to what we were talking about," Carl said. "I'm gonna talk with our connect in the next few days. I'ma try to swing something in the area of ninety-five hundred a brick."

Paul whistled.

"If I can do that," Carl continued, "or anywhere close to it, we're gonna purchase twenty bricks a week for the next six months, then do a one-eighty on that hustle. You down with that?" he asked, looking his partner squarely in the eyes.

"I'm game," Paul said, holding his friend's gaze.

"We're gonna cut back on a lot of the transactions and distribute the twenty bricks at one time. When everyone is finished, we'll collect our bread. I'm gonna let you coordinate the drop-offs and the pick-ups. We'll get the whole family together, so everybody will be on the same page."

"That's a bet. Let's wrap it up. Here comes Lil Chris," Paul said, nodding towards the door.

"What's up with my niggas?" Lil Chris asked as he strolled into the restaurant. The young brother stayed swagged up. He had on the whole Jordan hookup, with enough platinum and diamonds to make Baby from Cash Money proud.

Paul could tell the young hustler had been on his grind. His braids were fuzzy, and he had stubble on his face. Lil Chris usually stayed freshly shaved.

"We're chillin," Carl said. "What's up with you? Haven't seen you in a while." He stood to embrace his friend.

"Working harder than a motherfucker," Lil Chris replied.

"Ain't nothing wrong with a little hard work," Paul stated.

"Here's your shrimp basket," Sally said as she approached the table and placed a tray in front of Chris. When she walked away, he stared at her ass.

"I wouldn't mind getting some of that pussy! Sally is finer than a lot of these young bitches running around here. And I know that pussy is ten times better!"

Paul and Carl laughed at that.

"Check this out," Lil Chris said. "Paul said you didn't have shit planned. Y'all need to head out to Lake Travis with me and jump on them jet skis. It's gonna be so many hoes out with two-piece bathing suits on, you old niggas might go crazy!"

"I'm going crazy, because I'm down," Carl said.

"Me too," Paul agreed.

••••••

Federal Briefing

"How's everyone doing this morning? If some of you don't remember me from the last briefing, I'm Deputy Director Alexander; the lead investigator on this probe. This gentleman to my right is my assistant, Calvin Scottsdale. Every agent in this room will be a part of the investigation of Carl Fredrick and Paul Atkins' illegal activities. At this time I'll turn this briefing over to Agent Scottsdale. He will explain to you what we'll be doing on this probe. He'll also be reassigning some of you. Agent Richards," he said, looking her in the eyes, "I'd like to speak with you in my office, please..."

The two of them left the briefing room, while Scottsdale took over the meeting. When they got to his office, Alexander took a seat behind his cluttered desk.

"Have a seat, Ms. Richards," he said. "Could I have my secretary bring you a beverage or a pastry?"

"No, thank you, Mr. Alexander," Asha replied. She looked her supervisor directly in the eyes.

"I guess I'll get on to the business at hand then," Alexander said. "We plan to use a woman to try to infiltrate Atkins' and Fredrick's organization. That's the only method we haven't tried yet. We did a background check on all of the female agents that are part of this troop, and I, as well as the rest of the strategy team, feel you are best suited for this operation."

"Why is that, sir?"

"Because of your educational background and the fact that you graduated from Clark University. That tells us you've interacted with a lot of black folks."

They both chuckled at that.

"I told the strategists that you're also the hippest," Alexander stated, "compared to the other female agents. Not to mention you're a very beautiful and classy young lady."

That statement coming from her supervisor put Asha on guard. She didn't like the idea of being used for her looks.

"We learned from the last probe that Mr. Fredrick only keeps company with sophisticated, beautiful, voluptuous women," Alexander told her.

"Excuse me, sir..." Asha squeezed her eyes closed and shook her head slowly. "You make this assignment seem cheap and classless. I didn't sign up with the bureau because I had a nice ass and a pretty smile."

Alexander raised his hands in a defensive gesture. "Ms. Richards, let me explain something to you; something that should have been explained to you in the academy: Being an agent is like being an actor or actress. When you're undercover, you have to dress up and play a part. When I was in the academy many moons ago, my instructor made us take theater classes. That's how serious they treated the craft in my day.

"We're trying to apprehend drug dealers, Agent Richards. You have to enter their world when you're undercover. And the only thing they like is money, beautiful women and fast cars. So if you have to talk with Ebonics, wear short skirts and sashay until your ass falls off to get the job done, dammit, that's what you have to do!" Alexander raised his voice to hammer the point home to his young agent.

Asha glared at him unblinking. She was caught off guard by his bluntness.

"I've played a pimp in Oakland," he revealed. "I played a dope fiend in Miami. What I'm saying is, when we go undercover, some of the roles we play may be demeaning." He could feel the tension leave the office as he spoke.

"I'm sorry, Mr. Alexander."

"There's no need to apologize," he replied. "We needed to get that out in the open. I like to understand my agents. Looking at a person on a dossier can only tell you so much. Agent Richards, I believe you are perfect for this assignment, but the ball's in your court. What'll it be?"

"I'll take the assignment," she said, although she still had her reservations.

"Good. Now that that's out of the way, let me fill you in on Mr. Fredrick. He's a very impressionable man. What I mean by that is he's well-off, and if you're able to infiltrate, he'll spoil you rotten."

"Are you implying his gifts may cloud my judgment?" Asha asked, leaning forward in her seat.

"I never imply when it comes to the job. I just cover all the bases. I'm very thorough. One misstep and this operation is up in smoke. He's a dangerous man – with everything to lose. If he took you for a fed, you'd be dead before we get a chance to help you. Do you understand what I'm saying?"

"Yes, sir."

"I'm not trying to grill you, but the safety of my men is more important than the outcome of any case."

"I understand."

"This will be my last time asking you this: Can you handle this assignment?"

"Yes." This was Asha's first real assignment since joining the bureau a year and a half ago.

"Good," Alexander said. "Let's rejoin the others."

The agents headed back to the auditorium, where the briefing was taking place. Asha took a seat with her colleagues, while Deputy Alexander strode up to the podium and whispered something to Scottsdale.

"I just got word that Agent Richards will take on the task of infiltrating their network by way of Fredrick," Scottsdale announced.

Everyone applauded, but the female agents were envious. Every woman in the auditorium wanted Asha's assignment. Some of them smacked their lips and rolled their eyes. Asha was used to the jealousy.

"And we've had a change of plans," Scottsdale continued. "We will be monitoring Fredrick's home in Manor. The strategists think we may see him associating with certain people on our watch list – or maybe even making drop-offs close to his home. This investigation is officially up and running. Good luck."

Scottsdale abruptly left the podium with Deputy Alexander right behind him.

CHAPTER THREE

"Is everything in place?" Carl asked.

"Everything's on point, my nigga," Paul told him. "I hired the off-duty police officers, I took care of the limousine arrangements, hotel reservations, and I made sure our VIP booths are real plush and stocked with plenty of Cristal and Dom P. So quit trippin and chill."

"I don't know what I'd do without you, my nigga. You keep this motherfucking train on the track!" Carl bear-hugged his friend.

"If we don't look out for each other, who will?"

••••••

"This is your first night on the job, Agent Richards. Are you nervous?" asked Scottsdale.

Asha shook her head. "Not at all."

"That will probably change if you get the opportunity to interact with Fredrick."

"You act as if I'm a seventeen year old virgin going on her first date. I'm good, Agent Scottsdale."

"You should get used to being called Beverly Joyner."

"I'm attending the concert tonight with a friend, and she's been calling me Beverly for the past three days."

"Is your friend with the bureau?"

"No, but don't worry yourself. I already got clearance from Deputy Alexander."

"That's a cardinal sin at the agency," Scottsdale informed her. "But that's on Mr. Alexander. He's the supervisor. We'll have a couple of agents posted in the club posing as couples to watch your back."

"This man isn't going to acknowledge my presence the first time he lays eyes on me. There's no need for backup, unless the bureau likes giving away free concert tickets," Asha said smiling.

"They might spot something. A lot of dealers like to make moves under the cover of bustling, public places."

"That's fine with me. If we're through here, I need to be leaving. I have to stop by the mall and pick up something to wear."

"You're free to go, Beverly," Scottsdale said. He watched her as she exited the room.

••••••

"*How's it going tonight, Austin, Texas*?!"

The crowd responded with loud roaring and catcalls.

"Everybody knows me," the man behind the mic said. "But for those who don't, I'm *Donnie Motherfucking B*! I'm here tonight to host this motherfucking concert – not tell a million motherfucking jokes!"

The club erupted in laughter. Most of them were familiar with the popular comedian.

"The owner of this restaurant is spending a lot of bread to put Austin on the map," Donnie continued. "When people talk about Texas, they usually bring up Houston or Dallas, but what about Austin? I must say it looks nice in this cozy lil' city."

The crowd cheered loudly.

"I'll be sure to tell everybody I know that *Austin* is definitely a place to visit. Shit, I think I wanna buy me a house here!"

Donnie had the crowd eating out of his hands.

"All these Gucci boots and designer dresses... Take a look at this chocolate princess sitting up here in this front row! She's wearing this flower up in her head like she's on some throwback 70's shit! That's some classy shit, woman!"

"Thank you," Asha mouthed.

"You niggas up in this bitch representing, too!"

The men in the crowd barked in response.

"Gator shoes, Versace shirts," Donnie noted. "I'm really digging this brother here, with the Armani suit on, snuggled up with baby at your side. Yeah, I'm definitely feeling the Austin scene..."

●●●●●●

"It looks like you got a packed house out here tonight," R. Kelly said to Carl. The two of them met a couple of years back at an NBA all-star weekend event. Since then they continued to hook up, sometimes to play basketball, when time permitted.

"They came to see *you*," Carl said, looking over the club from his VIP spot. "All the ballers out tonight, ain't they, Paul?"

"You know niggas live for shit like this, so they can show their naked-asses!" Paul said, and everyone laughed.

"I like how y'all got the VIP booths set up around the stage and how y'all got the booths separated," R Kelly commented.

"We set it up like that so people can have a party while they're at the club," Carl replied.

"It's a nice set up," R Kelly said as he sipped a glass of Hennessey.

"Look out, Carl," Paul said. "Check out those two sweethearts sitting to the right of the stage."

"I peeped them already," Carl said. "The one with that pink get-up and that rose in her hair is shutting it down! You know who she is?"

Paul shook his head. "I never seen the broad before."

"I know one way to find out," Carl said as he dialed a number on his cellphone.

"What's the deal?" Lil Chris asked when he answered.

"I need you to do me a favor."

"Anything, baby."

"I need you to go over to that nigga selling those roses and buy a pink one. Give it to one of the waitresses and have her take it to the lady with the pink rose in her hair. She's sitting in the front row, to the right of the stage. Let her know it came from management, and tell her anything she wants is on the house. And if she'd like, her and her friend can come join me in VIP."

"That's a done deal, big homey," Chris said as he disconnected.

"You smooth, baby," R. Kelly replied, still sipping on his drink.

••••••

"Are you ladies enjoying the show so far?" the waitress asked when she stopped at Asha and Gwen's table.

"Yes," said a smiling Asha/Beverly.

"Well, someone thinks you're a special lady tonight. Here's a rose for you, and I was asked to read you this note." She handed Asha a rose that was identical to the one in her hair. "You two ladies are to receive everything on the house, compliments of management. And if you'd like, you can come join them in VIP."

"Who's the management?" Beverly asked, smiling like a school girl.

"The owners are the only management I'm aware of," the waitress said. "And if I had to guess, I'd say the rose came from Mr. Fredrick." She smiled at Beverly. "Just call it intuition."

"Well, could you tell Mr. Fredrick that I will accept his generosity but decline his invitation to join him in VIP?" Beverly stated.

"I'll let him know. You ladies enjoy the show," the waitress said as she strolled off to another table.

"Beverly! *Bitch*!" Gwen said as they both started giggling. "I told you before we left the house that all eyes were gonna be on you as soon as I saw your outfit."

Beverly had on a simple ensemble; a super short skirt with a light pink blouse. Her blouse wasn't skin tight, but it did plunge into her more than ample breasts. She had on six-inch platinum stilettos that added to her already statuesque frame. All you could see was chocolate legs and a whole bunch of ass. She had her hair pressed straight back, with the rose pinned on the left side.

"Shut up, Gwen. You look just as good as me."

"You don't have to lie to me. I'm not a hater. I know you're the baddest bitch up here!"

"Thank you."

"It seems like your job of getting next to Mister Drug Kingpin just got easier."

Beverly snapped on her friend while she was still wearing a smile. "Don't bring up anything about the investigation again!

The only reason I told you about it was because I was bringing you to the concert with me, and you had to know my alias. Now let's get our drink on, lust over R Kelly, then take our black asses home!"

As pissed as she was, no one watching them could tell she was upset. Asha was becoming a great actress.

"I've been to a lot of different cities across the nation," the comic on stage said. "And everywhere you go, you can identify people by their actions or their cultures. In L.A. most of the women are braided up, and the niggas talk like white boys. They gangsta, though!" Donnie B added. The crowd erupted in laughter.

"In Chi-Town, the niggas be Timbed-up and wear their clothes all off they asses. Them niggas super hard, too. I know y'all watch the news!"

The crowd responded with more laughter.

"When I'm in New York, I don't know what to expect," the comedian said. "It's so many ethnic groups up there. A motherfucker might walk up to you and start talking *Swahili*!"

After the laughter died down, he said, "Sweet Soul, Austin, Texas, my throat dry. I need to go get my drink on. It's about time we brought out the main event. Give it up for R. Kelly!"

CHAPTER FOUR

Federal Briefing

"How's it going this afternoon, Ms. Joyner?" Deputy Alexander asked. He reclined in a high-back chair with his hands folded in his lap.

"I'm fine, sir. If you don't mind, when I'm in the office, do you think you could drop the alias?" Asha asked.

"*Yes, Ma'am,*" her supervisor replied sarcastically.

Asha overlooked the slight. "I see that I'm reporting directly to you on my debriefings," she stated, crossing her chocolate, well-toned legs.

"Either me or Scottsdale," he answered flippantly. "So what happened last night at the concert, Agent Richards?"

"I was approached by management. They invited me and my friend to come and party with them in VIP. I turned down the invite," Asha said, smiling at her boss.

"I can't believe you passed on an opportunity to be in Fredrick's company." Alexander leaned forward in his chair, with his elbows on his desk.

"It was too soon," Asha explained. "I'll have to let him see me again – probably a couple more times before I set my trap. If I would've taken him up on that invitation, he would've looked at me as an easy conquest. No progress would've been made at all."

"I suppose you're right." Alexander leaned back in his chair and brought a cup of coffee to his lips. He sipped it slowly. "You sound like a professional seductress, Agent Richards. What's all this talk about setting traps?" He had a big smile plastered on his face.

Asha smiled at her boss' attempt at humor.

"I'll talk with the strategists and have them set up another chance meeting between you and Fredrick," he stated.

She shook her head. "I have my own strategy in mind," Asha stated matter-of-factly. "I don't need any help orchestrating another meeting with Fredrick."

"You're a stubborn young lady," Alexander noticed, "and I have no problem with that. It's insubordination that I will not tolerate. You're not talking to your friends when you come into the office, but with your supervisors and peers. Watch your tone when you speak to me. Is that understood?"

"Understood." Asha was livid, but she didn't show it.

"I'll let you control the reins on this one, Agent Richards. Just make sure that you hold on tight."

"I can handle it," she said smiling. Dealing with her supervisor kept her on an emotional rollercoaster.

"Just to steer you in the right direction, Fredrick and Atkins spend a lot of time at their Sweet Soul restaurant."

"I'll file that in my mental rolodex, sir."

"There's one more thing that I'd like to share with you before you leave today," Alexander said. "When I'm the lead investigator on a case, I do everything by the book, and I expect the same from my agents. I could've easily had a couple of kilos planted on Fredrick years ago and been done with it, but I'm not wired like that. If we get him, great. If our case crumbles, he walks. End of story. Everything by the book, Richards."

"I understand, sir." She stood and reached across the desk to shake his hand before leaving the office.

Alexander waited a few moments before calling his assistant. "Scottsdale!" he yelled through his open office door. "Get your ass in here!"

"What's going on?" his assistant asked as he stepped into the room. He wasn't fazed by his boss' insolence. He'd been Alexander's right hand for over twelve years.

"Make sure nothing happens to that girl," the deputy director said. "If she slips, make sure one of our people is there to catch her. I'm letting her freelance on this one. What do you think?"

"She made contact with Fredrick fairly easily, so that tells me she's a very alluring and intelligent woman. I trust your judgment. I believe she'll hold."

"That's what I wanted to hear," Alexander said, mostly to himself.

••••••

Someone rang Carl's doorbell repeatedly. He took his time getting to it and answered with a smile.

"Hello, Charlene." He greeted her with a kiss on the cheek. "What brings you to my humble abode?"

"Where'd you learn your manners, Carl?" Charlene asked. She stood with her hands on her hips.

"Forgive me," Carl said as he stepped aside and let Charlene and her husband Paul enter his home.

"I don't have the slightest idea why Paul wanted me to bring him way out here," she stated as she looked around the house.

"I'ma ride to the park with you," Paul told his friend.

"*I know you didn't*," Charlene said with feigned attitude. "I could've dropped you off at the rec and been at the mall shopping already."

"I needed to discuss a couple of things with him before we went to the park," Paul explained.

"I bet you did," Charlene said as she turned her attention to Carl. "You must have a woman staying here with you."

"What makes you think that?" he asked as he leaned against the island in his kitchen.

"It's too clean and organized," Charlene noticed.

"Are you saying men can't be meticulous?"

"That's exactly what I'm saying, Carl." She laughed.

"I hate to burst your bubble, but there's nobody staying here but me."

Charlene turned to her husband and asked, "Why can't you be neat and clean up after yourself?"

Paul grinned. "I have a wife and kids for that."

He and Carl dapped each other. Charlene rolled her eyes and perched her hands on her hips again.

"You best believe that's gonna change," she told her husband. "If Carl can clean up after hisself, so can you. Now let me get out of here. I'm going shopping. I'll see you when you get home tonight."

Charlene stepped into her husband's arms. They shared a quick, passionate kiss, and she was gone.

Carl smiled at their show of affection. "You a lucky man," he told his friend.

"I'm definitely blessed," Paul agreed. "You should have a good woman in your corner by now. But you always find a way to run them off."

"Name one." Carl had a smirk on his face.

"Damitra."

"Demanded too much of my time."

"Alright. What about Katrina?"

"What about her?" Carl answered.

"She was a Christian woman, and she could cook her ass off."

"She kept too many people in our business."

"The excuses never run out, my nigga," Paul said, shaking his head. "If you start focusing on a woman's good qualities instead of her flaws, that might help some."

"I appreciate you trying to look out for me, but right now I have too much shit on my plate to be thinking about a woman."

"It's a woman out there who'll make you change your way of thinking."

"I'm sure there is. Let me get back in here and finish writing Ghetto, before I put it off again," Carl said.

"I know you sending that nigga some flicks from the concert."

"You know I am. That's all a nigga in the penitentiary wants, pictures of bitches and cars and money on their books."

"He's gonna like them then. Lil Chris was flicking up nothing but bad bitches. I'm going out back and fuck with your dogs while you finish that letter," Paul said as he stepped through a pair of French doors that led to Carl's back deck.

January 18

Kinfolk,

What's da damn deal? Hopefully all is good when this letter reaches you. I'm sending some bread with these flicks. It should be enough money to hold you over until you hit the black-top. If not, just hit me up and I'll send you some more. I know it takes awhile for me to write back, but ya kinfolk is busy. I'm tryin to keep it 100% with you.

On other notes, everything is on point out here. The club and restaurant are paying the bills, and you already know that we got the streets on lock! The only thing that you've missed is a couple of good movies. And of course some of this good pussy that's walking around here!! SMILE.

Kinfolk, get yourself together mentally and physically. Be ready to hit the streets running, my nigga. It's gonna be like you never left. You know me and Paul are going to break you off. So just stay out of trouble and come home.

I'll get back at you later. Tell them A.T.X. gangstas I said what it do!

One Love,
Carl Fredrick

Carl stepped out on his deck and saw that Paul was feeding his dogs. "I just fed them this morning," he told him.

"My bad. They looked hungry," Paul replied.

"Let's ride. I'm ready to get my hoop on," Carl said.

"You ain't got a motherfucking thing on the court!" Paul joked.

But he was wrong about that. Everyone knew Carl Fredrick was the hood version of LeBron James.

CHAPTER FIVE

Carl sat behind the desk in his plush office at the Sweet Soul restaurant doing what he hated most: Paperwork. This was where he spent most of his idle time. If someone was looking for him, they knew they could find him there. Carl laid his pen on the desk when his do-it-all attorney walked into his office.

"What brings you by this afternoon?" Carl asked.

"I just finished jury selection for a murder trial," Robert Ganne said as he made his way to Carl's wet bar. "The judge recessed until tomorrow morning. We'll start our opening arguments then. That left the rest of the afternoon open, so I decided to drop in on my favorite client."

"You didn't come to see me. You came here to drink up my expensive Cognac," Carl said seriously. "That shit you're pouring up is five hundred dollars a bottle."

Mr. Ganne ignored his most influential client. He took off his jacket and laid it over the arm of the sofa. He took off his tie and unhooked his cufflinks. He then folded back the cuffs of his shirt. All of his movements were pronounced. That came from being a defense attorney for over thirty years. They had to be good actors in the courtroom.

Mr. Ganne finally sat down and sipped the expensive liquor. "For a black man, you sure have good tastes."

"What's on your mind, cracker?" Carl asked, not missing a beat.

The lawyer laughed and sipped his drink again. "Carl, I've been your attorney since you were a smalltime dealer selling crack rocks on a street corner. I've watched you grow from a boy to a man. A very successful man, I might add. There have been bumps in the road, and I've been there through it all. I've even done things that my colleagues would probably deem unethical."

Mr. Ganne swallowed the rest of his drink and went to the bar to pour another.

"What's up with the trip down memory lane?" Carl was busy and didn't feel like entertaining his lawyer.

"I think it's time you started investing more wisely."

"You don't think a restaurant is a smart investment?" Carl asked as he waved a hand around his office. "And what about my residential properties? What are those?"

"They keep money in your pockets. But I'm thinking of something on a larger scale, like corporate stocks and investing in start-up tech companies, things of that nature."

"Get the fuck outta here. Haven't you been watching the news? Those CEO motherfuckers and inside traders are always stealing folk's money. They'd label me a terrorist, if I was involved with that. And you'd be my first victim, for bringing that shit to my door."

Mr. Ganne laughed, but Carl was dead serious.

"I've been checking into a couple of start-up companies that I'm interested in investing in."

"Are you trying to turn a profit off my dollars?" Carl wondered what angle his lawyer was playing.

"Why do blacks always undervalue themselves?" Mr. Ganne asked. "I can invest my own money. I wanted you to look into these tech companies for me." He reached into his leather satchel and extracted papers containing information about the tech companies he was interested in. "I know you're tech-savvy and one helluva businessman. I'm an old dinosaur, and all I know is being a lawyer."

Carl rubbed his chin while he watched him. His lawyer was looking for help, and he thought he was trying to play an angle. *It's still better to stay ahead of the curve*, Carl thought.

"Excuse me for a second," he said as he stood and looked out over his restaurant. He then removed his phone from his pocket and dialed a number.

He watched as one of his employees in the waitress station answered. "Sweet Soul."

"This is Mr. Fredrick calling from upstairs."

"How can I help you, sir?"

"Do you see the lady that just sat at table four?"

"Yes, sir."

"I'll be down to wait on her table personally."

"That's fine, sir."

"Something came up, and I have to leave," Carl told his lawyer. "I'll look into those tech companies in a couple of days. Until then..."

He shook Mr. Ganne's hand and dismissed him.

••••••

"Welcome to Sweet Soul. I'll be taking your order today," Carl said as he handed the lady two menus. One was for entrees, and the other was for beverages.

Damn, this Negro has it going on! Asha said to herself. She was unable to break eye contact. *Tall, dark and handsome*! She was at a loss for words.

"Is there anything in particular you'd like to order?" asked a smiling Carl.

"I've never eaten here before," Asha stammered. She had to break eye contact. His gaze was intimidating. "I was here the other night for a concert, but I didn't get a chance to eat. A friend told me this restaurant has the best soul food she's ever tasted." Asha gradually regained her composure.

"Your friend spoke the gospel," Carl said, still smiling. "Would you mind if I ordered for you?"

"No, not at all."

"Our meatloaf is mouth-watering, and the collard greens are always fresh. The little lady who bakes for me... Umm! I'll let you be the judge of her cornbread and desserts."

"I'm sold. I love meatloaf," said a smiling Asha.

"We also have a very vintage wine collection," Carl added.

"I'll have unsweetened tea, instead of wine. Thank you."

"Let me turn that order in."

A few moments later, Carl returned with her tea. "Here's your drink, Ms..."

"Beverly," she said smiling.

"I'm Carl Fredrick. I own this establishment."

Beverly feigned surprise. "Do you usually wait on tables?" She sipped her tea, looking over the rim of her glass.

"No, but I had to get a closer look at you."

"Excuse me?" She sat her glass down and glared at him.

"I had to meet the mysterious lady who wore the pink rose in her hair the other night."

It wasn't possible for someone with a complexion as dark as Asha's to blush, but her cheeks definitely felt heated. "Did I draw that much attention to myself?"

"I saw you. Do you mind if I sit with you?"

"I'd enjoy your company."

"I'm the one who sent you the rose at the concert," Carl said as he sat across from her.

"I figured that much already," Beverly said. "My question is out of all the beautiful women at the concert, why'd you single me out? And don't give me that *you're so beautiful* shit, either."

They both laughed.

A waitress arrived with two plates. She sat one in front of each of them.

"I hope you don't mind me eating with you," Carl said. "I'm starving."

"I don't have a problem with it." *This man has the full-court press on*, Asha said to herself.

"When's the last time you looked in the mirror, Beverly?" Carl asked.

"This morning."

"Then you know you're a very attractive woman. And you also know that you stand out in a crowd. And the fact that I've never laid eyes on you before piqued my curiosity even more. I know you're not from here. You weren't born in Texas."

"Hold on a second, Mr. Fred–"

He held a hand up. "Carl. If you don't mind."

"Carl it is. How did you come to the conclusion that I'm not from Texas – by simply watching me?"

"I didn't know you were from out of town until today," he revealed. "Your accent is more southern. Mississippi or Alabama, maybe. If I was to bet on it, I'd say you were from Georgia."

Asha was taken aback by how easily he could read her. She knew that she had to keep her guard up around him. He was very perceptive. "Are you a psychic or something?"

"Nope. Just cultured," he said before he took a bite out of his meatloaf.

Asha dug into her meal as well.

"How long have you been in Austin?" he asked.

"Right at four months."

"Where are you from, Beverly?"

"Macon, Georgia."

They shared a hearty laugh.

"What brought you here?"

"The booming economy," she said. "Austin is supposed to be the fastest growing city in America."

"It's grown drastically over the last ten years. Where are you working?"

"That's actually why I'm in here today," she said. "I interviewed at an insurance company a couple of blocks over. I decided to stop and sample the food here, since I was in the area."

"So you're unemployed?"

"Right now, yes."

Carl watched her for a few seconds. "When people migrate to cities, the city has a tendency to turn in on itself. Are you following me?"

"There's so many people fighting over a few good jobs, or the jobs they think they're the only ones qualified for," Beverly answered.

"Exactly. Do you know how to curb that problem?"

"Obviously not. I'm still unemployed," she said sarcastically.

"Sometimes you have to take a job you're *over*-qualified for, until what you're looking for comes along."

"I'm not flipping no burgers at Mickey D's," she said rolling her eyes.

Carl kept his mask on. He was always serious when he talked finance. "Managers at fast food joints make good money. Did you go to college?"

"Yes."

"I'd be willing to bet that with that degree of yours, you could get a manager's job at one of those places. If you're not willing to go that route, I'm sure you'll humble yourself when that refrigerator gets empty, and your stomach is touching your back."

"Those aren't encouraging words, Carl."

"Encouraging words don't pay bills. Jobs do."

"Something tells me you've never worked in fast food."

"I got one of the good jobs right after college," Carl said as he reached across the table and took hold of her hand. They smiled at each other.

"I'm going to take your advice," she said.

They sat at the table for over an hour after they finished eating. They talked about everything from politics to religion and fashion. Their personalities were compatible, but their livelihoods weren't.

"I'm glad we had an opportunity to meet, Beverly."

"I am too. It's definitely been an enlightening couple of hours."

"Time flies when you're enjoying yourself." Carl gazed deeply into her eyes.

"It does." Beverly took his hand in hers and squeezed it softly. "I have to be up early again tomorrow, so I can put in more applications. I hate to, but I have to bring this lunch to a close. Could you grab my check, please?"

"It's on the house."

"I don't mind paying for my lunch. That meal and your insight was too good to be free."

"If you insist, I'll get your check."

When he returned moments later, Beverly was standing. With heels on, she was almost as tall as Carl, which was impressive, because he was six-feet, four inches. As he approached, he took in every detail of her voluptuous body. The swell of her hips was intoxicating to him.

"Here's your check. Hopefully I'll see you around."

"Something tells me we'll see each other again." She turned and headed for the exit.

Carl had his share of dime pieces, but he was blown away by Beverly's body. She was strutting like a show horse, and that ass was super fat!

"Be sure to get your tip off the table," she said over her shoulder. She knew he was zeroed in on her ass.

She left a five dollar tip and a note:

"I really enjoyed this afternoon. You're a very charming and genuine individual. When you're not too busy, call me. Bev"

Her number was scribbled at the bottom.

"You'll be hearing from me real soon, pretty lady," Carl said as he folded the paper and slipped it into his pocket.

CHAPTER SIX

"What's up?" Paul said, answering his phone.

"I need to see you ASAP! Something's come up," Carl said. Paul could tell he was upset.

"I'll meet you at the spot in thirty minutes. But in the meantime, you need to calm down," he said before disconnecting.

Carl called Beverly while en route to the spot. The call went straight to voicemail.

"Beverly. How are you? I haven't been able to get you off my mind. It's been a while since I was able to sit down and have a worthwhile conversation with a woman, like we did the other day. All I felt was positive energy when I was with you. I hope I picked up on the right vibes, because you definitely grabbed my attention, and I look forward to seeing you again. I hope that when you hear this message it brings a smile to your beautiful, chocolate face."

He made it to the spot before Paul. His friend showed up a couple of minutes later.

"What's up, nigga?" Paul asked when he walked inside Music Mania. They always met there when they wanted to talk about something private. There was always loud music playing.

"Hector couldn't swing the deal," Carl told him. "Somebody close to him got busted, and he said he can't touch twenty bricks a week. He said if he *did* do it, ninety-five hundred would be out of the question. Thirteen-five is as low as he would go."

"I see why you're so upset. Hector's bitch-ass is trying to choke us with that price. We're paying fourteen and getting five at a time, and we're only scoring every couple of weeks at best. You told him twenty a week, and he don't wanna show no love?"

"That's what I'm fucked up about," Carl said as he picked through some CD's.

"You wouldn't have called me if you didn't have something else planned. What's up?"

"I called H-Town and talked to Rome. He said he wouldn't have a problem putting his hands on the bricks, but he'd definitely have to do some negotiating to get the price we're looking for."

"Why'd you call me tripping, then? We been fucking with Rome for years. He's always been about his business."

"It's not him I'm worried about. It's that highway. It's been years since we've been to Houston. The laws have a lot of new technology that can detect what's in a nigga's car. It's dangerous out there on that open highway with a bunch of money. Then we have to turn around and come back with fifty bricks..."

"I see you trying to sneak that shit in, nigga. What happened to the twenty a week that we agreed on?" Paul was getting agitated.

"I figured if we have to go all the way to H-Town, we might as well get as many bricks as we can, so we can cut down on the trips."

"Yo funky ass is always figuring something without running it by me first," Paul said, mugging his friend.

"Ain't no difference between twenty and fifty. If something goes wrong, our asses are out there anyway. So stop crying, nigga. On top of that, Rome said the only way he could even *think* about getting the price as low as we want it, was if we buy fifty. You in or out?" Carl asked.

"You knew I was gon' roll with it before you called me over here."

They paid for their CD's and left.

• • • • • •

"It's been a while since you two niggas been down to the H to fuck with ol' Rome. It sure is good to see you, though!" Rome embraced Carl and Paul as soon as they stepped inside his condo. "How was the trip?"

"That was the most uncomfortable ride I've ever been on in my life," Paul said as he sat on the sofa.

"Why was that?" asked a smiling Rome.

"I had five hundred thousand reasons to be nervous!"

Carl and Rome laughed at him.

"It surprised the shit out of me when you said you were bringing the money yourselves," Rome said. "I was expecting y'all to send somebody."

"When you're on short notice, sometimes you gotta do the job yourself," Carl said.

"I can feel that. You niggas hungry?"

"We're good. We ate before we hit the highway," Carl said.

"What about something to drink?"

"Let me get a stiff shot of that Hennessy," Paul replied. "Carl's the designated driver for the return trip."

Rome walked over to his bar and made a drink for himself and Paul. "I been running all over town, trying to put this deal together since I got that call from you," he told Carl. "My people didn't wanna touch it, but they sent me to somebody else. The Columbian said he could do it for that price, since y'all was buying so many. It threw me for a loop at first. Nine a brick is an eighties, nineties number."

"I thought they were going for ten a piece," Paul said, looking at Carl.

"Ten is what *I'm* charging," Rome said. "I got bills to pay. I know you don't want ol' Rome to work for free."

"Never that," Paul said. "I'm tripping 'cause this nigga never tells me what's going on," he said, eyeing Carl.

"It's all love," Rome said. "I fuck with you niggas because it's always business. It's always real. Never any shit in the game."

Everyone sat there for a moment in their own thoughts.

"I got something else for you niggas..." Rome was a true hustler. He migrated to Austin in the late nineties and got rich. He never left any stones unturned when it came to making money.

"What's that?" Paul asked.

"Safe passage from my apartment to the outskirts of Austin."

"Get the fuck outta here!" Paul said excitedly.

"Twenty thousand a trip, and it comes outta my end," Rome said. "My cousin is a DPS officer, and he's gonna shadow y'all the whole trip. You're on your own, as far as getting that money down here. But I'm sure y'all will come up with a bullet-proof plan to protect that bread."

"You better believe it," Carl said.

"Let me grab that work for y'all, so you can get on that highway," Rome said. "My cousin's shift started twenty minutes ago."

He brought the bricks and helped load them in the car.

"Look out, Rome," Carl said before they left. "Lil Wayne is having a concert at Club Link. Why don't you and some of your boys fly down and represent? Everything's on me."

"That's a bet."

••••••

"Rome is about his business," Paul said when they got on the highway. Even though they had an escort, he was still nervous. They were sitting on a bomb.

"To last as long as he has in the game, you have to be on your game," Carl said. He was nervous too. His eyes surveyed everything on the highway. A state trooper kept pace with them, half a mile back. "We've been on top of our game too, nigga," Carl said to his best friend.

"Real talk," Paul said. His eyes never left the road.

••••••

"How are you this morning, young lady?" Deputy Alexander asked when Asha strolled into his office.

"I'm great. How about yourself?"

"I'm good. Has there been any progress?"

"I made contact with Fredrick yesterday at his restaurant."

"That's good. Real good. I may have underestimated you. How did you come to be in each other's company?"

"I didn't do much. I sat down, and he came to wait on me."

"He waited on your table?"

"Yep. That was his way to introduce himself. He said he remembered me from the concert."

"I'm sure he did. One of the other agents said you were dressed to the nines and looked beautiful."

She frowned. She knew there would be other agents at the concert, but she wished they had trusted her to handle it on her own.

"What transpired between you and Fredrick?" Alexander asked, ignoring her irritation. "Tell me verbatim. Don't leave anything out."

Asha sighed deeply as she stared at her supervisor. She told him what happened at the restaurant.

"It was like a first date?" he said.

"It felt like a first date," Asha agreed.

"What's your next move, Agent Richards?"

"Whatever it is, it has to be something spontaneous. Nothing scripted. He's a different kind of animal. I left him my information, and he's already left a message on my voicemail. I'll just let him drive for now."

Deputy Alexander looked at his junior agent for a moment. It was hard not to admire Asha. She was going about her job like she'd been with the agency for a decade, instead of only a year and a half. "I never thought this probe would accelerate so quickly," he said. "Make sure you proceed with caution."

"Of course," she said. "Will that be all?"

He nodded and dismissed her with a wave of his hand.

Scottsdale entered his office a few moments later. "How's she doing?"

"She's made contact with Fredrick," Alexander told him.

"So quickly? She's good."

"She's everything I expected and more. In the meantime, we need to get that informant into interrogation and see if we can add more profiles of Fredrick's and Atkins' associates."

"You mean Tracy McDonald?"

"Yes. Agent Richards needs to be aware of Fredrick's associates while she's in his company."

"Yes, sir. I'll get right on it."

CHAPTER SEVEN

Asha answered her cellphone. "Hello, Carl."

"Hello to yourself," he said with a deep voice. "How you doing?"

"I'm doing fine. Better now, since I'm talking to you."

"Oh yeah?"

"Yeah," she said with a giggle.

"Did you get that message I left on your voicemail?"

Asha liked the sound of his voice. "I did, but I've been extremely busy. I apologize for not returning your call."

"That's cool. Do you have any plans for this evening?"

"Nope. I'm just sitting here chatting with my girlfriend."

"Would you and your friend like to attend a Lil Wayne concert with me tonight?"

"Gwen has a prior engagement, and I'm bone tired. I appreciate the invite, though."

"You'd be in VIP with me. It'll be relaxing."

"I don't know, Carl."

"Just say yes. Tell me where you live, and I'll be there at eight to pick you up."

"Okay," she said.

"Where's he taking you?" Gwen asked when she got off the phone.

"A Lil Wayne concert."

"Bitch! I don't have a prior engagement!" Gwen was heated.

"I already told you that I'm not letting you get dragged into this investigation," Asha said. "I know you want to go to the concert, but I'm working. We'll have plenty of time to bop when this is over. Now help me find something to wear. He'll be here at eight."

"Wear those suede pumps you bought a couple of weeks back," Gwen said. "Match it up with a blouse and some skin-tight jeans. You know how niggas are infatuated with big asses!"

They laughed and Asha gave her a hug.

"I am fine, ain't I?" Asha said. She put her hands on her hips, turning side to side.

"All bullshit aside, Asha, you're the only friend I have in this world, and I love you to death. Take care of yourself."

"I love you too, Gwen."

They hugged again.

• • • • • •

"Who is it?" Asha asked, responding to a knock on her door.

"Carl."

"You're a little early," she said as she opened the door.

"I hope you don't have a problem with my promptness." The smile on Carl's face melted her every time.

"Make yourself comfortable. Let me grab my purse." She went back to her bedroom.

"This is a nice apartment," Carl called from the front room.

"Thank you."

"You're too young to have a jazz collection like this."

"Aren't you being nosey," she said as she walked up behind him.

"I'm just admiring your selections. I'm a jazz enthusiast myself," he said and turned to face her. "You look stunning." He pulled Beverly into his embrace and kissed her softly on the lips.

When they got outside, she noticed his BMW. "Nice car."

"I've been paying a hefty car note for the past four years."

They both laughed at his lie.

"Look in the CD case and find something to listen to," he said. "Are you hungry?"

"I ate earlier."

"You don't seem to be as tired as you said you were."

"You're refreshing," Beverly said. She looked over at him as Trey Songz started belting from the speakers.

"If you'd like, when we get to the club, we can watch the show from my private quarters."

"Lil Wayne's not my favorite, but I do want to at least see him."

"I'm glad you feel that way. I wanted to show you off anyway," he said gazing deeply into her yes. "I need you to tell me one thing, though."

"What's that?"

"What's your last name?"

She chuckled. "Beverly Nicole Joyner."

They arrived at the club and headed for the main entrance. Carl dapped it up and embraced more than a dozen people before they made it inside. All of the females were shooting daggers at Beverly, wishing they were in her place. She ignored them as they walked arm in arm.

Beverly could see why everyone loved Carl. He was one of those rare, average people who just happened to have a lot of money. He was a millionaire, but here he was, wearing faded jeans, Jordan's and a hundred dollar watch.

They made it to the VIP booth, where his friends were already partying.

"Beverly, I'd like to introduce you to a few people. This is Paul, my best friend and business partner. And this is his lovely wife, Charlene."

They exchanged pleasantries.

"This is another good friend of mine," Carl said. "His name is Rome."

"How do you do, pretty lady?" Rome said as he cupped one of her hands in his and kissed it.

Beverly smiled.

"And this is the man of the hour," Carl said. "The best rapper alive! *Lil Wayne*!"

The tattooed entertainer stepped forward. His diamond-studded grill gleamed as he smiled. "Get off the gas!" he told Carl. "It's nice to meet you," he said to Beverly as he shook her hand.

She was star struck. "The feeling's mutual."

"Ms. Beverly, you must be a very special lady," Charlene said. "I haven't seen Carl on a date in well over a year."

Everyone laughed at that.

"Make yourself comfortable," Carl told her. "I need to discuss a couple of things with my partner." He kissed her cheek before walking away.

"Okay. Take your time."

Carl, Rome and Paul walked to a secluded area.

"I'm glad you made it down for the concert," Carl said to Rome.

"You knew I was coming as soon as you asked."

"Did everyone get their packages?" Carl asked Paul.

"I passed out twenty-five bricks, like you said. When I told them the price on the ticket, they were happier than a motherfucker."

"What you letting them go for?" Rome asked.

"Thirteen," Paul answered.

"*Thirteen*? You niggas done wigged out," Rome said. "You could've put sixteen on the ticket. Y'all giving these niggas H-Town prices."

"I know I could've put a higher price on them," Carl said. "But we're trying to lock down the city for the next six months. We're gonna force the competition to score from us."

"What you think, Paul?" Rome asked.

"I don't like it. It's gonna bring a lot of heat to us. I signed up for it, though. It is what it is."

"I feel what y'all are saying," Carl said. "But by the time any heat comes our way, we'll be out of the game. Can you boys count?"

"I count good than a motherfucker," Paul said. "That's right at four million to split after six months. If everything goes as planned."

Carl was ecstatic. "And we don't have to sell one ounce, just get it and pass it out. Only a fool would come up short with our money. Y'all with it or what?"

"You pretty much made up our minds for us," Paul stated.

"Let's get this money," Rome said. He stood between the taller men with his arms draped over their shoulders.

"You fellas enjoy the concert," Carl said before he returned to Beverly. "I have a guest to entertain." He approached her and asked, "How do you like the VIP treatment?" They stood together, looking out over the club.

"It's real plush up here, and you get to interact with the celebs all the time."

"I've come to find out they're everyday people, like you and me."

"You're a celebrity yourself," Beverly said, flirting with him. "Everyone gravitates to you, hangs on your every word."

"I appreciate the flattery," he said, putting his arm around her waist. "But at the end of the day, I'm just a local club owner, trying to make an honest living." He kissed her softly on the lips.

She smiled. "I bet when it's just you and the boys, y'all have women escorted up here all the time."

"You'd lose that bet. Paul is happily married, and I try to stay as professional as possible. When I sent that waitress over to you, that was the first time I've ever done that."

"I suppose you expect me to believe that," Beverly said as she looked up at him.

"I don't want you to just believe me. Trust is something that's established over a period of time. I think you'll trust me later." He wrapped her up in a tight embrace and kissed her more passionately.

"You're just too confident for me," she said, trying to catch her breath.

"I'm persistent."

"Why'd you kiss me like that?"

"You look so inviting." His eyes peered into her soul.

Beverly initiated the kiss this time. It was almost too sensual for public. They were oblivious to their surroundings.

"Where'd he meet her?" Charlene asked her husband as they watched them.

"At the R. Kelly concert," Paul said.

"They've connected pretty good in such a short time."

"He never gets attached to women. After a week or so, he probably won't see her again."

"I think you're wrong this time. He's all over that woman."

"I wish the best for him. He'll figure out before long that money won't buy him happiness."

Charlene agreed with that.

● ● ● ● ● ●

"Wayne, I think it's time for you to set it off."

"I'm on it. I'll be back in an hour," he said before taking the elevator down to stage level.

"Watch how crazy it gets when he walks out there." Carl stood behind Beverly with his hands wrapped around her waist. "Those young niggas start firing up blunts and everything else. Do you like his music?"

"I like him, but I think he bashes women too much."

The crowd erupted as soon as Lil Wayne hit the stage. The club became hazy from all of the weed smoke. The DJ started them off with "Rich as Fuck," before going through a dozen more hits in the artists' catalogue.

Although Beverly wasn't a fan, she couldn't help but notice how the crowd reacted to him.

"They're going crazy out there."

"They feel him because he's a gangsta like most of them. He's from the dirt," Carl said.

Lil Wayne went through song after song and quickly had the audience worked up in a frenzy. The women started bouncing their asses and pussy popping. Beverly shook her head as she watched them with a smile.

After a while, Carl whispered in her ear, "Let's get out of here and go somewhere private."

"What about the concert and your friends?"

"They'll understand."

She smiled. "Okay. Let's go."

"Let me tell Paul I'm leaving."

"What's up homey?" Paul asked when Carl walked up to him and Charlene.

"I'm outta here. Can you handle everything?"

"He handles everything all the time," Charlene interjected, and they laughed.

"Look out Lil Chris," Carl called.

"What it do, big homey?"

"Let me get the keys to the eleven hundred. You can take my Beamer."

"That's a bet," Chris said as he threw Carl the keys to his bike.

When they made it outside, Carl asked Beverly, "Have you ever ridden on a motorcycle?"

"No. Where's your car?"

"Just get on," he said as he straddled the bike and turned it on. He revved the engine a couple of times.

"It's too chilly to be on a motorcycle." She appeared worried.

"Zip up that leather, and you won't feel a thing."

They left downtown and headed for the hills west of Austin. Carl sped up Mt. Bonnell, taking curves at unsafe speeds. When they made it to the top of the mountain, Beverly was happy to get off the bike.

She looked around and said, "It's beautiful up here. Where are we?"

"Mt. Bonnell," Carl said as they looked over the city. "This is where all the wealthy, white folks live."

"Where do you live?"

"East."

"That's telling me a lot," she said sarcastically. "Do you stay in a house, an apartment?"

"I live in a home." All of the stress from the day left his body. Standing at the highest point in Austin gave him a tranquil feeling.

"You probably have a wife and kids staying there." Beverly was just playing the role. She knew he was single from his profile.

"I don't have any kids, Bev, and there's no woman in my life."

She stared at him, thinking about the investigation that would take him down.

"Why are you looking at me like that?"

"It's nothing," she said and then asked, "What's that building left of the capitol?"

"The UT Tower."

"That's where that sniper shot all those people, back in the day?"

"Yep." He kissed her on the nape of the neck. She moaned softly.

"It's easy for a woman to fall for you, Carl. You're successful, handsome and definitely a charmer."

He chuckled. "I'm looking for those same attributes in a woman: Ambitious, beautiful, well-spoken and smart enough to help me take my life to the next level. If a woman can't bring that to the table, I don't have anything to do with her. If hard times ever hit, I want to be able to lean on my woman for support."

Beverly turned and looked up at him.

"I don't know why you're looking at me with those big, doe eyes," he said. "Niggas look for security in a relationship, too."

She laughed and pecked him on the lips.

"I think we should slow down a little," she told him.

"Just let it take its natural course, Bev. I haven't felt this way about a woman in years, and I'm not about to put a cap on my feelings."

"You're difficult," she said and laid her head on his chest.

"Just persistent."

They kissed passionately. He sucked softly on her bottom lip before he slid his tongue inside her mouth. She was on fire. Juices were flowing between her legs.

"Would you like to get something to eat, before I take you home?" he asked.

"I could eat a sub sandwich or something."

"Let's ride."

They rode down the mountain, leaving west Austin, headed east. They rode down Koening Lane for a few miles. When they made it to HWY 290, Carl told Beverly to hold on tight. It was two in the morning, and there were only a few cars on the road. Carl roared past them at speeds over a hundred miles per hour. Beverly held on for dear life. Everything passed her in a blur.

It seemed like only minutes passed before Carl began to downshift. They turned off the highway, onto a road that ran behind Manor High School. They followed the road to Blue Bluff and rolled down a dark, tree-lined street until they reached a clearing and Carl's home came into view. The house was brightly lit. Carl pulled into the circular drive and stopped in front of the door.

"This is the biggest sandwich shop I've ever seen," Beverly said as she climbed off the bike. The vibrations from the motorcycle had a river running in her panties. "You told me you had a home, not a *mansion*."

When they entered the house, Beverly took her time looking around, taking in everything. "How long have you stayed here?" she asked as she followed him into the kitchen.

"I built it two years ago."

"You've been here two years? This house is virtually empty," she said as she sat on a stool.

Carl leaned on the counter, looking her in the eyes. He stepped to her and turned the stool until her back was against the counter. He stood between her legs with his hands on her waist. They gazed into each other's eyes, waiting to see who would make the first move. It was Carl.

He kissed her violently, and she was receptive. She wrapped her legs around him, so he couldn't back away. She broke the kiss. Carl moved to her neck and began to bite and suck, causing her to moan loudly. He ripped her blouse open and stared at her ample breasts. She wore a lace bra. Her flood gates were open, and there was nothing she could do to close them. Carl could do whatever he wanted to do to her, and he knew it.

He took her by the hand and led her to the bedroom. He turned the lights on and then dimmed them. Beverly sat on the bed, and Carl helped her out of her skin tight jeans. He pulled off his shirt, while Beverly worked on his belt and unbuttoned his pants. He took his pants and boxers off at the same time. Beverly scooted to the middle of the bed and bit her bottom lip as she stared at his long, hard piece.

"I hope you have a condom." Her voice was barely above a whisper.

He walked to his dresser and came back with a box of magnums. Beverly took off her bra and then lay back on the bed. She lifted her hips so Carl could remove her lace panties. She reached up and took his piece into her hand. She had to. She was mesmerized by his size. The feel of her hand on his meat made Carl groan. He kissed her gently on the lips. She lay back, and he crawled between her legs.

They kissed again. Her tongue darted between his lips. He bit her gently on the cheek, down her neck and slowly made his way to her beautifully rounded, dark melons. She moaned softly, running her fingers through his wavy hair. He gave her breasts serious attention. He kissed down to her navel and then back up again. The sensations caused her to arch her back. Her breathing was erratic.

He knew she was primed and ready. He reached for one of the condoms. She then took it from him and tore the package open with her teeth.

"Stand up," she said. She stroked him a few times before she slid the condom on. She laid back and opened her legs for him.

Carl went in. Her pussy was tight like a new glove and well-maintained, as he had expected. The first moments were awkward, until they found a rhythm. When he felt her body had adjusted to his size, he turned up the heat and started putting the pound game down. Beverly cried out and bit him on the shoulder. She scratched up and down his back as she moaned loudly in his ear.

"*I'm cumming, baby*!" she yelled. She wrapped her long legs around him.

Carl hiked one of her legs over his shoulder and tried to knock the bottom out of her pussy.

"*I'm cumming! I'm cum– Damn!*" Lust dripped off her lips.

Carl stroked a few more times before he started grunting. After he climaxed, he continued to stroke the pussy for another minute. He lowered his body onto her, and she didn't complain. It took a moment for them to catch their breaths.

"Are you okay?" Carl asked as he rolled and lay beside her.

"That was the best experience of my life," she breathed. "But we should have waited."

He put a finger on her lips and then kissed the corner of her mouth. "Let it take its natural course. I'm not going anywhere. I plan on seeing a lot of you, Ms. Joyner."

"Is that so?" Beverly asked as she turned on her side to face him.

"Yeah."

"I'll tell you this much," she said. "The dick is good. That's the best sex I've ever had." Their relationship was all smoke and mirrors, but Beverly wasn't lying about that. "But you have to bring more to the table." She started to caress his manhood again.

"That's a conversation for another time. Let's enjoy this moment."

"You're right. I hope you're not finished for the night." She already knew the answer to that. His dick was as hard as steel in her hand.

"I'm just waiting for you to recuperate," Carl said.

"I'm ready. Go wash up," she suggested.

She stared at his bare ass as he left the bedroom. When he returned, she rolled him onto his back and slid another condom down his shaft. She straddled him and lowered her body onto his. She let out a long sigh as he penetrated her. "*Ummmmm.*" She put her hands on his muscular chest and started to ride him slowly.

After a while, Carl couldn't take anymore. He wanted to fuck this beautiful, black woman doggy-style. "Lay on your stomach," he instructed her. "I wanna hit it from the back."

Beverly rolled to her stomach and raised her big ass in the air. She looked over her shoulder as Carl positioned himself behind her. He palmed her cheeks and entered smoothly. He continued to pull her cheeks apart, so he could watch himself work. He slammed in all the way.

"*Carl*!" she screamed. "*Oh, baby*!"

He was oblivious to her pleas. He knew they were cries of ecstasy. He saw her thick, creamy juices coating his dick with every stroke. She let out one last shriek, "*Ahh! Ahhh*!" and Carl exploded again.

He collapsed on top of her. They were both covered in sweat.

"Don't hurt me, Carl," were Beverly's last words before they slipped into a coma. At the time, she didn't realize how ironic that comment was.

CHAPTER EIGHT

Blocker Unit
Maximum Security Prison

"Look out, D Watt!" called Ghetto.

"What it do?" answered D Watt, his homebody from Austin.

"I just got a busload of flicks from my kinfolk, Carl Fredrick. Tell all the Austin niggas and the rest of our homies to come up to three-row dayroom and check them out."

"I got you. I'll be up there on the first thing smoking. I'ma bring the coffee too."

When they got to the dayroom, D Watt was impressed with his friend's pictures.

"Yo kinfolk is keeping it 100 with you while you're on this lil' vacation."

"He ain't just keeping it real with me. He's keeping it real with all the Austin niggas on lock," retorted Ghetto.

"Right," D Watt replied.

"This nigga got all this money and still in the game," one of their other homies named Snootie said. He was a little Crip with a hot head.

"Carl ain't in the game no more, nigga," Ghetto lied. He didn't feel that was their business. "My kinfolk got a club, a restaurant and rent houses all over Austin."

"I don't give a fuck what you say, and I don't give a fuck about you getting mad," Snootie said as he mean-mugged Ghetto. "Carl and Paul still slanging them bricks, nigga!"

"You on some ho-shit, Snootie," Ghetto said, getting upset. "Carl must have fucked one of your bitches or something."

"You need to chill, Snootie," said another thug named Rosewood. He was a shot-caller for a Blood gang in Austin. He and Snootie were cousins. "This nigga take pictures with R. Kelly and Cedric the Entertainer. He ain't hustling no more. Carl is balling out of control!"

"Snootie, go put us a stick of that green in the pipe," Rosewood said, trying to pacify him. He didn't want any shit to jump off amongst his friends. "When I hit the black top next year, I'ma try to jump in the real estate game with Carl and Paul. My mama passed and left me some bread and two houses. I'ma try and turn that into something."

"That's what I'm talking about," Ghetto said. "That's the realest shit I've heard in months." He and Rosewood dapped it up with a handshake only Austin thugs knew. "I know my kinfolk will help you get on your feet, if you got your head on straight."

Ghetto had over a hundred pictures in all. The penitentiary niggas loved pics with scantily dressed women and whipped-out rides. Twenty or thirty inmates gathered to look at the pictures. Almost all of them had a cup of coffee in their hand. They daydreamed about when their time would be up and what it would be like when they got back to the streets.

●●●●●●

Federal Briefing

"Agent Richards," Scottsdale said with a smile when Asha walked into his office.

"Agent Scottsdale," she replied as she sat down.

"We haven't heard from you in a couple of days. Is there anything new?"

"Fredrick is definitely interested in me," she told him.

"What makes you say that?"

"He took me to a concert the other night, and then to Mount Bonnell. Afterwards we went to his place."

"Is that where you flew off to on that motorcycle? Agent Collins wasn't able to keep up with you, once you and Fredrick left the downtown area."

Asha felt like she was the one under investigation. They had people watching her at all times. She didn't let her irritation show.

"So Fredrick took you to Austin's best known freak-um spot?" Scottsdale asked.

"Is that what his place is known for? He wanted to be alone with me, so we could talk and get to know each other."

Scottsdale smiled at the beautiful, young lady who sat before him. "He could've taken you to a restaurant, if all he wanted to do was talk."

"You know how you men are," Asha said. "Y'all try to be romantic, always wanna show off your expensive things."

"Understandable. So how was his home?"

"I must say it was an immaculate house. Rather empty, but nice."

Scottsdale nodded.

"We listened to music and talked for a couple of hours," Asha reported. "He's a great listener. We kissed a couple of times, and then his gentleman nature kicked in. He showed me to one of his guest bedrooms, and I retired for the night." Asha wasn't sure why she decided to lie about their sexual exploits.

"I have to commend you on the job you're doing," Scottsdale said. "We've never been able to get this close to Fredrick. Keep your eyes open, and always remember that your sole purpose is to gather enough evidence to attain a federal indictment."

"I understand my assignment, sir."

Scottsdale reached into his desk and removed a manila envelope that contained a lot of pictures. "These are pictures of known associates of Fredrick and Atkins. If you see any of these men in their company, try to determine what role they play in the organization."

"I've met this guy already," Asha said as she studied the pics. "He owns the motorcycle we were riding."

"Good. Anything else?"

"Not at this time, sir."

"Deputy Alexander thinks you should cut out the visits to our office, unless an emergency arises."

"I agree," Asha said, sliding the packet of pictures across the desk.

"Those are for you, Agent Richards."

"I've recorded them to memory. I wouldn't feel safe walking around with pictures of Fredrick's associates."

"I understand. That will be all for now. You have a nice day. Be careful."

"Thank you. I will."

Asha stood and left the office. A moment later, Deputy Alexander appeared in the doorway. He had been listening to their debriefing from another room.

"What do you think, boss?" Scottsdale asked.

"It's going smoothly now and way ahead of schedule," Alexander said. "But I have a feeling things are going to get dicey."

"Why do you say that?"

"Do I have to spell it out for you?" Deputy Alexander asked angrily. "Agent Richards is young and inexperienced. And the magnitude of this case would be trying for a veteran agent." He turned and walked out of the office.

"You hand-picked her yourself," Scottsdale said to an empty room.

●●●●●●

"Where are you?" Carl asked Paul on his cellphone.

"At the White Swan, shooting pool, kicking it with these clowns," Paul answered.

"Who you calling a clown?" someone yelled in the background.

"Fast Black got his punk ass up there?" Carl asked.

"He's up here somewhere," Paul said. "His car is parked around the back."

"I'll be up there in an hour," Carl said. "I wanna look at him on that chess board."

The White Swan was a legendary bar in East Austin, located at the intersection of E 12th and Chicon. Carl made it there forty-five minutes later.

"What's up, Dre? Fast Black?" he said as he greeted his friends.

"Out here chasing this paper, nigga," Dre said as the two dapped it up. "What's up with you? I haven't seen you on the streets in a while."

"I'm trying to get nigga rich, like everybody else."

Everyone within earshot laughed at that.

"Black, set up that chess board," Carl said. "I'ma get on that ass as soon as I get through rapping with Paul."

"I'll be waiting," Fast Black replied.

"What it look like?" Carl asked his friend.

"Everything's going as planned. That shit is almost gone," Paul answered.

The barmaid, Ms. Florene, brought Carl a beer.

"You bullshittin'," Carl said to his friend as he turned up the bottle.

"You know I don't play. That boy Sweets went through twenty bricks by himself. I believe him and Dre done teamed up, though. Sweets already talking 'bout buying a brand new Suburban and putting twenty-two's on it."

"That ain't good," Carl said. "He's young, though. He'll have to live and learn. We should have hit Dre up with some of that work. That nigga is the one who put us on our feet back in the gap."

"I already got at him. But he told me he was gonna keep eating like he's been eating," Paul said.

"I can feel that."

"Big Pat is moving slow, as always."

"What?" Carl couldn't believe it. "He should've been done. He got the whole north side sewed up."

"I was thinking the same thing."

"After I play a couple of games of chess, we'll drop in on Pat and see what he's up to."

"That's a bet."

"Is Donna ready to hit that highway tomorrow?"

"Yeah. But she wanted her ten grand up front."

"Bet. It's a done deal."

••••••

"Something sure has your mind occupied," Gwen said to Asha.

"I'm just enjoying your company," said a spaced-out Asha.

"You need to tell that lie to someone else. Usually when we come back from shopping, you're full of energy. I've been talking to you for the last thirty seconds, and you haven't heard a word I said. So let me hear it."

"Give me a second," Asha said as she called Carl's cellphone.

"What's up, Bev?" he answered.

"What's up with you?" she asked in her sexiest voice.

"On 12th Street, chilling with my boys."

"I can't stop thinking about you," she said.

"I love it when a plan comes together."

"Boy, if I was standing next to you, I would bop you upside the head. You know you crazy," she said laughing.

"If me having feelings for you makes me crazy, then I'm a loon!" he replied. "Where are you?"

"I'm walking through the door of a restaurant downtown."

"Cancel that. Catch 12th Street and 35, and come east to the second stop light. You'll see my car parked in front of the club. I'll be waiting for you."

"Carl–"

"Carl, nothing. I'll see you when you get here." He disconnected.

The girls returned to their car and hit the road.

"I guess you'll be a part of this investigation after all," Asha said to Gwen.

"What are you talking about?"

"Carl wants me to meet him at some club on 12th Street."

"Bitch! He's trying to turn you into a hood rat."

"Fuck you, Gwen!" Asha laughed. "Need I remind you of my alias?"

"I'm on top of my game, *Beverly Joyner*."

"You better be. There's his car," she said as they neared the intersection.

There looked to be a hundred niggas standing on the street corner. They were hustlers, dopefiends, peddlers and patrons of the club. Beverly pulled in right behind Carl's BMW. She and Gwen had all of the hustlers' attention as they stepped out of their car and made their way inside the club.

"Who are you beautiful ladies here to see?" someone asked.

"They're here to see me," Carl told him.

Beverly and Gwen walked to the table where he was playing chess.

"I should've known they were here to see the black Hugh Hefner!" Buck commented, and everyone laughed.

"Carl, this is my friend Gwen," Beverly told him.

"Hello, Gwen. It's a pleasure to meet you."

"When did you become a bitch-ass gentleman?" exploded Fast Black. "You need to be figuring out your next move."

"Do you mind if I finish this game for you, baby?" Beverly asked.

"Do you know what you're doing?" Carl said.

"Somewhat."

"We're playing for three hundred a game."

"I'd love to win that money for you, baby," Beverly said as she sat down at the table.

When the game resumed, everyone crowded around the table to see the outcome. Every time Fast Black moved a piece, Beverly had an immediate counter-move.

"Why you looking at me like that?" she asked him with her game face intact. "You need to be studying the board."

She checkmated Fast Black in three moves. Everyone was shocked, because they knew Black had a good, if not great chess game.

"I believe you owe my lady friend three c-notes," boasted Carl.

"You act like I got a problem paying!" Black said loudly. "I wanna play her again," he said as he handed over three crisp one hundred dollar bills.

"Some other time, chump. Let's go, ladies."

They walked outside and jumped in Carl's ride and took off.

"Here's your money," Beverly said, offering him the cash.

"You won it. Keep it. Go buy yourself something nice. You ladies wanna get something to eat?"

"Sure. But we're not starving," Beverly answered for both of them.

"Good, because I have to make a stop first."

"This is a nice car," Gwen called from the back seat. "It looks like you can eat off the floor!"

They all laughed.

"Where are we going?" Beverly asked.

"I have to stop at a site where I'm having a house built. Then I'll take y'all to get something to eat."

Gwen sat back and listened to Frankie Beverly & Maze playing softly on the radio.

"You're looking lovely as always," Carl said, sneaking glances at Beverly.

"Thank you. But I don't feel beautiful. I'm tired as hell. Nobody's hiring."

"You were out job-hunting when you called me?" he asked.

"Actually me and Gwen were shopping."

"Can you put on some rap music?" Gwen asked. "This Frankie Beverly shit is depressing!"

Carl put The Game's new CD in and turned up the volume. Gwen started to rap along with the lyrics.

"I don't think I should've played that chess game for you," Beverly said. "Your friend was pretty upset."

"Don't pay Fast Black no mind," Carl said. "That's typical Fast Black. He tries to intimidate people, especially if he doesn't know you."

"He scared the shit out of me."

"I'm glad you stood your ground. He'll respect you now."

They pulled up to the building site, and Carl told everyone to get out of the car.

"How's it going Mr. Milton?" he asked as he approached the contractor.

"It's going. How do you do?" Milton asked the ladies.

"Fine," they said in unison.

"That's my bad," Carl said for not introducing them. "Milton, these are my friends Beverly and Gwen. Ladies, this is my contractor, Mr. Milton."

"It's nice to meet you ladies," Milton said.

"Do you mind showing me what work you have left?" Carl asked.

"I don't mind at all," Milton replied.

Everyone followed him inside the home.

"I see you got the cabinets handcrafted, like at your other house," Beverly noticed.

"They look better than those manufactured cabinets," Carl said.

"This is a beautiful home you're building," Beverly said, "especially for this part of town."

"I'm trying to spearhead the urban revitalization," Carl explained.

Beverly looked at him with admiration in her eyes.

"How much will we need to finish the house?" Carl asked the contractor.

"Twelve thousand."

"Okay, I'll write the check. What color should the carpet be in here, Beverly?"

"A light beige color. The kitchen tiles are the same, so those mahogany cabinets will stand out."

"You heard the lady," Carl said to his contractor.

"Yes, sir," Milton replied.

"Let's get out of here and grab something to eat," Carl said and the three of them left the house.

CHAPTER NINE

"I thought you forgot what we had to do, when you just up and burned off with that broad," Paul said.

"I did forget, until I saw your truck parked up here when I dropped Beverly off. My bad."

Paul didn't respond to that.

They pulled into Big Pat's apartment complex twenty minutes later. He had four whipped up cars parked directly in front of his unit. As soon as they stepped out of Paul's truck, they smelled marijuana and heard loud music coming from his apartment.

Paul knocked on the door eight times.

"Who is it?" barked Big Pat.

"Paul."

"Why is you knocking on my door like the law?" Pat said when he snatched the door open. "Come in," he said with an attitude. "Let me get rid of my workers and these ho's."

His workers and the young ladies filed out of the apartment.

"What brings you two niggas by my house?"

"We were in the neighborhood and decided to stop by," Carl said.

"You ain't never been to my shit, Carl. And you've only been here once, Paul. So what's up?"

"For starters, we stood outside and knocked on that motherfucking door for at least two minutes," Paul said. "So now you know why we were knocking like the law." His voice was rising with every word. "Then we fall up in this bitch, and you're having a motherfucking party!"

"You act like you trying to regulate what goes on up in my shit!" Pat said, matching Paul's intensity.

"Look at this shit, Paul," Carl called from the kitchen. "This stupid-ass nigga got the lab set up. You don't think these ho's will have your silly-ass robbed?" Carl was hot.

Big Pat had cookies of crack stacked up on the kitchen counter. He had Purex and measuring cups full of powder ready to go in the microwave.

"We told you not to cook this dope up. We told you to wholesale the shit!" Paul was so angry, he was on the verge of violence.

"Nigga, you can't–" Before Big Pat could finish his sentence, Paul slapped him to his knees.

Paul was usually laid back, but when provoked, he had a deadly temper. He was the enforcer for his and Carl's enterprise. Paul stood six foot even and weighed 290 pounds. He was built like Warren Sapp in his prime.

"You done lost your mind, putting your dick beaters on me," Pat said as he got to his feet.

"You gon' beat him up?" asked a smiling Carl.

"I don't see a motherfucking thing funny, nigga!" Pat said, rubbing his jaw.

"The only thing I see is you trying to be greedy," Carl snapped. "And that shit is slowing me up. Sweets done went through twenty bricks, and you're still on the first ten!"

"Nigga, go in there and get my motherfucking bread," Paul told him.

When Pat returned from his bedroom with the money, Paul greeted him with a Desert Eagle.

"It's like that? You gon' draw down on me in my own shit?" Pat said, throwing the duffel bag to the couch.

"I was making sure you didn't try nothing slick," Paul said as he put his gun away. "Is that all the money?"

"Thirty-nine thousand. All I owed you was three more bricks."

"You should've been done with that shit a week ago," Paul said.

"I'm glad we dropped in on your fat ass," Carl said, "so we could see how you're conducting your business. You're a liability, the way you're handling up. Let's ride, Paul."

They were both quiet when they got back in Paul's truck. Big Pat was like family, and they both hated doing him like that. But business is business.

"Are we going to drop that nigga another package?" Paul asked, breaking the silence.

"Hell naw! If he wants some work, he can buy it. He had about two ki's in that kitchen, so he's good. When he wants to score, we'll keep it at the same price."

"We can't afford for nothing to go wrong, and that Negro is an accident waiting to happen."

"I feel you on that, Paul. But you best believe I'm not gonna go out there and sell it," Carl said.

"It's time for Lil Chris to get his status up. He's been under my wing for two years. He's ready," Paul boasted.

"I knew you were gonna bring Chris into the fold. I was just fucking with you, though. If I had to put my shoes on and hit the streets, I would," Carl said, looking over at his best friend.

"I know you would," Paul said before he turned the volume up on the radio.

• • • • • •

"Hello?" Beverly answered her phone with sleep in her voice.

"May I speak with the lady of the house?"

"I'm everything in this house, Carl."

"Did I wake you up?"

"Yes, but I needed to get up anyway."

"What has you so worn out this morning?"

"Gwen and I went to a club called Mid-Town last night. I didn't get in until three-thirty in the morning."

"Go back to sleep, and call me when you get up."

"It's okay. I can talk."

"I had plans to spend the day with you."

"Now you don't want to?" Beverly pouted.

"It's on you."

"What do you have planned?" she asked eagerly.

"A shopping spree, so we'll have something to wear to the Spurs game tonight. LeBron is coming to Texas. Then tomorrow we'll fly to Dallas for the Beyoncé concert."

"I thought the plans were for today," she said nonchalantly, trying not to show her emotions.

"My bad. I meant I planned something for the whole weekend. Are you going to be a part of my plans?"

"You don't hear it?"

"Hear what?"

"I'm already running my bath water!"

They both laughed.

"You'll have to pick me up," she said. "I don't feel like driving anywhere."

"I'll be there in an hour," Carl said and disconnected.

●●●●●●

"The door's open," Beverly said, responding to the doorbell.

Carl walked into her apartment.

"You need another watch, Carl. That's the fastest hour I've ever seen," Beverly told him.

"I tried to catch you half-naked," he said, peeping into her bedroom.

"Boy, you mannish!" she said as she stepped into his arms and kissed him. "I see you're Jordan-ed down," she said, giving him a once-over. "And you smell good, too."

He didn't respond to her compliment. He just smiled and held her gaze. He took her by the hand and led her out of the apartment. He couldn't help but notice the short skirt she was wearing.

"Is this your car?" she asked, noticing his new Cadillac.

"It's a rental. It's gonna be a long drive to Dallas, if that's alright with you."

"That's fine by me," she said as they got in the car. As he drove out of her apartment complex, she said, "Carl, this relationship is starting off at break-neck speed, and we really don't know anything about each other. I think we're setting each other up for failure. I know what you said about the natural course and everything. But the things we're doing don't usually happen on a third date."

Carl kept his eyes on the road. "I don't know what to tell you about what usually happens. That shit you're talking about is for a regular, a square-ass nigga. I'm on a different plateau." He was speaking the truth, not bragging.

She stared at him. "I didn't mean to upset you. I just want to get to know you a little better. We don't have to slow down, but we should be more forthcoming with each other."

Carl continued to watch the road. Beverly didn't know if he was listening or not.

"Where did you work, before you had the club and the restaurant?" she pressed.

"Domino's Pizza."

"*Domino's*? You didn't come up with the money to start all of your businesses working at Domino's. You can tell that to someone else." She glared at him.

"What's up with these questions?" Carl asked, glancing her way.

Beverly continued to stare at him. She could tell he was irritated, but she had to continue spinning her web. "I walked out of a bad relationship a year ago, and I gotta be careful now. I need to know what I'm getting into."

Carl didn't respond, so she continued.

"He was a serial cheater. I'd threaten to leave him, and he'd do good for a while. Then in a couple of weeks, he'd be right back cheating. He fathered a baby with my first cousin." Beverly had tears in her eyes. She needed an Academy Award for this performance. "That was the breaking point for me. I suffered from depression after that." The tears were streaming down her face now.

Her story put Carl at ease. "I started hustling, selling drugs when I was in college," he told her. "I took the money I made and started building houses with this old cat. Paul was balling out of control, so we hooked up and bought the club on 6th Street. Why did you want to know?"

"Your friends at the bar seemed like ballers and thugs. On top of that, you hang out in the seedy part of town every day."

Carl sneered at that. "What the fuck you mean by seedy part of town? Where the fuck am I supposed to hang out? That's where I was raised. That's where I build most of my houses. I love niggas. I love my people, *period*."

Beverly put her hands to her mouth. The outburst scared her. They pulled into the mall's parking lot. Carl sat, looking straight ahead. He'd already counted backwards from ten to one to calm himself.

"Are you gonna ask if I'm still indulging?"

"Are you?" Tears were still streaming down her face.

"Yes. But in an advisory role."

"I don't know what that means, but I don't date ballers."

"You had a bad experience with a baller?"

"A man like you, in your position, could have countless women at his disposal."

"Are you saying you don't want to date me anymore?"

"Don't put words in my mouth," she said. "Are there any other women in your life? And don't lie."

"You're the only one," Carl said with a devilish grin on his face.

"I'm not laughing," she said. "I love hard. And I'm feeling you something serious."

"I'm feeling you too, Bev."

"I want to represent Carl Fredrick." She reached over and rubbed his crotch.

"I guess we're both going to get what we want then." He leaned over and kissed her softly on the lips.

CHAPTER TEN

"Hello!" snapped Deputy Alexander as he answered his cellphone.

"Good morning, sir. This is Agent Collins."

"You'd better have one helluva reason for disturbing me on a Saturday morning."

"Yes, sir. I have an update on the target."

Alexander grunted rather than respond.

"We followed Fredrick and Atkins to an apartment on Northeast Drive," Collins continued. "As soon as they entered the apartment, a group of people left. Fredrick and Atkins were there for fifteen minutes. When they left, Fredrick was carrying a large duffle bag. We checked to see who the apartment was rented to. Patrick Lewis is the occupant. He's on our watch list, sir."

"You're doing a fine job. Is there anything else?"

"Yes. Fredrick and Agent Richards are spending a lot of time together. They met at a bar on 12th Street. She had her friend with her again."

"I'm going to grill her ass!" Deputy Alexander exploded.

"They're together now," Collins reported. "Fredrick picked her up at nine this morning. We followed them to the mall on the north side of San Antonio."

"Is there anything else?" Alexander was ready to get back to his family.

"No, sir."

••••••

"You're the first man I've met who doesn't mind shopping with a woman," said a smiling Beverly. "We've been to at least twenty stores, and I've tried on a bunch of outfits. But you haven't complained one time."

"There's nothing to complain about. You're smiling, and I'm here to keep you happy," Carl replied, which scored him a kiss from Beverly.

"Let's get something to eat," she said as she carried her outfits to the counter at the Gucci store.

"That's a good idea. I'm hungry too."

••••••

Mary J Blige's newest jam was bumping from the speakers at the Mid-Town night club. Paul and his wife Charlene stood together at a table near the bar.

"Why you staring at me like that?" Paul asked his wife.

"Can't I admire my man?" Charlene said seductively. "We haven't been out in months."

"We both been busy. You at the hospital, and I been managing the club and these streets. But I felt like I needed to show you off tonight."

He gave her a slap on the ass, and she chuckled.

"We've been together for fifteen years and married eleven of those," she said. "Everybody knows I'm Big Paul's woman." She kissed him passionately.

Charlene was a big-boned, yella, with small eyes. She turned her back to Paul and started bouncing that ass for her husband. Paul stepped back so he could enjoy the show – and so he wouldn't spill his drink.

"Mid-Town is jumping tonight!" Charlene said as the song ended.

"That it is. A lot of new faces, younger faces." Paul pulled Charlene into a tight embrace. She was grinding her ass against his dick. She felt his hard-on.

"Speaking of young faces, look who just walked in," Paul said.

"Y'all put him in the family, huh?"

"Our hand was forced. Me and Carl wanted to wait a lil' longer, but we couldn't."

"He's gonna take care of his business," Charlene predicted.

Lil Chris' dress code had niggas tipping their hat to him and women making eyes for him. He had on a black Gucci sports suit, with a light pink, heavily starched, cuff linked shirt that was open at the collar. He wore black gator shoes and a black Dobbs that covered his fresh braids. He had ten thousand in his ears and twenty thousand hanging from his neck.

"What's up, Paul? Charlene," said a smiling Chris.

"I'm just chilling. I had to pull my Benz out of the garage," Paul said, referring to his wife. Charlene kissed him on the cheek.

"That's what it do," Chris remarked.

"Let's find a table," Charlene suggested. "You should come join us," she told Chris.

"I'll do that," he said as he took off his hat.

"Donna came to the club with us, Chris," Charlene said as they sat down.

"Quit trying to play match-maker," Paul told her.

"Where is she?" Chris asked.

"She's on the dance floor."

"Her old ass gon' pass out," Chris said.

He and Paul laughed.

"Donna's thirty-one, boy," Charlene said defensively. "And can't none of these young ho's hold her – or me, for that matter."

They all laughed.

"Here she comes now," Charlene said.

Chris turned to look her way. "Damn. Donna still got it."

"Close ya mouth, nigga. You embarrassing me," Paul said.

"It's hot in here," Donna said as she approached them.

"You sho' are!" Chris said.

Donna was the spitting image of Charlene, except she was slim. She still had a fat booty. They were both high yella, with chingy eyes. "Who invited you to sit at our table, lil' boy?" Donna said, giving Chris a once over.

"Charlene invited me to kick it with them. Now I'm kicking it with you too, beautiful lady," he replied.

"It's really hot now," Donna said, fanning herself again. Chris was no longer the dirty, little boy she grew up with in the projects.

Charlene doubled over in laugher at her sister's antics.

"Here's a towel," Chris offered.

"Boy, is that towel clean?" Donna asked.

"Brand new." Lil Chris reached and patted her face with the towel.

"Excuse me," Paul said to a passing waitress. "We need some drinks over here. Keep the sour martinis coming, and bring us half a gallon of Hennessey. This is going to be a night to remember." He clapped Lil Chris on the back.

"What's so special about tonight?" Donna asked.

"Girl, Paul and Carl put him down with the family," Charlene told her.

"I guess you a baller now," Donna said mockingly.

"I'm a business man," Chris corrected her.

"Excuse me, Mr. Business man."

Everyone laughed at that.

"Let's drink up!"

Everyone lifted their glass to Chris. They drank, danced and chatted until the club closed. Lil Chris was immediately accepted into the tight-knit family.

"Where are you parked?" Paul asked him when they left the club.

"Next to your Suburban."

"Let's hit up I-HOP," Paul said.

"I don't feel like waiting in no line. Let's go to my house. I'll cook breakfast for everybody," Donna volunteered.

"That's even better," Paul said.

"Are you gonna ride on my bike with me?" Chris asked Donna.

"Think I'm not – The way you been feeling me up all night," Donna said sassily.

When they made it to their cars, Big Pat rolled up on Paul with his entourage. Before Paul knew what was going on, Big Pat jumped out of his ride and hit him with two staggering blows to the jaw.

Big mistake.

Charlene started swinging at Big Pat like a nigga. Donna jumped in too. She went straight for his eyes with her nails.

"What the fuck?" Chris said. He jumped off his bike and pushed the women out of the way. Chris was only five-eight, but he'd been boxing since he was nine. He began to throw combos at

Big Pat. Pat saw that he couldn't handle the young nigga, so he retreated to his car and sped off.

"Is Paul alright?" Chris asked as he caught his breath.

"He's okay. Follow us to Donna's house," Charlene said.

"What about you, Donna?"

"I'm good. But that punk busted my lip, though."

Chris kissed her and sucked on her bottom lip. "Does it feel better now?"

She was speechless.

"Follow us to Colony Park," Charlene said as she jumped in the driver's seat of the Suburban.

• • • • • •

"You need to quit yelling, Paul." Charlene was becoming irritated as she tried to calm her husband down. "I left a bunch of messages on Carl's voicemail. What else you want me to do?"

"I can't believe you don't know where he is," Donna said.

"He's in Dallas with his girlfriend," Paul said through clenched teeth.

"If he's in Dallas, what the hell am I calling him for?" Charlene shouted.

"Everybody just chill," Chris said. "What are we arguing for? Paul got hit in the mouth. It's over with."

"Where my gun?" Paul asked his wife.

"What you need a gun for? Ain't nobody gonna come over here messing with you, and your stupid ass ain't leaving! You need to start thinking about your kids, before you go around shooting people."

"She's right, big homie," Chris said. He was trying to get everyone to loosen up. "I thought you were gonna cook breakfast, Donna. I'm hungry."

"Okay," she said. "Let me get in the kitchen."

• • • • • •

"Something happened at home," Carl told Beverly when he saw all of the missed calls from Charlene. He called Charlene's cellphone.

"What took you so long to return my calls?" she shouted.

"I was out of pocket. Lower your voice. Now tell me what's up."

"Big Pat ran up and beat for my husband last night when we were leaving Mid-Town."

"Is Paul alright?" Carl slurred. He was tipsy from all the alcohol he and Beverly had been drinking.

"He has a swollen jaw, but other than that he's fine, Carl. You should have seen me and Lil Chris and Donna get on that Negro's ass!" Charlene laughed. "His fat ass took off running."

"Was anyone else hurt?"

"No, but this fool husband of mine is talking about getting his gun–"

"Put him on the phone," Carl said, cutting her off.

After a moment, Paul came to the line. "What's up?"

"You better leave that gun where it is. I'll be home in three and a half hours."

"Don't worry. I'm gon' chill till later on today. Then I'm gon' let that nigga have it!" Paul said and disconnected.

"I'm gonna take a shower," Carl said to Beverly. "We gotta head home."

She waited for him to get in the shower, and then she picked up his phone and called Charlene back.

"What?" she answered.

"Is this Charlene?" Beverly asked.

"Yes. Who is this?"

"This is Beverly, Carl's girlfriend."

"What's up?"

"I'm calling to let you know that me and Carl partied hard last night and this morning. We had a lot to drink, and I don't think it would be safe for us to drive home right now."

"Tell Carl I said for him to get some rest before he gets on the highway. He can take care of this later on today."

"Thank you. I'll tell him."

"So it's official?"

"Is what official?" Beverly was smiling.

"Don't play with me, girl."

"We're a couple," she confirmed.

They both smiled.

"I'll see y'all later today," Charlene said and disconnected.

Beverly walked into the bathroom while Carl was showering. She stripped off her clothes and opened the glass slider and stepped in. "You don't mind, do you?"

He pushed her gently against the shower wall and started kissing her. When they broke for air, she said, "I called Charlene back and told her we'd been out drinking, and I didn't think it would be safe for us to drive home tonight. She said for us to get some sleep and come later today. You're not mad at me, are you?"

If he heard her, he didn't respond. He was sexually charged, and he wanted to get up in her goodies. Beverly caressed his hardness while he palmed her ass and bit her on the neck. The louder she moaned, the harder his dick got.

Carl picked her up and went inside of her. She had one foot on the rim of the tub, helping him support her weight, and he had his arm under her other leg. He had his face buried between her breasts, lowering her up and down. This wasn't lovemaking, but a liquor-induced fuck-down. Carl shot his seed inside her, and she cried out at the same time. She wrapped both legs around his waist and he stepped out of the tub with her.

"Don't take it out, baby," Beverly pleaded. "You feel so good inside of me."

Carl was going limp as he lowered her. She stared into his eyes.

"I love you, Carl."

He grabbed a towel and dried himself off, and she did the same.

They lay in bed and Carl asked, "Did you enjoy yourself this weekend?" He ran his fingers through her dark hair.

"I had the time of my life. I never experienced happiness like this before," She said honestly.

Carl smiled at her as he drifted off to sleep.

Later, he was the first to wake up. It took an act of congress to wake Beverly up. She rolled out of bed to wash her face and brush her teeth.

"Come here," Carl told her.

She walked between his legs wearing only a g-string.

"I have something for you," he said.

Beverly grabbed his piece.

"You a freak," Carl joked. "I have a present for you." He reached under the pillow and came out with a long jewelry box.

Beverly gasped and her hands shot to her mouth. Carl opened the box. When Beverly saw all the ice, she almost fainted.

"Put your left foot between my legs."

She did, and he clasped the bracelet on her ankle. Beverly was still in shock. "It looks expensive."

"Do you like it?"

"I love it." Tears glistened in her eyes.

Carl stood and pecked her on the forehead. "Get dressed. We have to head home."

CHAPTER ELEVEN

"Wake up, sleepy head." Carl shook Beverly's leg softly.

"We made it back already?" she asked, wiping sleep from her eyes.

"Yep," he said as they turned on the rural road that led to his house.

"I slept all the way. I wasn't good company at all." She pretended to pout.

"I enjoyed watching you sleep. Plus Frankie, Beverly & Maze kept me company."

They both laughed.

"I have some things to do this afternoon," Carl said. "Take the rental car home and rest. Or you can stay at my house and get some sleep."

"I need to go home, so I can change clothes and pay some bills."

"Can you meet me at the restaurant at five-thirty?"

"Of course. Don't get in trouble. I heard the conversation you had with Charlene this morning."

"I'll be a good boy."

She smiled. They kissed and then he got out of the car and walked to his BMW that was parked in the circular drive.

Carl's first stop was at Givens Recreation Center. A lot of ballers in the area went there to hoop every Sunday afternoon. He knew Big Pat would be there. When he got inside, Carl walked to the middle of the court and interrupted the game that was in progress.

"Goddamn, Carl! You just gon' fuck off our game like that?" asked Johnny Bee with his hands in the air.

"I need to holler at ya," he said pointing at Big Pat.

"I know you didn't come up here to trip–"

Carl spun around quickly, so he could face the young nigga that was talking to him. It was one of Big Pat's cronies named Pill. "I'll beat the brakes off yo bitch-ass. What's up, pussy-ass nigga!" Carl exploded.

Pill didn't say anything. Carl turned back to Pat. "Nigga, let's go outside."

"Somebody take my place. I'll be right back," Pat said as he followed Carl to the lobby.

"You know you tripped out," Carl said without raising his voice.

"That nigga tripped out when he put his hands on me," Pat replied. "I ain't no ho-ass nigga." Big Pat was mugged up, but Carl wasn't fazed.

"He shouldn't have did that."

"You should have said that then, but you went along with that shit!"

"Paul was right. He just handled it wrong. You know I'm gonna back his play, wrong or right."

"Well, I did what I did." Pat wasn't backing down.

Carl knew there wasn't anything soft about him. "All this could have been avoided, if you would've listened. We asked you not to cook that work up. We told you and everybody else to wholesale that shit. You got 'em for thirteen, Pat. You could easily turn around and sell the bitches for seventeen."

"Now you counting my money again. As long as you get your money, that's all that should matter."

"We have to get that dope moved in a certain amount of time. That's why we were able to get the shit at the price we got 'em for." Carl felt his temper rising.

"You should've told me that from the beginning."

Carl sneered at him. "You know you scratched Charlene up and busted Donna's lip."

"I wasn't trying to hurt them, but they took off on me," Pat said defensively.

"What did you expect? That's Paul's wife and his sister-in-law. They'll die for that nigga."

"I'ma get Lil Chris. That nigga bloodied my nose and broke my chain," Pat snapped.

Carl waited for him to calm down. "You know I'm not gon' let you touch Lil Chris. But enough about that. You gon' get back down or what?"

"I ain't never went nowhere. We just had a misunderstanding. I could've brought some gunplay into this shit, but I didn't."

"It's all good. Let me call Paul and Charlene, so you can apologize."

"I'll apologize to Charlene and Donna, but I ain't got nothing to say to Paul right now."

"I feel you on that," Carl said as he dialed Charlene's cell.

"Hey, Carl." She was still in a sour mood.

"You alright, baby girl?"

"That shit last night still got me stressed."

"It's over. I'm standing here with Big Pat. He wants to apologize to you and Donna." Carl put Pat on the phone.

"You alright, Charlene?"

"I'm fine. What the fuck got into you last night?"

"Ask your hubby to fill you in. I just wanted to apologize to you and Donna."

"Donna," Charlene called, "Big Pat is on the phone. He wants to apologize for busting your lip."

"I ain't trying to hear that I'm sorry shit!" Donna said, still angry. "He needs to send a bitch to the beauty shop, so we can get our hair and nails redone. And he need to pay for that $125 blouse of yours that he ruined!" she shouted.

"Did you hear that?" Charlene asked Pat, chuckling.

"I heard her. I'll give Carl $400. That should take care of both of you."

"That's real. I'm sure you and my husband will patch it up. Now put Carl back on the phone."

"What's up Charlene?" Carl asked.

"Where did you find his fat ass?"

"At Givens."

"You must have left Dallas at six this morning."

"Seven."

"You and this Beverly chick are pretty serious, huh?"

"I got to get off this phone. I'll get at you later," Carl said before returning to the gym. He walked on the court again and told Pat's friend, "What's up, bitch-type nigga!" He posted up in his fighting stance.

"You got me fucked up!" Pill talked loud, but Carl saw in his eyes that he was scared.

"I'm gonna teach you ho-ass niggas about getting in my business," Carl said calmly.

Johnny Bee had the same hood status as Carl. "Everybody back up, so these niggas can check paper," he said, widening the circle.

Carl shot a hard, left jab that Pill had to use both hands to block – which was what Carl wanted him to do. A kick to the sternum followed right behind the jab. Pill stumbled back a step. The kick stole his breath. Carl moved in with a left, right combination and finished him off with a left elbow that landed under Pill's right eye. He was out cold in the middle of the court. Carl kicked him in the face one time for good measure, and then he glared into Big Pat's eyes.

When he was little, Carl's father had a friend named Bennie Mays who gave him backyard karate lessons. All these years later, he still remembered his training. He could definitely hold his own.

The spectators moved aside so Carl could walk by.

"Let's ride, Ced," Carl said to his young cousin who had been sitting in the bleachers before he arrived.

Ced and three of his gang-banging friends stood, tucked chrome pistols in their waistbands and then walked out with him.

Carl knew he was respected in the streets, but he wasn't a dummy. He was always prepared for every situation. That was another lesson he learned from Bennie Mays, back in the day.

• • • • • •

"What have you been doing for the past two days, where you couldn't return my messages?" Gwen asked as she plopped down on Asha's couch.

"The last time I checked, I was grown," Asha countered.

"When did you start keeping things from your sister?"

"Alright. I've been with Carl all weekend. My voicemail specifically said, "*Gwen I'll be out of town until Monday morning*. That should have been enough to keep you off my case."

"Wait a minute, bitch. I just wanted to know where he took you."

They both smiled. Gwen was the polar opposite of Asha. She was ghetto without faking it.

"Let's go in my bedroom, so I can fill you in."

When they got there, Gwen saw designer clothes and bags strewn everywhere.

"Bitch, where did he take you, *Italy*?"

"He spent thirteen thousand on me, just at the mall."

"I suppose you don't think strings come with that money..."

"My job is to get close to him and build a bond."

"Just make sure you don't forget you're the police," Gwen said as she sorted through her clothes.

"Why you going through my shit?"

"Finding me something to wear. So where did y'all go?"

"We went to a Spurs game. We sat right behind Cleveland's bench. We took pictures with LeBron after the game. That man is *sooo* fine! And he looks better in person. Then we drove back to Austin and saw Trey Songz perform at Top of the Mark. Gwen, you should've seen us. We were late, and when we walked in, all eyes were on us. We were escorted to a table in front of the stage. I felt so special."

"So your gangster boyfriend is a romantic?"

"That he is," Asha said thinking of him. "After that, we went to his house and went to sleep, so we could rest up for the next day."

"Hold 'em up. Back up, bitch," Gwen said and stopped looking through her clothes. "You spent the night at his house?"

"Are you going to let me finish telling you what we did for the rest of the weekend?"

"Go ahead, Asha."

"We drove to Dallas and went to *another* concert."

"I know you're not talking about Beyoncé," Gwen said excitedly.

"You know it!" Asha was just as excited as her friend.

Gwen stared at her in awe. "Damn. You done hit the jackpot!"

"I'm not done. We went to an exclusive after party, and I met Beyoncé in person! Plus Tamia was there. She opened up for her. Carl and Tamia's husband, Grant Hill, played in a summer basketball league a couple of years back. Gwen, this Negro is *major*!"

"I guess being a federal agent has its benefits."

"Sometimes. But for the most part it's a stressful job. A bunch of paperwork, debriefings, surveillances... That shit can get old. I just happened to get the lead on this one. This case does have a little excitement."

"Girl, what's that on your ankle?"

"What does it look like?" Asha said. She moved her left foot forward, so her friend could inspect the anklet.

"It looks expensive. That's what it looks like."

"I've been parading around in my panties for the past 45 minutes, and you're just now noticing my ankle bracelet?"

"I know for a fact you're fucking him now!"

"You don't know anything."

"Since I don't know, then tell me. Are you sleeping with that nigga?" Gwen asked seriously.

"*Yes*. Are you satisfied?"

Gwen was shocked. She sat on the bed shaking her head in disbelief.

"Gwen, you're my only friend," Asha said as she sat next to her and started to cry. "I'm telling you this because I'm in love with Carl."

"You need to step down from the case then, before your emotions and your bad decisions get you killed," Gwen said softly.

"I'm not stepping down. I have a job to do."

"How are you going to be able to do your job, if you have feelings for this man? If you love him, how can you send him to prison? You got me confused now."

"He already admitted to me that he indulges in the drug trade." Asha covered her face and cried harder.

Gwen wrapped her arms around her.

"I'm going to have to save his black ass!" Asha bawled.

"I got one question."

"What?"

"Is the dick *that* good?"

Gwen's question took them from a somber mood to laughing.

"I can wrap both of my hands around it, and he can go all night," Asha said seductively.

"Um, um, ummm," Gwen sighed, biting her bottom lip.

CHAPTER TWELVE

"Hello sweetheart." Carl greeted Beverly when she walked into his office at the restaurant.

"Hey," Beverly said as she walked around the desk and kissed him. "What you up to?"

"Business as usual. What about you? What you been doing since I left you this morning?"

"I went and paid my cellphone bill and did some grocery shopping. After that, I just lounged around with Gwen, filling her in on what we did this weekend. Have you been to sleep?"

"No."

"When do you rest?" Beverly asked, looking worried.

"I'll probably slow down when I hit sixty."

They both laughed and shared another kiss.

"Why'd you ask me to meet you here?" Beverly asked.

"I need to talk to you about some things," Carl said. They walked to the window that allowed him to look out over the restaurant.

"It's a lot of business in here for a Monday," she said.

"Beverly, this is the Sweet Soul. This is the hottest soul food restaurant in Austin. Even the white folks flock in here to see what all the buzz is about." He wasn't boasting, just stating a fact.

"Those women over there sure seem to be enjoying themselves," Beverly said.

"They come in every Monday."

"Have you met them personally?"

"I think so. The one with the brown scarf around her neck is my mother."

Beverly's eyes widened. "Are you serious?"

He didn't answer. He just smiled. "Why are you looking at me like that, Bev? I didn't call you down here to meet my mom. I asked you to come by so I can offer you a job."

"What job are you offering?" She didn't want to sound too excited.

"I need a club manager."

"I thought you and Paul were the managers."

"Our contracting business is starting to overwhelm us. He agreed that I should offer you the job. Actually Charlene thought I should offer you the job."

"I really don't have any choice here," Beverly said. "My bills are piling up, and I can't keep asking my dad to pay them."

"You do have a choice," Carl said smiling.

"What choice is that?"

"I could pay all your bill–"

Beverly put a hand up to cut him off. "Like I said, I don't have a choice. I'm not going to depend solely on a man to take care of me. If I sit on my ass now, I'm not going to want to get up later."

"You're hired then."

"When do I start? What are my hours, and what is my salary?" she asked, smiling at the last part.

"I'd like you to come in at seven a.m., and you'll get off at four p.m. I'll need you available when I have functions here. I'll start you off at $25 an hour and give you bonuses when you oversee additional duties."

"I'm cool with that. Now take me to meet your mother."

"Are you sure you want to do that? She can be a handful."

"I'm sure."

"You've been warned."

They walked hand-in-hand to his mother's table.

"Hello, ladies. Is everyone enjoying their meals?" Carl asked.

"We're fine, Carl. Why are you interrupting my social gathering?" his mother asked. Her friends laughed at that.

"It's nice to see you too, Mom," he said sarcastically. "I wanted to introduce my girlfriend."

"Girlfriend?" Jo Ann was shocked. She had to crane her neck to get a good look at the statuesque figure standing over her table.

"Her name is Beverly Joyner. Beverly, this is my mother, Miss Jo Ann Fredrick."

"It's nice to meet you, ma'am," Beverly said while extending her hand.

"You must be a special young lady," Jo Ann said, accepting her handshake. "I haven't met a girlfriend of his in a while." She gave Beverly a quick onceover.

"I take it you're not going to introduce us," Ruth, a friend of Carl's mom, asked.

"Beverly, these are my mom's friends Janice, Ruth, Mary and Cynthia," Carl said.

"It's nice to meet you ladies," Beverly said with a warm smile on her face.

"I guess that means Carl is off the bachelor's list," Cynthia said. She was the youngest of his mother's friends.

"Yes, he's officially off the list," Beverly replied.

"Damn! I made my move too late," Cynthia said. Everyone at the table erupted in laughter.

"Son, why don't you bring Beverly to the house sometime, so we can get better acquainted?" Jo Ann said.

"I'll do that." Carl stooped to kiss her on the cheek before he and Beverly walked away.

They returned to Carl's office so he could familiarize her with the security system and show her how to do the books.

"Your mom is beautiful and very outspoken," Beverly said.

"I told you she's a handful."

"Thanks for giving me a job."

"I try to help people when I can," he said.

Beverly walked into his arms, and they held each other's gaze for what seemed like an eternity.

She told him, "I love you, Carl," and they shared a light kiss.

Rather than profess his love for her, he said, "Let's go to my house and order a pizza and watch some movies."

"Sounds like an excellent idea to me." She was a little disappointed, but she didn't mention it.

●●●●●●

Federal Briefing

"What brings you in today, Agent Richards?" Deputy Alexander said. "You've never come in without being summoned."

"I thought I'd bring you up to date on my progress," Asha said, helping herself to one of his fresh pastries.

"I'm all ears," he said, leaning back in his chair.

"I'd like to let you know that I'm officially Mr. Fredrick's girlfriend."

"That's great."

"He has his hands in the drug trade. I don't know what role he's playing, though."

"Let me ask you this, Agent Richards, have you seen any triple-beam scales, excessive measuring cups, baggies, razor blades or any other kind of drug paraphernalia at his home?"

"None, sir."

"How many microwaves does he have?"

"One."

"They're not cooking crack at his house?"

"I think he's just the money behind it. He may be purchasing the drugs and distributing amongst his friends. But he's not doing any dirty work himself. Neither is Mr. Atkins."

"What brings you to that conclusion?"

"They spend a lot of time at their restaurant and their club. And they're really hands-on with their real estate ventures. But I've never seen them around drugs."

"What about guns?"

"I haven't seen any, not even on his associates."

"That's odd. Most dealers are armed to the teeth."

"Carl is different. You said so yourself. He's trying to take his squeaky-clean image to the next phase. He trusts his inner circle to keep him clean and to protect him."

"You're a very productive young lady," Deputy Alexander said. "The agency is proud of the job you've done thus far. Keep your eyes open." Switching gears, he said, "You seem to be pretty upbeat and rosy today."

"Carl's good to me."

"Oh is he?" Alexander smirked.

"He's everything a woman would look for in a man. He's handsome. He has money and a home that's paid for. And most of all, he's considerate and knows how to treat a lady."

"Those feelings sound pretty deep and personal, Richards."

"They might be, for some. Just trust me to walk this line, sir."

His eyes narrowed. "I'll see you at the next debriefing, Agent."

• • • • • •

"What's on your mind?" Paul asked. He and Carl stood in line at Sam's BBQ, waiting on their lunch.

"Some weird shit's been happening."

"Weird shit, like what?" Paul asked looking over at him.

"I've ran into this young, black nigga out by my house twice in the last few days."

"What's weird about that?"

"The nigga is out of place," Carl said through gritted teeth. "I got his license plate number and had it looked up. The car is registered to *Trent Collins*. That ain't nobody I know."

"What you thinking, the feds in our business again?"

"I think they are," Carl said. "I've been followed leaving the restaurant. At first I dismissed it as paranoia. But after seeing this Trent nigga around my place, I'm positive now. But I'm not fazed by it. If it is the feds, I don't have nothing for 'em. Since we made that trip to H Town, we've backed all the way up."

"I feel you on that. But if it is the feds, we might bring the heat down on our people," Paul said.

"You think we need to call Rome and tell him we're going to chill for a minute?" Carl asked.

"We don't have to go that far. But we may need to pull back from our runners until this unfolds or blows over."

"What we need to do is change our plans from six to three months," Carl said. "That gives us another month and a half, then we're out the door."

"How do you think those hoes got onto us?" Paul asked.

"There's a number of possibilities. You know that nigga Tracy McDonald got hit."

"We haven't fucked with that nigga in years."

"I'm just throwing his name out there. The heat could've come from anywhere. These niggas out in the streets are dropping like flies. And they don't have no problem rolling over on a nigga when they get popped. My bet's on Tracy, though. That nigga has always been shady."

"You sho' right." Paul was so upset, he couldn't eat his BBQ. He had his family on his mind.

"The heat could be coming from Rome," Carl said. "Ain't no telling who he's been fucking with down there in the H."

"Ain't gon' do us no good speculating," Paul said. "Let's just keep our guards up and be extra cautious." He threw his untouched meal in the trash as they left the restaurant.

• • • • • •

"Hey, baby," Beverly said answering her cell.

"What you doing?" Carl asked.

"I'm on my way home from work."

"What's on your agenda for the rest of the evening?"

"I don't have any plans."

"I thought we might spend some time at my house. Do you have a problem with that, Ms. Beverly?"

"Two nights in a row? No, I don't have a problem with that at all. I wanted to talk to you about something anyway. I'm going to stop by my apartment to grab a couple of things, and then I'll head your way."

"Bring something to wear to work tomorrow," he said, "and a pair of jogging shoes."

"You're inviting me over for the night?" Beverly purred.

"Yes."

"I'll be there in an hour."

An hour later he invited her into his home, and she followed him to the kitchen.

"What you cooking? It smells delicious," Beverly said. She noticed Carl had an apron on.

"It's crawfish etouffee." They pecked each other on the lips. "Grab a beer out of the fridge."

She got one and handed it to him to open for her. Carl dipped his spoon in the pot simmering on the stove and offered her a sample. Beverly blew on the spoon and then tasted it.

"Hmmm! It tastes just as good as it smells."

Carl opened another beer for himself. He sat on the stool next to her and admired her natural beauty for a moment.

"Who taught you how to cook Cajun food?" Beverly asked, turning up her beer.

"My mom is from New Iberia."

"Enough said." They both smiled.

"Why are you looking at me like that?" he asked her.

"I can't figure you out. You're so different from any other man I've dated."

"I hope that's good," Carl said jokingly.

"Of course it's good. No man has ever cooked for me – not to mention the other things you've done for me."

"I believe if the shoe was on the other foot, you would have done the same for me."

Beverly didn't reply. She just gazed into his eyes, trying to mask her conflicting emotions.

"Let me serve dinner," Carl said, bringing her out of her reverie. He had already set the table. All he had to do was light the candles.

Beverly's first bite was a heaping spoonful. She closed her eyes and savored the taste. "What's in this?"

"Smoked sausage, onions, fresh crawfish, garlic, lemon juice, parsley, a little celery and my mother's secret rue."

Beverly burst out laughing.

"What's so funny?"

"My man can cook better than me," she said shaking her head.

"How do you like your job?" Carl asked.

"It's probably the best job I've ever had."

"Oh yeah?"

"Everyone is so professional. That makes it so easy to manage. And I get the chance to meet Austin's most influential people."

"I'm glad you're enjoying yourself. Is there anything that needs to be upgraded?"

"I looked at your upcoming events. You might want to bring more neo-soul and jazz artists to the restaurant."

"I'll give you the numbers for my road managers and agents, and you can handle that."

"You don't think that's too much responsibility for me?" she asked placing her hand on top of his.

"You're up for the job. If you have any problems, me or Paul can help you. Do you want seconds?" he asked, noticing she was almost done with her bowl.

"I'm stuffed, Carl," she said rubbing her stomach.

"Did you leave room for desert?"

"Depends on what it is."

"Pound cake with vanilla ice cream."

"I'll pass. I'd rather have you for desert," she said as she stood.

"You must be reading my mind. But first, go put your jogging shoes on."

She returned minutes later wearing a halter top, tennis skirt and sneakers. Carl led her out of the French doors that led to the back of the house. When she saw all of the dogs, she stiffened.

"Are those pit bulls?" She was terrified.

"Yes, they are."

"I'm scared. Take me back in the house."

Carl pulled Beverly to him and kissed her deeply on the lips. When they finished, his cocaine white pit walked up.

"Why is this dog lying on my feet?" she asked nervously.

"Her name is Cocaine. When I'm happy, she's happy. All the other dogs listen to her. Now let's go."

"It's so beautiful out here, walking under the stars," she said. "It's serene."

"Anytime I get stressed out, I come here and take a walk."

"I can't even stay mad at you," she said as she took his hand.

"Why were you mad at me?"

"I hardly hear from you. I call, and you never answer."

"I call you back when I can. I leave you voicemails, if you're sleep."

"I know, but it's not the same as talking to you. But I'm not going to ruin this evening complaining."

Carl stopped and turned to her. "I want you to move in with me."

Her eyes widened. "It's too soon, Carl. I'm sorry."

They held hands and kissed again, but the rest of their walk was in silence.

CHAPTER THIRTEEN

"Boss, I think it's time we start rattling Fredrick's cage," Scottsdale said.

He and Deputy Alexander were playing golf at a country club.

"So soon?" Alexander asked.

"We might get him to make a misstep."

"I think we should wait and see what Agent Richards comes up with," Alexander said as he teed up for his shot.

"I don't think she's going to come up with anything significant," Scottsdale said. "If she does, I don't believe she'll give us the information."

Lawrence stopped in mid-swing and looked at his assistant. "What are you insinuating, Scottsdale? Do you think Agent Richards has crossed the line?"

"I'm not insinuating anything. I don't think we should give her a chance to cross the line. If we move now, her hand will be forced."

"What type of move are you suggesting?" Alexander asked as he took his shot. "Shit! I missed the green."

"We need to get our informant to try to buy from Fredrick or Atkins."

"You know damn well neither of them are going to make a transaction personally, especially to Tracy McDonald."

"I thought you'd say that. That's why we should send him at Patrick Lewis, AKA Big Pat. We know he's tied up with both of them."

"I agree that we need to make a move. But if we send our informant to this Big Pat guy, and he gets suspicious and doesn't do the deal, a red flag will be raised. Our whole operation will be in jeopardy."

"You might be right," Scottsdale said. "I just want us to be on the same page. I'll talk with the strategists and see what they think. I'll see if they can help us come up with an offensive. Fredrick is too cocky. We need to knock him down a peg or two."

••••••

"I have a lot of running around to do this morning," Carl said.

He was on his back, staring at the ceiling. Beverly's head rested on his chest. She had her leg draped over him.

"Me too," she said. "I have to go to the restaurant. I have a mountain of paperwork."

"I'd like to treat you to breakfast before you head to the office. There's a lil' diner in town. The cook, her name is Lesabre, makes the best omelets I've ever tasted."

"Let me take a shower and try to do something with my hair."

Carl smacked Beverly's ass as she scooted out of bed.

Forty-five minutes later they pulled up to the diner. Carl ordered two omelets and orange juice. One of the things he liked about Beverly was she wasn't ashamed to get her eat on. Most women tried to be modest when they went out to eat. Her meal was almost gone before they said anything to each other.

"You were right. This omelet is great," she said, wiping her mouth with a napkin. "The biscuits and gravy are delicious too."

"You've been smiling since we got out of bed," Carl said. "Do you mind telling me what's causing that beautiful smile?"

"You. I've never known happiness like this."

"I don't know how they do it in Georgia, but in Texas when a nigga sees something he likes, he snatches it up." He was smiling now.

"Yeah, well you better be good to me, Texas nigga."

••••••

"Look at this ho-ass shit!" Carl exploded as he slammed his fist against the steering wheel of his car.

"What is it?" Beverly was caught off guard by his sudden anger.

"This motherfucker in the black car is watching me or something!" he shouted as he stared at the rearview mirror.

"What reason would he have to be watching you?" Beverly asked. She already saw who it was.

"I don't know, but I'm gonna find out," Carl said as he got out of his vehicle and walked briskly towards the black car. "How's it going this morning, Trent?"

"Do we know each other, homey?" Agent Collins asked.

Carl laughed at his attempt to be hip. "That's what I'm trying to figure out. I've seen you a couple of times roaming around this area. I know a lot of folks named Collins, but I don't know you, *homey*!"

"I stay in Austin," Collins said. "I'm on my way to Manor Downs."

"I think you're lying. The horses don't start running until eleven."

"I don't know who you are, big homey, but I–"

Carl slapped sparks from his ass. A lot of the customers in the diner were watching the incident. Lesabre and a couple of others stepped outside to see what was going on.

"What the fuck you hit me for?" Agent Collins asked. He was woozy from the blow.

"Because you're not telling me what I want to hear." Carl was about to hit him again when Beverly stepped to his side.

"What's going on?" she asked him. "Why'd you slap that man?"

"Get back in the car," Carl said through clenched teeth.

"Not until you tell me what's going on," she said, holding her own. She wasn't about to let Carl get in more trouble than he was already in.

"Lesabre, this guy's name is Trent Collins," Carl told her. "Do you know him?"

She shook her head. "I've never seen him before"

"Let's go," Carl said to Beverly. He yanked her hard by the arm, leading her back to the car. "The next time I catch you out by my house, I'm gonna do more than slap your bitch-ass!" he told Collins.

When he and Beverly drove off, she was shaking like a leaf. "You scared me back there, Carl. I've never seen you that angry before. Do you want to tell me what that was all about?"

"I'll explain it later. I'm taking you to your car, so you can go to work."

"What are you into, that has you thinking someone is watching you or following you?" she asked, hoping to draw attention away from herself.

"I'll come to the restaurant later. We'll talk then," Carl said. He leaned across the seat and kissed her, trying to calm down. "And quit being so damn scary."

●●●●●●

Federal Briefing

Asha was livid at Collins. He was nowhere near prepared for the confrontation he had with Carl. He looked and acted like a rookie with the agency, instead of a senior agent with twelve years experience.

She called her superior and said, "Deputy Alexander, can you please tell me what's going on?"

He smiled. "You were there. You witnessed the assault, Agent Richards."

"There's a good chance Agent Collins screwed up this whole operation," she said. "He was a sitting duck out there. Who does that – orders surveillance in a secluded area like that?"

"I'm contemplating having Fredrick hauled in for assault on a federal agent."

"That's your decision to make. That's all we'll probably get him for anyway. His guard will be up now. Damn it! Have we lost focus on what our objective is? We're supposed to be trying to tie him to illegal activities in the drug and gun trade, not arrest him for slapping an agent."

"I agree with you partially. If he took Collins for a fed, he's going to shut everything down."

"No offense, sir, but what this boils down to is you and the agency not trusting me. I'm the manager at Fredrick's restaurant. I have complete access to his computer system. I do the books for his club. I was in the process of looking for irregularities in his cash flow. I'm at his home almost every night, and I've stumbled across a lot of money."

Asha threw in the last part because she knew it would pique his interest. Hopefully it would give her time to map out her next move.

"How much money, Richards?"

"I'm not sure. It was in a large, military-style duffle bag. I know it was all hundred dollar bills."

"Why didn't you get a better look?"

"He was in the house with me. He likes me, but he's not going to let me snoop around his home, not yet anyway. Sir, he could be hiding money and drugs at his home and his restaurant; places I have access to. But if you want to pull the plug on this operation, go right ahead."

"We're so close, I can taste it," Deputy Alexander said. "If this operation falls apart, I'm going to have the strategy team's ass in a sling! They should have never questioned my judgment by putting agents near his home." It took him a moment to calm down. "Keep your eyes open, Richards. If you find any drugs to go with that duffle bag full of cash, let me know, and we're coming in."

"Yes, sir," she said before disconnecting.

•••••

Carl went up on the streets to talk to his best friend. Paul was in the middle of a pool game when Carl entered the White Swan. Carl took a seat at the bar and asked the barmaid to bring him a beer. He sat there in a daze listening to Johnny Taylor sing about a *Disco Lady*. Paul signaled for the barmaid to send him a cold one also.

"What's wrong with you?" he asked as he sat next to Carl. "You look like somebody stole your dog," he joked, turning up his beer.

"I know for a fact that the feds are in our business," Carl said without emotion.

Paul looked at his friend and asked, "What happened?"

"Do you remember me telling you about that young nigga that I've been seeing around my house?"

"Yeah."

"I confronted him and asked if he was following me."

"What'd he say?"

"He said he didn't know me, and he was out there to go to the horse track. But the horses don't start running until eleven. This was seven-thirty in the motherfucking morning!"

"You told him that?"

"Yeah."

"What'd he say then?"

"He didn't get a chance to say anything, because I slapped the shit out of him."

"You what?" Paul asked angrily.

"You heard what I said."

"I did. And I know you tripped out."

"I'm tired of these bitch-ass white folks getting in our business."

"Nigga, that's what they get paid to do. You cracked under pressure. You exposed your hand. Operation shut down has to go into effect right now."

"I know. We need to get rid of those thirty bricks and lay low for awhile. Where's Lil Chris?" Carl asked.

"He's out to Donna's house."

"Get everything from him. I don't want him to get looked at because of me."

"Chris is damn near through with that shit," Paul said as he drunk the last of his beer.

"That's good. We can get Big Pat and Sweets to run through the rest of it."

"I'm outta here. I'll get back with you later," Paul said as he exited the club.

CHAPTER FOURTEEN

"Who is this?" Big Pat asked as he answered his cellphone.

"This ya boy, Tracy."

"Why is you calling me from a restricted number?" Pat asked in his deep drawl of a voice.

"It's just a habit of mine. You know a nigga got ho problems," Tracy said.

"I feel you on that. What it do? I haven't heard from you in a minute."

"I been laying low, trying to fly under the radar." Tracy hoped Big Pat hadn't heard about his arrest. "I need to holler at you about some business."

"Meet me at Clicks on Lamar in an hour."

Tracy checked-in with his fed contact before he headed to the pool hall. They tried to persuade him to wear a wire. Tracy wasn't feeling that, but he promised to set up a transaction with Pat and deliver him gift wrapped.

He pulled into the parking lot of Clicks about an hour later. Big Pat was standing next to his car talking to a young, white girl. She looked like a prostitute or dopefiend. Tracy didn't want to make an appearance. He didn't want to take the chance of getting seen by someone who knew of his arrest. He was driving his baby-mother's Infinity. He pulled next to Pat and lowered the passenger window.

"Come on. Ride with me," he said.

Pat walked to the car and looked through the open window. "I didn't recognize you, creeping up on a nigga in this new whip."

Pat got into the car, and Tracy dashed out of the parking lot.

"What you trying to do, Tracy?" Big Pat asked, getting straight to the point.

"One of my homies said you got the bricks going for fifteen."

"I got 'em, but they lied to you about the price. They're sixteen-five."

"You trying to hurt a nigga's pocket with that price. My lil' bitch Sandra told me you sold her brother one for fifteen."

"Nigga, I'm not doing no negotiating. If you want 'em cheaper than sixteen-five, you need to take ya ass to H Town or to Tone," Pat said looking at Tracy sideways. "Besides that, you been in the game too long for that price to hurt you."

"I ain't gon' lie to you, my nigga. Between them dice and my trick bills, I'm spread thin."

"I don't care about ya problems. But on the strength that you used to fuck with my sister, I'll let you get two of them for thirty-one."

"I appreciate it. You a real nigga, Big Pat." Tracy knew that he and Pat were going to have the same problem pretty soon. The feds were in their life!

"Meet me at Springdale Shopping Center at three-thirty," Pat said. "I'll be in front of the Chinese store. Now drop me back off."

●●●●●●

Federal Briefing

"How's everyone doing this morning?" Deputy Alexander asked, looking over his agents in the tactical room. "I hate doing this on such short notice, but a transaction has been set up with one of Fredrick's and Atkins' primary pushers. Patrick Lewis is going to sell our informant two kilos of cocaine. We're going to crash the party after the buy. Once we get Lewis in custody, we'll try to squeeze him for information implicating our two targets. If everything goes as planned, we should be able to tie Fredrick and Atkins to the conspiracy."

"How do we know Lewis will cooperate?" one of the agents asked.

"If he doesn't, then we'll book his ass and let the prosecutor stack levels on him. I don't have time for any more questions," Alexander snapped.

"I'm sorry, sir, but it's imperative that I ask a few more questions," one of the veteran tactical agents said.

Alexander worked with him before and respected him to the fullest.

"Go ahead, Duran."

"If Lewis doesn't cooperate, do you think our operation and the identity of our informant will be compromised?"

"We've already taken that into consideration," Deputy Alexander said. "If Lewis doesn't talk, we're going to move in on Atkins and Fredrick anyway. Agent Richards informed me that Fredrick keeps large sums of cash and possibly drugs at his home. If that's the case, it will probably be the same for Atkins. We'll keep Lewis under lock and key, so he can't tip off either of our targets.

"Furthermore, we chose Patrick Lewis because of his lengthy criminal record. With this arrest, he'll be facing a life sentence under federal guidelines. He may be loyal to Atkins and Fredrick, but when facing over three hundred months in prison, I've seen the toughest men succumb to the pressure."

The deputy took a sip of water before he continued. "This take down has to be as efficient as possible. The location of the transaction is a highly public area. The less people who witness the bust, the better our chances are to achieve our goal. Are there any more questions?"

No one said anything.

"Scottsdale, do you have anything to add?"

"No, sir."

"Let's roll," Deputy Alexander said, and they all filed out of the tactical room.

• • • • • •

Tracy made it to the rendezvous spot before Big Pat. There were several nondescript sedans scattered all over the crowded parking lot. There were three agents in each car. Big Pat pulled up minutes later in a Camry. He pulled into a parking spot in front of the Chinese store, as he said he would.

Tracy exited his car with a backpack draped over his shoulder. Pat saw him through his rearview mirror and unlocked the passenger door for him.

"What's up, my nigga?" Tracy asked as he got in the car.

"Open that bag and let me look at the money." It was always business with Big Pat. Tracy complied. "Get the bag out of the backseat and inspect your work," Pat told him.

Tracy grabbed the bag from the backseat and unzipped it. The ki's were wrapped in airtight bags. Pat knew there was no way for Tracy to truly inspect the packages. He had to trust him.

It was time for Tracy to give the signal to put everything in motion. He scratched his right ear, and half a dozen agents suddenly converged on the car. A van pulled up behind them and pinned the car in. All four doors of the Camry were yanked open at the same time. The agents pulled Big Pat out and threw him to the ground. They put riot cuffs on him and pushed him in the back of the van. They ushered Tracy to one of the tactical vehicles. Both of their cars were driven off by agents.

"That bitch-ass nigga set me up!" Pat said angrily.

"Shut up!" yelled one of the agents. He then kicked Pat in the ribs.

"We got the drugs, and we found a pistol in the car," one of the agents said, talking to someone on his cell.

"Take both of them to the Twin Towers building on Cameron," Deputy Alexander told him. "Take Lewis to interrogation, and put McDonald in a holding cell."

"Yes, sir," the agent said and disconnected.

••••••

They left Big Pat in the interrogation room for more than three hours before Scottsdale decided to go in and talk to him.

"How's it going, Mr. Lewis?"

"How you think it's going?" screamed Big Pat.

"I hate to see you in such a foul mood. I'm here to tell you that blowing your cool will not be beneficial to you. The reason we brought you here is to give you a chance to cooperate."

"I ain't no snitch!"

"If you don't know by now, Mr. Lewis, you're up shit creek without a paddle," Scottsdale told him. "Need I remind you that you already have three felony convictions and a host of misdemeanors? With that and those two kilos *and* the pistol we busted you with today, they'll give you so many years, you'll never touch your kids again. I don't mean to be harsh, but you were well aware of the consequences when you decided to play the game. Mr. Lewis, you can terminate this interview, or you can cooperate. It's your choice. What will it be?"

"What's on the table if I decide to cooperate?" Pat asked sullenly.

"We'll ink a deal when your lawyer and the federal prosecutor are present. But we need to know if you're going to help us, before we consider helping you."

"Who y'all trying to get at?" Pat asked.

"We want something on Carl Fredrick and Paul Atkins."

"I'd like to invoke my rights. This interview is over!" Pat said clearly.

"I think you're making a big mistake," Scottsdale told him.

"Fuck you ho's! Gon' and book me." Pat was done talking.

••••••

"Yes?" Asha said as she answered her cellphone.

"Can you talk?" Deputy Alexander asked her.

"I'm alone. I'm on my way from work. What's going on, sir?"

"We arrested one of Fredrick's associates; Patrick Lewis. He's on your watch list."

"I've seen him before."

"He had two kilos and a semi-automatic pistol on him."

"Okay..." Asha was tired and didn't feel like dealing with her supervisor.

"We tried to get Lewis to cooperate and give us something on Fredrick and Atkins, something that would link them to a conspiracy. But for some reason, this Lewis fellow has a strong sense of loyalty to those two." Deputy Alexander was at an all-time low. His case wasn't looking good at all. "We're going to close in on Fredrick and Atkins. We're gonna raid Club Link and the Sweet Soul. Do you have any input, Agent Richards?"

"What do you want me to say? I told you everything at the last debriefing."

"Is the money still at his house?"

"Yes, I think so."

"What about drugs or anything else that will help bolster our case?"

"I haven't had the chance to look around thoroughly. Fredrick has never left me at his home alone. I'm on my way there for dinner. If I have a chance, I'll do some looking around. When I leave for work in the morning, that would be a perfect time for the raid. That would give me enough time to make it to the restaurant. I want to be there when the raid takes place."

"That makes sense."

"If I find anything tonight, I'll let you know in the morning."

"Alright. I'll talk to you then, Agent Richards."

••••••

"What's up woman?" Carl asked as Beverly walked into his kitchen.

She stepped into his arms and they shared a kiss. They looked into each other's eyes for a few moments.

"I'm tired," she said. "I was looking forward to unwinding, talking to you. You seem to be headed out the door, though."

"I'm going to hang out with the boys for awhile. You wanna come?" He kissed her on the lips again. This time he sucked on her bottom lip.

"I wanted to talk to you about something."

"I apologized for that incident this morning."

"You didn't have to apologize to me. I wasn't the one who got slapped." Beverly smiled.

"Then what do you want to talk about?"

"I've asked this question before, but I have to ask you again. What am I getting myself into?" She sat down at on an island stool. "You're not telling me nowhere close to enough about what's going on around me."

"I guess I'll stay home and tell you whatever it is that you'd like to know." Carl looked deeply into her eyes.

"Go ahead and hang out with your friends," Beverly said. "I'm going to jump in the Jacuzzi, sip on some wine and unwind a little. When you come home, we'll have our talk."

"I'll be in around midnight. I love you, Beverly."

"I'll see you when you get back, baby." She stood up and kissed him.

When Carl walked out of the house, she sat back down on the stool and stared into space. That was his first time professing his love for her.

Let me line up my priorities, she said to herself. *Carl is a young, black, successful business man. He has to be worth at least three million on paper. There's no telling what his illegal stash looks like. And he certainly knows how to treat a woman. A ten inch dick, and he knows how to serve it up. Mmm mmm mmm.*

On the other hand, I have my career as an FBI agent. I don't have any strong family ties, and I have a best friend who has no direction in her life. Last, but not least, I have thirty-five hundred dollars in the bank, and I still owe on a ten year old Honda that's on its last leg.

If this shit blows up in my face, I'll lose my career and my man. This is crazy. Why do all the good men have to be thugs? She shook her head and made up her mind. *For whatever it's worth, I'm keeping my black, handsome thug!*

Beverly took a quick shower and slipped into a teddy. She poured herself a glass of wine and went on the prowl. She started in his guest bedroom, where she saw the money last time. She stepped into the walk-in closet, and it was full of bags of money.

Look at all this damn money! What if this fool has some cocaine stashed somewhere in the house or on his property? Then all this James Bond shit I'm doing will be in vain. At least I'll have a bunch of money, she said to herself.

Beverly dumped all of the bags of money on the floor in the bedroom, and it was a good thing she did that. At the bottom of one of the bags, she found ten kilos. Beverly put the drugs and the money she was taking in the trunk of her car. She left only one bag. That was the one she told her supervisor about.

She briskly went through the rest of the house. She even went into the attic. She didn't find anything else.

She took off the teddy because she sweated too much during the search. She took another shower and decided to wear only a G-string this time. Carl made it home at a quarter till twelve. He walked into the bedroom. Beverly had dimmed the lights and put on some jazz music. Carl walked to the bed and pulled the sheets back. Beverly got up on her knees, so they were eye to eye.

Carl was sexually charged at the sight of her sensual chocolate body. Beverly kissed him and started undoing his jeans at the same time.

"Have you been smoking weed?" she asked as she fumbled with his jeans.

Carl didn't respond as he took off his shirt and pants. He was completely naked.

"Damn," Beverly said looking at his soldier standing at attention. She was still on her knees. She grabbed his dick and started to stroke it.

Carl pushed her until she lay on her back in the middle of the bed. He climbed on top of her and they engaged in a violent kiss. Beverly turned to the side to break the kiss. Carl bit her hard on the neck, and she cried out in ecstasy. He kissed his way to her breasts and gave them a lot of attention. Her areolas and nipples were wet with his saliva.

"*Carl! I love you, Carl.*"

He made a line down her torso with his tongue until he reached her love nest. He could feel her arching her back. He pulled the moist, well-maintained pussy lips apart and licked the top of her clitoris.

"*Oh my God*!" Beverly moaned.

She had her hands on his head, rubbing his waves. He pulled the hood back on her clit and licked it directly. Beverly started fucking his face and moaning harder. Carl's lips were drenched with her juices.

He made his way back up and they kissed. Beverly's tongue darted all over his mouth. He tried to lift her legs and get in the pussy, but she stopped him. She reached down and stroked his hard, throbbing piece.

"Lay on your back," she demanded. Her eyes were full of lust.

Carl did what he was told. Beverly took him in her mouth. She started licking his mushroom and stroking him at the same time.

"Look in my eyes, while I'm sucking this dick," she demanded.

She was on her knees between his legs, looking in his eyes while deep-throating him. She cupped his jewels and sucked harder while stroking him. His warm, thick cum gushed into her mouth. Carl grunted, pulling her hair.

Beverly didn't want to waste one drop. Carl's toes curled up while she continued to suck his dick. He started to go limp, but she was determined to suck it until it was hard again. Once his dick was back at full attention, she rolled to her stomach and pushed her round, black ass in the air. She reached between her legs and parted her wet pussy with her fingers.

Carl went in. He wasn't making love. He was fucking her, slamming all of his manhood in her.

"I'm cumming baby! Fuck this pussy! This pussy is all yours, daddy! Umm! I'm cumming!"

It didn't take long for her tight pussy and her encouragement to take him over the top again. He pulled out and came all over her ass. Beverly turned over and started stroking his dick and sucking it again. She wanted to taste him again. She collapsed on the bed, and he lay next to her. It took her ten minutes to catch her bearings.

She went to the restroom and got a warm towel and soaped it up. She came back and cleaned Carl's genitals off. She then dried him with another towel.

"Don't worry about getting up in the morning," she told him. "Sleep in and get some rest. I'll grab some breakfast on my way to work..."

Carl didn't answer.

"Did you hear me?" she asked, squeezing his dick again.

"I heard you." He smiled. He was exhausted.

"I love you, baby."

"I love you too, Beverly."

Carl fell into a coma. Beverly fell asleep next to him.

In the morning she showered and left the house before dawn. She wasn't about to stick around and let her supervisor double-cross her and catch her with all that shit in her trunk!

CHAPTER FIFTEEN

"All personnel converge now!" echoed through all of the agents' radios and earpieces.

They broke through the French doors that led to Carl's bedroom. They hit all of the other entrances to his home. Before Carl had a chance to respond, the agents had him restrained with guns trained on him. He heard multiple gunshots in the backyard.

"What you bitches doing up in my shit?" Carl yelled as he fought against them.

"For starters, try assault on a federal agent!" retorted the agent in charge. "We also have you on conspiracy and organized crime charges. I'm sure when we get through tearing up your house, your clubs and your partner in crime's house, there will be more charges added," he boasted.

"Do I get to put clothes on, or am I going to jail with my dick swanging?" Carl had the stone face on now.

"Mr. Fredrick, you seem to have a good sense of humor, for someone who's going to prison for a long time."

"That remains to be seen," Carl said as they helped him into his boxer shorts. "If y'all arresting me for that punk I slapped the other morning, I know you don't have no case." He laughed at them.

They escorted Carl out of his house through the broken French doors. He saw all of his dogs had been shot to death. That put a strain on his heart, but he didn't show it.

An agent walked up and spoke to the man in charge. "We found a bag with large bills banded with bank tape in one of his bedrooms. We also found a loaded semi-automatic pistol, a triple beam scale and other things that could be considered drug paraphernalia."

"Is there anything you'd like to say for yourself, Mr. Fredrick?" asked the smiling agent.

"Book me in. Then get Robert Ganne down there to bond me out!" There was nothing else that could be said.

••••••

"Fill me in on what we got in the raids, Scottsdale," Deputy Alexander said.

"We found $410,000 at Fredrick's home."

Alexander whistled. "That's a lot of money to just have lying around the house." He shook his head. He thought Fredrick was smarter than that. "What else?"

"Seventeen thousand at his restaurant."

"That's nothing. It's common for thriving businesses to have large sums of money in the safe."

"I thought the same thing, sir."

"What about guns and drugs, the hard shit?"

"The only gun we found was a registered 9mm. We found a scale, but nothing else that would constitute a drug conspiracy."

"What about at Atkins' house?"

"Nothing. No guns, excessive money. Nothing. We didn't even take him into custody."

"They should've brought him in anyway, so we could press him. Anyway, what about their phone records? Can we tie them to the dealers we busted?"

"Surveillance always sees him talking on the phone, but nothing's listed under his name."

"He's using pre-paids and throwaways," Alexander said, mostly to himself. "Did you check his mother, Scottsdale?"

"She's clean, sir."

"Hmmm. I hope we didn't jump the gun on this one. We should have let agent Richards gather more information. She had the inside track."

"I disagree, sir. It was now or never, especially with that incident with Agent Collins. I've already spoken to the prosecutor. He told me we can put him away for ten years for the assault, coupled with the money."

"If that happens, I'd say we were successful," Alexander said. "But what if he can account for the money?"

"The IRS is running an audit as we speak. Every penny that can't be accounted for will warrant a tax-evasion charge and possible conspiracy," Scottsdale said.

"I'm pleased with the way you've taken the lead on this," praised an exhausted Alexander.

"Thank you, sir."

••••••

Three hours earlier…

Asha called her best friend Gwen as soon as she pulled out of Carl's driveway. It took awhile for Gwen to answer the phone at five-thirty am. Asha told her to meet her at the corner of 7th Street and I-35. Gwen didn't want to get out of bed, but Asha told her it was a matter of life and death.

Gwen was already pumping gas when Asha pulled into the gas station. Asha walked up to the pump looking around nervously.

"Why am I downtown at six in the morning?" Gwen was in a sour mood.

"I need you to switch cars with me right now, and go get a hotel on the south side. Rent the room for three days. Make sure it's a nice hotel."

"Bitch! What's in your car?" Gwen snapped.

Asha didn't bother lying to her. "Money and drugs."

Gwen's face filled with worry. "Asha, what have you done?"

"They're going to raid Carl's house this morning. I took all the money and drugs and put them in my car."

"You have finally lost your mind," Gwen said as a nervous smile came to her face. "What do you plan to do now?"

"I don't know. I need some time to sort things out."

"Why didn't you just tell Carl you're a federal agent?"

"I was afraid of how he would react," she answered honestly. "Listen, I have to be at the restaurant before the raid goes down. Now get going," Asha said as she walked to Gwen's Corolla.

"How much money is in the car?"

"A million dollars and ten kilos."

"Bitch! We done hit the lottery!"

"We haven't hit shit! That's my man's money," snapped Asha.

"With that type of money, you don't need a man."

"That's just it, Gwendolyn. I want a man. I want Carl. Besides that, he's worth way more than a million dollars."

"I guess," Gwen said, giving in.

"Go straight to the hotel and get a room," Asha told her. "Make sure it's one that's facing the parking lot, so you can watch the car. Take the bags inside one at a time. Wait an hour between each trip to the car, in case someone's watching you. Now I have to go."

Asha got in Gwen's hooptie and sped off.

• • • • • •

Blocker Unit
Maximum Security Prison

"Look out, Ghetto," called one of his friends.

"What it do, Rosewood?" Ghetto was sitting on the bunk in his cell reading a magazine.

"Have you been to the library to read the Austin paper?"

"Naw. I just got off work in the kitchen. Those hoes are working a nigga like a slave up in that bitch." Ghetto walked to the bars.

"Ya kinfolk made the front page, and it ain't good, big homey."

"Get my cell door rolled, so I can go check it out."

Rosewood walked down the run to ask the officer in the rotunda if he'd open Ghetto's cell. Seconds later Ghetto's door rattled open. He and Rosewood headed for the prison library. Moments later Ghetto had the *Austin American Statesman* in hand.

The article wasn't very long: Carl Anthony Fredrick, a local black business owner, was arrested yesterday morning by federal authorities. He's been charged with tax-evasion and engaging in organized crime. He also has a third charge of aggravated assault on a federal agent.

They didn't release a lot of details, only that nearly half a million dollars was confiscated. They also raided his club and restaurant, and the home of his business associate, Paul Atkins, but he was not arrested. According to the article, Carl was waiting to be arraigned by a federal magistrate.

"That's fucked up!" Ghetto sat at a table shaking his head.

"I know it, my nigga." Rosewood knew Ghetto and Carl were as thick as thieves.

"I seen that paper," an inmate named Snootie said as he listened to their conversation. "I told you that nigga was still in the game."

"If you already knew about it, that means the only reason your bitch-ass followed me in here was to fuck with me!" Ghetto snapped. "I'm not in the mood for your hating."

The clerk and the rest of the inmates in the library turned to see what was going on.

"I ain't no hater, nigga," Snootie said, not backing down. "You was trying to make like Carl was all the way legit and on another level from the other gangstas on the streets. But I knew he wasn't."

"How many of them niggas you used to hang with send you pictures and money?" Ghetto asked him. "How many of them go by and hit ya mama off because she's doing bad?"

When Snootie didn't respond, Ghetto said, "I already know the answer, nigga. You don't have to say nothing. It's written all over ya face! Carl even hit D Watt up with a five hundred dollar spot, just because they played little league together. I'm through fucking with you, Snootie. Stay out my way, nigga, before I run over you!"

Ghetto and Rosewood mobbed out of the library.

•••••

"I'm so mad at my son, Janice," Jo Ann said to her best friend. "There's no way in hell Carl was supposed to have that kind of money just laying around his house."

"You have every right to be mad," Janice said. "But being mad ain't gon' help your son right now. He needs you to have a clear head. You can be mad later. When he gets out, me, you and the rest of the girls can get together and kick his ass!"

"That's why I love you, girl. You always make light out of every situation." Tears streamed down Jo Ann's face.

"Are they going to give him a bond?"

"His bond has already been set at five hundred thousand."

"That's a lot of money, Jo Ann."

"That's what his lawyer said. Carl wants to get out, though. He's putting up the deed to his restaurant."

"I read the newspaper. They said something about organized crime and assault. What's that all about?" asked Janice.

"They're trying to say that everything he owns was bought with drug money."

"I know that's not true. I co-signed so he could get the loan for the club," Janice said proudly.

Jo Ann knew that Carl took out a number of loans to start his businesses and keep the white folks off his back. Hopefully it would save his ass. "I know, Janice."

"What about the assault?"

"Carl told me that some guy had been following him for days. He said he confronted the man and they started arguing. Carl said he slapped him."

"I don't know, Jo Ann. All this stuff sounds pretty serious. I agree with him getting out on bond. He could probably handle things better than us. Besides, we can't kick his ass if he's behind bars."

Janice and Jo Ann laughed and hugged.

• • • • • •

"Hello?" A woman answered Rome's phone.

"Yes, could I speak with Rome?"

"Hold on a second."

"Hello?" Rome said in his deep voice.

"Rome, this is Charlene."

Rome's senses automatically went on alert. "What's up, baby girl?"

"Those people are down here tearing everything up," she told him. "Paul gave me your number and told me to call and put you on notice."

"What they find?" Rome asked.

"They got four hundred thousand from Carl's house."

"They didn't find nothing else?"

"Nothing."

"That ain't shit then. What's happening now?"

"They let Paul go. They didn't find anything at the club or at our house. Carl is being held on half a million dollar bond."

"That's crazy! A bond like that for some money?"

"He has three charges: Organized crime, assault on a federal agent and conspiracy," Charlene said sadly.

"They're just trumping the charges up, hoping he'll break," Rome said matter-of-factly. "But he's too smart for that."

"He won't talk," Charlene agreed.

"Thanks for calling, baby girl. When Carl gets out, tell him to get at me."

"Gotcha."

CHAPTER SIXTEEN

AUSTIN AMERICAN STATESMAN

Carl Fredrick, the local black business owner who was arrested on multiple federal charges three days ago, was released after paying a five hundred thousand dollar cash bond.

The arrest and the amount of the bond started an uproar in East Austin. The local black leaders have come out in support of Fredrick. They are calling the arrest a conspiracy within itself. These leaders believe the federal government is taking racial profiling to another level. They believe the government is trying to bring down a young, successful, black businessman.

Minister Edwin Delaney, of Mountaintop Baptist Church, was quoted as saying, "Because Mr. Fredrick has a $350,000 home and drives an $80,000 car, the federal agents think he's into something illegal. I'll agree that four hundred thousand dollars is a lot of money to have at your home, but I'll assure the public that Mr. Fredrick is involved in enough building projects to account for that money two or three times over.

"He's the owner of 23 rental properties. He has a construction company. He owns a social club and an upscale restaurant. I believe the federal probe and the arrest s a waste of tax payers' money and surely a travesty of justice. And I speak for the masses."

••••••

"Asha, your boyfriend has a lot of name recognition in Austin," Gwen said as she read the article in the newspaper.

"I told you he was special." Asha was counting the money she took from Carl's house.

"Why are you counting that money, when you already know it's a million dollars?"

"Because I don't know how much it is," Asha said with a grin on her face. "I only told you that so you wouldn't mess with it."

"You know I'd never steal from you, bitch."

"Help me finish counting this money. I don't have time to argue with you. I have too much shit going on, and I need to get to my job. Besides, any fool would know that's more than a million dollars." Asha laughed.

"I don't see a damn thing funny," Gwen said. She was getting heated. "I never even looked in those bags."

"Alright. I apologize for not trusting you. But I need your help. Dump that other bag out, and start counting the money. Please."

"You owe me big time for getting me involved in this shit."

"Whatever. You've been trying to get involved from day one."

"What's this shit taped to the bottom of this bag?" Gwen asked.

Asha peeked into the bag. "That's the cocaine I told you about."

"Ooh! This Negro is a real bad boy!"

"I know it," Asha said excitedly. "If they would have caught Carl with this dope, he would have never gotten out of prison."

"What's the plan now?"

"I'm gonna stay undercover."

"Carl's gonna want to know where the rest of his money and his drugs went to."

"I'll play dumb."

"He might even take you for a fed, bitch. Then what? I think you're playing with fire." Gwen knew the stakes in this game were high.

"I thought about that," Asha said. "If he does accuse me of being a fed, I'll come clean."

"Come clean? Are you crazy? This ain't no game. That nigga is out of a million dollars and a lot of dope. And you know that man adores you. He'll flip out."

"That's the chance I have to take. I knew what I was getting into when I decided to straddle the fence."

"Asha, you're crazy. Do you know that?"

They both laughed and went on counting the money.

"What do you plan on doing until this plan of yours materializes?" Gwen asked.

"I need you to go to Corpus Christi. I have a cousin who lives there. His name is Raymond Williams. He's going to let you stay with him, until you find us an apartment."

"Corpus Christi? Your cousin? You want me to ride all over Texas with this shit in the trunk of my car? You put this plan together without running it by the person who's taking the biggest risk." Gwen was speaking the gospel. If she got caught with that money and dope, there would be no saving her.

"I didn't have time to iron out all of the wrinkles in the plan. Things were happening so fast. You're the only person I could turn to, Gwen." Asha hated putting her friend in this spot, but she had no choice.

"You must trust this cousin of yours an awful lot, if you want me to go over there with all this money," Gwen said.

"Trust me on this," Asha told her. "I would never put you in harm's way. Raymond is my first cousin on my mother's side. We've been close all of our lives. Once you get there, give him one of those kilos. He's a baller, and he's gonna take care of you until I get there."

"You're not going to put me in harm's way, huh? Bitch, my feet are hanging off the side of a cliff. I'ma help you though. But I'm really helping myself, because when it's all said and done, you best believe Gwen is gonna get something out of this!"

"I love you, and I'm going to make sure you're taken care of when this is over," Asha assured her friend. "Now, how much money is in that pile?"

"Two-point eight million."

"That adds up, because this is one-point two million."

"Four million dollars," Gwen said in a daze. "This nigga is really official."

"It's time to roll," Asha said. "When you get on the highway, make sure you go the speed limit and use your blinkers. Put on those designer glasses and get out of here. As soon as you get to Corpus, call my cousin. He'll come and get you. Call me when you get to his house. I love you. Now be careful."

••••••

When Carl and his attorney walked out of the federal courthouse, they were rushed by a small group of reporters.

"Mr. Fredrick, are you the notorious drug dealer the media is making you out to be?" a reporter asked.

Carl just stared at her and shook his head. She must have thought he was stupid enough to give her a comment.

"What were you doing with close to half a million dollars in your home?" another reporter asked.

"Mr. Ganne, will you be seeking a plea-agreement for your client?" asked the first reporter.

"No, we will not," the lawyer said. "My client will be totally exonerated on all charges. The FBI is on a witch hunt again. There's no crime against being young, black and successful. At least there wasn't when I went to law school."

A few reporters laughed at that.

"That's the only question I'm fielding today," Mr. Ganne said. "My client is tired and wants to get home to his family."

Carl and his lawyer headed for a chauffeured Yukon. As they drove away from the courthouse, Ganne looked over at him.

"Well, Carl, it looks like you're a local celebrity now."

"This is a helluva way to gain celebrity status," Carl retorted.

Mr. Ganne said, "Well son, you have to pay the cost to be the boss. And at this level, the stakes are extremely high. But don't worry yourself. Just stay busy with your businesses and let me handle the legal stuff. Make sure you have a bottle of that Monsieur Cognac in your office for when I stop by."

"You got it."

"Things are already looking up for us."

"Why you say that?" Carl asked curiously.

"Some very influential community leaders have stepped forward as a public show of support."

When the chauffeur pulled into Carl's driveway, he saw Mr. Milton's truck parked in the drive. Milton was the contractor he hired for most of his building projects. Carl knew that Paul had sent him over to repair the damage the feds did to his house.

••••••

"Hey, baby." Beverly greeted Carl when he walked into the office at the restaurant.

"We need to talk," Carl said in a flat tone.

"Yes, we do." Beverly was scared to death.

Carl closed and locked the door to the office. It took all of Beverly's resolve not to scream. He grabbed her by the arm and pulled her to him. He stared into her eyes for a moment and then kissed her roughly on the lips. She never closed her eyes.

"I thought you wanted to talk, Carl."

"We can talk in a minute." He started biting her on the neck. "Take off your panties and bend over the desk."

Beverly stepped out of her G-string and watched as he pulled his pants down. His dick was rock hard from just staring at her. Beverly's pussy started to pulsate, anticipating Carl inside her.

He pushed her skirt up to her waist, and she laid her chest flat on the desk. She still had her heels on, and that was perfect. Carl pushed inside of her.

"*Damn, baby!*" she said as she bit her bottom lip. She looked over her shoulder, and they locked eyes as he beat the pussy up.

It didn't take long before she screamed, "*I'm cumming!*"

Carl looked down and saw that his dick was coated with her essence. The sight made him explode inside her. He could feel her pussy walls contracting with every stroke. He grunted and pumped a few more times before he pulled out. He was breathing like he ran a marathon.

Beverly pulled her skirt down and kicked off her heels. She went to the restroom and came back with a towel. She ushered Carl to the couch and pulled his pants all the way down to his ankles. As she cleaned him, she said, "You made me feel like a ho."

"How'd I do that?"

"You handled me too rough. You bent me over and – it just didn't feel right." A tear rolled down her face.

"I just wanted to touch you," he said truthfully. "I missed you so much."

"You act like you were locked up for a long time. It's only been three days."

"I thought about you and my mom the whole time. I felt helpless."

He stood up, and he and Beverly stared at each other.

"When the feds hit my house, there was four million in the closet of one of my bedrooms," he told her. "But they only confiscated–"

"I know what they took," Beverly said. "I read it in the paper. If you're asking me if I took it, the answer is no." She lied calmly.

"I didn't think you did, but I had to make sure. It's a dirty cop out there four million dollars richer, with ten bricks," Carl said looking off into space.

"What's a brick?" she asked.

He just looked at her and smiled. "Nothing you need to worry about, Bev."

"I need to tell you something," she said.

"What's that?"

"I won't be working at your restaurant any longer."

"Why? You found another job?"

"No, it's not that. There isn't a job out there that's as good as this one. But I'm moving back to Georgia."

"What?"

"Please don't be mad at me, baby," Beverly pleaded. "When the police came in here, they handcuffed all of the employees, like we were common criminals. I told you from the outset that I didn't want to have anything to do with drugs."

"Baby, let me explain."

"There's nothing to explain. One of the waitresses and one of the bartenders quit. The bartender said he was on parole, and he wasn't about to get caught up on a humbug."

Carl was speechless. Beverly could see that he was in turmoil, and so was she.

"You just gonna up and leave?" He was getting angrier by the second.

"Please don't make this harder than it already is. And don't think for a second that I don't love you. I love you with all my being." She stared into his eyes. "I'm not closing the door on this relationship. Men like you don't come along every day. I need to get my life together, and you need to straighten out this situation."

"It's gonna be hard for me to cope without you."

"Carl, you know you're stronger than that. You can still call me whenever you want, to keep me posted on everything."

"When this blows over, I'm coming to Georgia to get you," he said.

They embraced like it would be their last time seeing each other.

CHAPTER SEVENTEEN

"What's up jailbird?" Paul said as he invited his friend inside his home.

"I'm chilling. What's the word?" Carl asked as he stepped inside. He could smell something sweet in the air.

"The niggas on the streets are skittish," Paul said. "The feds have everybody leery. We still got our faithfuls, though."

"Who was that at the door, baby?" Charlene called from the kitchen.

"It's Carl."

Charlene walked into the den. She wore an apron that was dusty with baking powder. "Why did you have all that money in your house?" she asked with her hands on her hips.

"I don't know if it's cool to talk here," Carl said. "You know how those ho's are with those listening devices."

"I had the white boy Tim from Best Buy come and sweep the house," Paul said. "It's cool."

"I see you're on your stick," Carl said.

"Everybody was on their stick – except you, Mr. Airtight himself," interjected Charlene.

"You're right. But I need to fill y'all in on some more shit."

"I'm not sure I want to hear this," Paul said.

"I had way more than what they found at my house," Carl told them.

"How much more?" Charlene asked emphatically.

"Add four million to what they got and ten of them thangs."

"Get off the shit, nigga," Paul said angrily.

Carl just stared at his friend. There was no need to repeat himself.

"I thought you were smarter than that," Charlene said. "But after hearing this, I was sadly mistaken. You sat there and told us that someone was following you. Then you turn around and slap the shit out of that nigga – who just happened to be the law. And after all that, you leave that shit in your house? You're the silliest nigga I've ever met in my life!"

"Take your ass in the kitchen, Charlene," Paul told her. He didn't like for his wife to disrespect men, especially his friends.

"I'm not going anywhere, until I finish saying what I need to say!"

"Take your motherfucking ass in the kitchen! I'm not gonna tell you again!" he said through clenched teeth.

Charlene turned and walked to the kitchen.

It took Paul a moment to get his temper in check. "So where's the missing shit at?" He was so mad, he could barely get his thoughts together.

Carl hunched his shoulders.

"Did you ask your lil' girlfriend if she had it?" Charlene asked from the hallway.

"She said she didn't know anything about the money or the work," Carl said. "Bring your ass back in here, Charlene."

She came and sat next to him on the sofa.

"She left my house and went to work at the restaurant the day of the raid," Carl said. "She got handcuffed with everyone else at the restaurant."

"Bags full of money and dope don't just up and disappear," Paul said, eyeing Carl. "Somebody got the shit!"

"Do you think the feds are keeping an ace in the hole?" asked Charlene.

"The feds don't play like that," Paul said. "They would have put all their cards on the table and crucified Carl and probably me too."

"The only thing I can think of is a dirty cop," Carl said.

"Well," Charlene said to her husband, "it's time for you and Carl to end y'all's business partnership."

"This ain't the time for that!" Paul snapped.

"My sister ain't doing nothing else for you, Carl, so don't even ask her," Charlene said, ignoring her husband. "And you're wrong, Paul. This is the perfect time to part ways with Carl. You might not be counting your blessings, but I'm counting them for you. Carl's irresponsibility could have cost us big time."

"Let's not argue," Carl said, trying to calm everyone down. "I need y'all to stay level-headed. Charlene's right, Paul. I think we should split the businesses, at least on paper. It will look like you're disassociating with me because of my legal issues, and that's fine. You take Club Link, and I'll take Sweet Soul. I know the restaurant brings in more money, so I'll still let you draw a profit for whatever amount we agree on. As for the other properties, we can split those right down the middle.

"I'll get Ganne to draw up the papers and make sure the press gets word of us dissolving our partnership. In the meantime, I'm going to come up with a plan to turn Austin out this summer. We're gonna host concerts at both venues every week the entire summer. Are y'all down with that?"

"Let's go with it." Paul spoke for himself and his wife.

"You make me sick, Carl," Charlene said, but she had a smile plastered on her face.

"I love you too," he told her. "One more thing before I go: You have the best woman in Austin, Paul."

"Boy, get out of here! He already knows that," Charlene said.

They laughed. All was good once again.

••••••

"Hello, you've reached the Richards residence."

"Hey, Dad."

"Asha, is that you?" her father asked excitedly.

"The last time I checked, you only had one daughter," she said playfully.

"It's been awhile since I heard your voice, sweetheart," James sad. "You don't call and check up on your old man anymore, since you joined that damn FBI."

"Please, Dad. Don't start. Besides, I know your work keeps you pretty busy."

"I've never been too busy for my baby."

"I know, Dad."

"So what's going on? Or is this a casual call?"

"Maybe I just wanted to talk..."

"Or maybe you called to ask for something," her father said laughing.

"I need a favor, Dad."

James laughed harder. He could read his daughter like a book. "What is it, sweetheart?"

"Me and Gwen need to move in with you. I'm transferring back to the Georgia district."

"You know you don't have to ask to move back home. One day this will be your house anyway."

"There's more to tell, but I'll fill you in on everything when I get there."

"I guess I'll have to wait for that. When does your plane arrive?"

"I'm driving in."

"Do you still have your house key? You remember the alarm code?"

"Yes."

"Okay. I'll see you when you get here, sweetheart."

"Okay. I love you, dad."

"Love you too, Asha."

● ● ● ● ● ●

"What brings you to my office this morning, Agent Richards?" Deputy Alexander asked.

"I talked to the regional office about transferring back to Georgia. They said it wouldn't be a problem, but I'd have to get my supervisor to sign off on it," Asha said smiling.

Alexander sat back in his seat and glared at his young agent. He tried to compose himself before he spoke. "Why would you want to move back to Georgia, while we still have an on-going investigation on our hands? A probe doesn't end when Agent Richards says it ends."

"There's nothing else I can siphon out of Fredrick," Asha said calmly.

"Has your cover been blown?"

"No, but Fredrick is shutting everything down and shutting everyone out. He's not in a trusting mood now, which means he's unstable and capable of anything. I told him I was moving back home until he got his situation under control. I also told him that when the restaurant got raided, everyone was handcuffed like common criminals, and it scared me."

"I'm sure he was devastated to hear you're running out on him at the first sign of trouble. It's clear that he cares about you."

"He does care for me. But that's irrelevant. I'll be able to come back and testify, if needed. I'll still be in contact with him. If he confides in me and tells me anything that might bolster our case, I'll be sure to pass on the information."

"I don't agree with you transferring in the middle of an investigation, but I'll sign off on it." Deputy Alexander was without emotion. "Leave all of your contact information with Scottsdale on the way out."

"Thank you, sir."

He glared at her but didn't respond.

●●●●●●

"What in the hell were you doing with all that damn money in your house?" Jo Ann asked her son. She had been a nervous wreck since Carl's arrest. He was the only thing on earth that she truly loved.

"I don't feel like going through this again, Mama," he complained.

"Maybe if you would have brought your black ass over here two days ago when you were released, you wouldn't be tired of explaining it!" Jo Ann was hotter than a firecracker. "I should have been the *first* person you talked to when you got out."

"Calm down. Yelling at me won't get us anywhere. I had to pacify a lot of people who could've been hurt by my carelessness."

"Please don't tell me you're still involved with drugs." Jo Ann's heart was heavy, because she already knew the truth.

"I was, but I'm not anymore."

"I bet you're not," his mother said as she started to cry. "You have all these people in the community stepping up for you, putting their reputations on the line. And you're still out there in the streets fucking up!"

"I didn't come over here to argue."

"Why did you come over here, then?"

"I came to see you and let you see me, so you could see that I'm strong," Carl said, looking into eyes that were just like his.

"Boy, bring your ass over here and give me a hug! You're my only child. It would kill me to see you locked up. I can't function without you. You've been taking care of me since your father died."

"I'm not going anywhere," Carl promised as they embraced.

Jo Ann pushed her son away. She still had things she wanted to say to him. She wasn't letting him off the hook that easily.

"Are you willing to lose everything you have, chasing dirty money? You already have more money than you can spend. I know exactly what your problem is," she said. "You can't stand prosperity. You're never satisfied."

Carl sat down and rolled his eyes as he took his admonishment.

••••••

Paul walked into the office at the restaurant to find Carl sitting behind the desk.

"What you doing in the office this early?" Paul asked.

Since Beverly quit, Carl had to resume the bookkeeping duties.

"I'm trying to put some things together. When them white folks got in our business, that changed the whole complexion of the game. I don't know how long it will be before I go to court, but I need to make back some of the bread them hoes took."

"I feel ya. But how you gonna get it back with no work?" Paul wasn't about to touch any dope or even be around it. He was taking heed to his blessing.

Carl smiled. He wasn't mad at his friend for wanting to pull back. He wasn't about to touch any cocaine either.

"We're gonna do what we've been doing for years: Promoting concerts."

"We'll make some money," Paul said. "But that four million you're chasing is out the window."

"I don't know, Paul. You might wanna check out this list."

Carl handed him the papers he was working on. "The ones with the red check by their name have already been booked," he said smiling.

"Some of these concerts are on the same night," Paul said.

"The hip hop concerts will be at Club Link, and the R&B concerts will be at the Sweet Soul. This is the year Austin gets put on the map. I have houses going up on all of my vacant lots. I hired four new crews. Mr. Milton is going to oversee all of them."

"This is where we should have been focusing our energy in the first place," Paul said. "The dope game has been trash for years."

"I'm not gonna cry over spilled milk," Carl said. "What's done is done. Let's move forward."

Paul didn't reply to that. He decided to switch lanes. "If my math is right, you're gonna try to build over thirty houses. You'll be spreading yourself real thin. If something goes wrong, it could send you to the poor house."

Carl just smiled. He couldn't see how anything could go wrong, when it came to real estate. He was hands-on with all of his projects, and Mr. Milton was going to help him monitor the sites.

"How do you plan on financing the construction?"

Paul knew that Carl's reserves had to be low, maybe even empty.

"Home Depot is giving me a draft for all of the materials, and I'm taking a loan out on my house and the restaurant to cover the rest of the costs. And I'm selling half of my rental properties." Carl already thought it through, and his mind was made up.

"You lost your mind," Paul said. "Your whole decision making-process has been fucked up for the last couple of months."

Carl dropped his pen on the desk and stared at his friend. "I don't understand what you're upset about. You stand to lose nothing. You already signed the papers my lawyer drew up, splitting all of the properties."

"I signed the motherfucking papers, but those papers don't mean shit," Paul said. "I don't want to see my best friend lose everything the game has blessed us with, trying to chase money. We're young niggas. We got the rest of our lives to chase money."

"There's no need to talk about it anymore," Carl said. "It's a done deal. We're gonna split the money from the concerts sixty-forty, my way. I mean, if that's alright with you."

"I don't have a problem with the split," Paul said. "You've always put in more than I have."

Carl stepped around the desk and they hugged each other.

"I want to apologize for the way Charlene talked to you the other day," Paul said.

"She's only looking out for your best interests, Paul. There's no apology needed. Brothers and sisters have disagreements. Have you read the newspaper this morning? It's over there on the couch."

The new article wasn't very long. It indicated that business partners and life-long friends Carl Fredrick and Paul Atkins severed their business ties after Carl was arrested on multiple federal charges. The reporter said he tried to contact Fredrick and Atkins for a comment, but neither of them would give an explanation for the split.

"This nigga lying," Paul said as he read the article. "Ain't nobody tried to ask me about this shit."

"Me neither," Carl said. "Those hoes will do anything to push a story. I gotta get out of here. I'll get back with you later," he said as he headed for the door.

CHAPTER EIGHTEEN

"What's up, Carl?" asked a smiling Big Pat when Carl stepped out of his car.

"I'm tired," replied Carl. They dapped each other up.

"Let's fall up in Big Earls and get our eat on. I'm starving," Pat said.

They were greeted by a waitress as soon as they walked through the door. "What will you boys be having today?" The menu was plastered in big letters behind the counter.

"I'm not hungry, but I'll have two pieces of that peach cobbler and some vanilla ice cream," Carl said.

"And you, sir?"

"I want a plate of neckbones, cabbage, black-eyed peas and some hot water cornbread," Pat said. "And when I'm done eating, I want two servings of peach cobbler too."

"What would you like to drink?"

"Lemonade," Pat said.

Carl didn't want anything.

After the waitress left, Pat asked, "What's on your mind, Carl?"

"I wanted to see how you were holding up, since you got rolled."

"It's fucked up. Everywhere I go, niggas start acting funny, like a nigga snitching or something."

"You're not fucking with nothing, are you?" Carl asked suspiciously.

"Hell naw! These hoes already got me by the balls."

"Fuck what a nigga think then. You good. You've been fucking with some real nigga–"

"I'm on my way to the penitentiary, probably with a busload of time."

"I can't help that part. But I will make sure you're taken care of while you're gone. I got a house on 14th Street & McKinnley Heights. It's a small house and needs a lil' work. It's yours," Carl said. "Get the work done and get ya mama out the projects, nigga. Me and Paul are gonna give you fifty thousand apiece to put in a safety deposit box, so you'll have some money when you get out. The feds pay you to work, but we'll still hit you off when you need it."

"The only reason y'all are looking out is so I won't implicate you and Paul. I ain't no dummy."

Carl looked at the man like he was crazy. "That's exactly why we're looking out for you, because you kept it real, nigga. And since you're talking shit, you are a dummy. What in the world possessed you to fuck with Tracy McDonald? Everybody knows that nigga got popped."

"That nigga used to fuck with my sister. He has two kids by my cous–"

"That nigga don't give a damn about your sister, them kids or nobody else. He's trying to keep his ass out that penitentiary, at all costs!"

"I can see that now." Pat's voice lowered almost to a whisper. "Is that nigga locked up?"

"Naw, that bitch ain't locked up. He's on they payroll. He's out there trying to set somebody else up."

• • • • • •

"Damn, kinfolk, you sure have gotten fine," Raymond said. He was Asha's first cousin that lived in Corpus Christi.

"Boy, shut up," responded Asha. They shared a big hug.

"How long has it been, five, almost six years since we seen each other?" Ray asked.

"It's been awhile, and that's a damn shame," replied Asha. "I'm glad we stayed in touch when we were in college."

"You know I had to keep up with my lil' sister," Raymond said as he swept her off her feet in another big hug.

"Where's Gwen?" Asha asked when he let her go.

"She's in my bedroom asleep."

Asha walked into the bedroom and slapped Gwen on the ass. "Bitch, get up."

"How long have you been here?" Gwen asked, stretching her limbs.

"I just walked through the door."

"I haven't been able to find an apartment."

"That's cool. We're going home to stay with my dad anyway."

"You need to make up your mind," Gwen said. "I'm not riding all over the country with that shit in the trunk."

"She's right, Asha," Raymond interjected. "That ain't cool at all."

"Do you have the money to purchase the other nine kilos?" Asha asked Raymond.

"How much you want for them?"

"Give me $110,000, and they're yours."

"I'll have to patch up with a friend of mine."

"If you don't have six figures, you not a baller," Gwen said seductively.

"Don't pay her no mind, cousin," Asha said cutting her eyes at Gwen. "She has *zero* figures. Do you have a friend who can follow us to Macon? We don't need to be on that highway with all that money by ourselves."

"I don't know," Raymond said.

"You can do it yourself. I'll pay you ten thousand," Asha told him.

"You don't have to give me anymore money," he said. "It's time I get down to Georgia and see my people anyway. I just want you to take me and my homey to ATL and party with us. That will be payment enough."

"That's a deal," Asha said. "In the meantime, you need to try to get that money together while me and Gwen get some rest. I want to be on the road by seven in the morning."

"I can get that done in an hour or two."

"What about finding someone to ride with you?"

"I already got somebody in mind. After we buy that dope from you, we'll put it in storage until we get back."

"Now that we got that out of the way, I'm going to ask this one time," Asha said. "Do you trust this nigga? Because I know how to use this pistol, and I'm not taking no losses." She pulled a .45 automatic from her handbag.

"The nigga is official. He's the one who showed me how to hustle when I lost my job. We been getting it in ever since. That was over three years ago. Now put that heater up, before you hurt somebody."

Asha grabbed her overnight bag and headed for the shower.

••••••

"Let's get out of here. We need to be in position before the sun comes up."

"I'm just making sure my pistol is in working order."

"You been fucking with that pistol for the last four hours," said killer one. "If that gun doesn't work when it's time for us to take care of our business, I'm gonna bust you in the ass my gawd-damn self!"

They both laughed.

"Is the switch-out car in place?" asked killer one.

"You starting to piss me off, nigga," killer two said. "We done over fifty hits together. Has anything ever went wrong?"

"No, it hasn't. And that's the way I want to keep it. Now let's roll out."

Killer one was the shot caller of the two.

"This nigga sho' is paying a lot for this hit," killer two said.

"That's because we always work clean and don't run our mouth. We drop in a city, take care of our business, then disappear," killer one said.

"This is the first time I was paid all the money up front. We could just bail with the cash."

"Just like a no good nigga," killer one said. "Always trying to pull a fast one. Do you know who we're fucking with? If I pulled some shit like that, we'd be dead before the month was out. This nigga has graveyards across the nation."

They turned onto a tree-lined, residential street in a middle class neighborhood.

"We're here," killer one said. "I'ma go make the block one time, to make sure everything is cool."

"You see those old folks walking?" killer two asked.

"Yeah, I see them. That's good. Hopefully they can give the police a description of our car."

"Pull over. We'll walk to the house from here," killer two said.

"I'm gonna position myself behind those bushes on the side of the garage," killer one said. "After you make the alarm go off on that pretty Mercedes, position yourself on the other side of the house."

Killer two acknowledged the instructions without speaking. Seconds later the car alarm was blaring. A minute or so after that, a sleepy Tracy McDonald came out of the front door with a pistol in his hand, looking around.

"Bitch-ass cats, jumping on a nigga's shit," he said to himself. His pistol was relaxed at his side.

"Nah, homey. It's not a cat," said killer one as he stepped up behind Tracy.

"What the fuck?" Tracy was caught off guard. He tried to swing the pistol up, but killer one grabbed his wrist like a vice.

"We're more like thieves in the night," killer two said.

"Drop the pistol, before I smoke you," killer one said calmly.

Tracy complied.

"Look, man. I ain't tripping. Y'all caught me slipping. I got a hundred grand in the house. It's y'alls. Just don't hurt me or my family," Tracy begged.

"We don't want your money. We came here to rob you of your life," killer two said.

"It ain't gotta be like this!" Tracy was crying now.

"Shut up, snitch-ass nigga," killer two said as he shot Tracy in the face multiple times.

BLAK! BLAK!BLAK!BLAK!

Killer one dropped a kilo of cocaine that had a piece of paper taped to it. The note had the word "SNITCH" written on it.

Killer two dropped his pistol next to the dead body, and they jogged back to the awaiting get-away car. They drove right by the old couple that was out on their morning walk. The old folks eyed the car suspiciously, like killer one hoped they would. They drove ten blocks and switched to their personal car. They left the stolen car in the parking lot of a dentist office.

"Our work in Austin is done," said killer one.

"That was the easiest fifty grand I've ever made," said a smiling killer two.

• • • • • •

Scottsdale called his supervisor on his private line. "Sir, I think you'd better get down here to the office."

"This better be damn important, for you to be calling me at six-thirty in the morning," Deputy Alexander grunted.

"Tracy McDonald was murdered."

"Shit! I'll be there in thirty minutes."

Deputy Alexander walked through the doors at the bureau eighteen minutes later, and he was pissed. "Give it to me, Scottsdale."

"It was a professional hit. McDonald was shot four times in the face."

"Where'd it take place?"

"He was killed in his front yard. We talked to his wife. She said the car alarm went off, and he went out to see about it."

"He was ambushed," Deputy Alexander surmised, shaking his head.

"It gets worse, boss."

"Give it all to me, Scottsdale."

"The assailant left a kilo at the scene with the word '*SNITCH*' taped to it. We also found two pistols at the scene. Tracy's wife identified one of them as being his."

"The killer left the murder weapon," Alexander said. He was barely audible.

"That's what it looks like, sir."

"I take it we don't have any witnesses, since it happened so early in the morning," Alexander said.

"Actually we have two witnesses."

"I'm listening..."

"An elderly couple was out taking a walk when they saw a late model sedan pass them by. They didn't pay much attention to it at first. But a few minutes later they heard gunshots and the same car came flying back by them."

"Have we put out an APB–"

Scottsdale interrupted his boss. "We found the getaway car about a mile away in a parking lot."

“They had a backup car,” Alexander said. “We’ll probably never catch the killers. *Fuck*!” he screamed as he knocked over the coffee machine.

“Do you want us to bring Patrick Lewis in for questioning?”

“He’s too scared and dumb to pull off something like this, Scottsdale. Carl Fredrick orchestrated this murder.” Alexander sat on the edge of his desk rubbing his temples. “Don’t let the media bounce all over this.”

“Too late. McDonald’s wife had already spoken to a reporter by the time we got there.”

“So much for damage control. Our other informants are going to be reluctant to cooperate now. I’m going home. Get a hold of Agent Richards. I need to talk to her. I don’t give a fuck if she’s in China!” Deputy Alexander said as he stormed out of the office.

CHAPTER NINETEEN

Blocker Unit
Maximum Security Prison

"Look at you! You done came to prison and got some muscles," Carl said to his cousin Ghetto.

"You looking good yourself."

"What's up, Carl!" said one of the guys who was waiting on the Greyhound bus to take them home.

"I'm chilling, lil' homey. All you niggas going to Austin?" Carl asked.

"Yeah," replied the group. They had just been released from prison, Ghetto included.

"All you niggas can't fit in my car, but I'll tell you what, meet me over there at those cab vans," Carl said. "How much are y'all gonna charge to take these fellas to Austin?" he asked one of the drivers.

"We charge $25 a head," answered one of the cabbies.

"It's ten of them," Carl said. "Five in each cab." He gave each of the men a hundred dollar bill. "Use some of that extra money to stop and get something to eat. I know they feed y'all like shit in that bitch-ass prison."

"You sho' right!" the group answered.

"Look out, lil' homey," Carl said to the man who spoke to him first. "You Mee-Mee's lil' brother, ain't you?"

"Yeah. I didn't think you knew who I was."

Carl gave him another two hundred dollars. "I'll see you boys in Austin." He and Ghetto walked to his car.

"I been reading all this bullshit they been writing about you in the paper," Ghetto said. "What's up with it?"

"They ran up in my shit and found four hundred grand."

"That ain't shit. With all the businesses you got, I know you can account for that."

"My lawyer is trying to work that shit out right now. The feds have a hard-on for me, though."

"What are you and Paul tripping on? The papers say y'all split up your businesses. You been knowing each other too long for some punk shit like this to break y'all up."

"Me and Paul are still tight. We split the businesses to keep him out of harm's way."

"That's some real shit."

"Yeah, but enough about me. I hope you ain't been down here in the pen getting fucked!" Carl joked.

"You got Ghetto fucked up! I been down here repping that ATX to the fullest!" boasted Ghetto.

Carl looked over at him and smiled. "I know you a real nigga. That's why I fuck with you. It's a whole different ballgame now, though. You gonna have to represent Austin on a national level. After this summer, everybody's gonna have Austin dripping off their tongues," he bragged.

"I'm feeling that. What role am I gonna play in all this?" Ghetto was serious.

"I need a restaurant manager at the Sweet Soul. My girlfriend quit on me. I'll start you off at $25 an hour."

"*Twenty-five dollars an hour*?! I ain't never made that type of bread on no job before!" Ghetto was crunk. Fresh out of prison with a legit come-up.

"Elevators, baby," Carl said. "If they ain't going up, we ain't riding! And I want you to host all the rap concerts at Club Link. Can you handle all these responsibilities right out of prison?"

"Something's telling me I don't have a choice."

"You must be a mind reader, 'cause you're going in." Carl had the utmost confidence in his cousin. "Your dress code has to be on point. Gators, dress slacks and dress shirts. That's at both venues. A lot of these niggas come from cities faster than Austin. At least they *think* they're faster than Austin. We have to show these niggas how to hold. We have to demand respect. When they leave Austin after the concert, they gonna tell everybody that them niggas down there are live! Are you with me?" Carl asked. He wanted to make sure Ghetto was keeping up.

"I'm soaking it up," Ghetto replied.

"You better have one helluva sponge," Carl said, "because you start tonight."

"Tonight?" Ghetto didn't know if he could handle it so soon. "Is it a concert?"

"Luda and Lil John," Carl said, bobbing his head up and down. "Don't worry about clothes. We wear the same size. You can go to the mall tomorrow and do some shopping."

"I don't know what to say, kinfolk." Ghetto was in a daze. "This shit is way too real."

"Just handle up. And this last shit that I'm fixing to tell you, I'm only gonna tell you one time: Ain't no dope selling *whatsoever*. If you jump back in the game, I'm cutting you off."

"That chapter of my life is sealed. We going to the roof!" Ghetto had tears in his eyes.

••••••

Macon, Georgia

"Dad, that food sure smells good," Asha said as she stepped up and gave her father a hug and a kiss. "What's the occasion?"

"I haven't seen my daughter in over a year. That's reason enough," James said.

"I made it in about eleven o'clock last night and waited for you till twelve," Asha said. "Where were you?"

James smiled at his daughter's attempted invasion. He tended to the food he was cooking for a few moments before turning to her. When he did, she was sipping on a glass of orange juice, waiting for an answer.

"The last time I checked, I was a grown man," he said smiling. "Besides, *I'm* the father. I ask all the questions."

"Okay, Mr. Secretive."

They both laughed.

"I'm dating someone, Asha."

"Yeah? Who is she? And why haven't I met her?"

"I didn't feel like the time was right. I wanted to make sure both of us were comfortable and it was a relationship, instead of telling you I was just seeing someone."

"You're telling me about her, so that means it's serious."

"Her name is Dianne, and our relationship is blossoming beautifully." Asha's father was glowing. "That's not going to be a problem with you, is it sweetheart?"

"Why would it be a problem? You're my father. I want to see you happy. You're too young and handsome to be alone."

"Thank you, baby. I needed to hear that." James kissed his daughter on the forehead. "Now I believe there's some things you need to tell me. Out of the blue you just move back home and bring Gwendolyn with you..."

"My situation is a little more complicated than yours, Dad. I think you need to brace yourself."

"You haven't gotten into any trouble, have you?" James asked nervously.

"No. Just listen. We were doing a federal probe into this local, black businessman for conspiring to sell drugs and other things. His name is Carl Fredrick, and he's been under federal investigation before. The first investigation was suspended due to lack of evidence. We busted a guy a couple of months ago, and Carl's name came up again.

"The informant said Carl was purchasing large amounts of cocaine every month. With that news, my supervisor decided to open another probe into his illegal activities. Just for the record, Dad, I wasn't involved in the first probe."

"Okay..." James said, waiting for her to get to the point.

"Because of the information the agency obtained the first time," Asha continued, "they knew it would be virtually impossible to infiltrate his organization with a snitch. He has a bullet-proof circle around him, and he'll never make a transaction or even set up a deal personally."

"He seems like a smart man to me," James said. "Now let me guess. That's where you come in."

"Exactly. It wasn't hard at all for me to get acquainted with him," smiled Asha. "We went out on a couple of dates. He gave me a grand tour of Austin. He even gave me a job at his restaurant. Carl fell head-over-heels in love with me, Dad."

"Let me ask you this: How do you feel about him, sweetheart?"

Asha walked to the kitchen window and looked out at their small backyard. Tears started to stream down her face. She turned back to her father and said, "I'm deeply in love with him. I may have jeopardized my whole career for him." She was bawling now.

James stood to hug her. "Calm down, and finish telling me what happened"

"A number of things happened," Asha said. "My supervisor started pressing me for information, because I was going out with him and spending a lot of time at his home. I told my supervisor that I found a large sum of money at his house. I told them about the money to appease them, to get them off my back. But the confusion started to set in. My emotions were running wild. I knew Carl was in the drug trade. But his good deeds outweighed his bad ones."

"You put your life in danger, while you were straddling the fence," James said. "Not just yours, but your fellow agents." He was still fairly calm.

"I realize that. Can I finish, before you pull out your belt?" Asha joked.

She and her father hugged again.

"One of the agents doing surveillance got a little too close," she said, "and Carl noticed him. He confronted the agent at a diner near his house. It turned into a heated argument, and Carl slapped him."

Asha told her father everything. She had to because she gave Carl their home number, and James would probably be the one to answer if someone called.

"My supervisors felt the investigation was slipping away," she said, "so they organized a raid on Carl and his best friend's home, their club and the restaurant. They took a shot in the dark, to see if they could come up with something.

"But an hour before the raid, I loaded four duffle bags full of drugs and money into my car. I purposefully left behind a bag of money that contained four hundred thousand dollars. Carl was arrested and charged with organized crime and assault on a federal agent. Come on, Dad. Let's go out to the garage."

Asha showed her father the money in the trunk of her car.

"How much is it, Asha?" James was shocked.

"Four million."

"*Four million dollars*?! Have you lost your damn mind? You know he's going to try to track down that money."

"When he got out on bond, he asked me if I took it. I told him no."

"So I take it he still doesn't know you're a federal agent."

"No, he doesn't."

"What excuse did you give him for leaving town?"

"I told him I didn't want to be involved with the lifestyle he was living. I told him that when he got his shit together, I'd be waiting for him."

"Four million dollars, and his drugs are missing. Then you just up and leave town. He's going to put two and two together, and all fingers are going to be pointing at you. I wouldn't be surprised if he's in the living room right now waiting to kill us both."

James walked out of the garage and went to the kitchen table and sat down.

"I know he's happy that someone took it," Asha said. "If I wouldn't have, he would have gotten a life sentence in federal prison."

James stared at his daughter. It was clear that she didn't understand her logic was screwed up.

"It's a good thing you didn't get pulled over with all that stuff in the trunk. Then *your* dumb ass would've been the one in federal prison for life."

●●●●●●

Houston, Texas

"What's up, boy?" Rome said. "I haven't seen or heard from you since you got ran in on two weeks ago."

"I been throwing myself into my work," Carl said. "I lost four, almost five million dollars. I won't be able to make it all back, but I'll get some of it back with what I got planned." Carl was pretty upbeat, for someone in his situation.

"You been in the game too long to let something like that roll off your tongue," Rome said. "When gangstas lose something, they don't try to chase it down. They charge it to the game. On to the next one. The only way you'll get that money back is if the feds return it. And we know that's not gonna happen." He watched his friend. "I talked to Paul. He told me you're selling some of your rental properties and trying to build twenty houses at a time."

"Something like that," replied a smiling Carl.

"Those rent houses are bringing in *for sure* money," exclaimed Rome. "Let's just say they bring in five hundred a month. Nigga, that's damn near two million a year."

"Since everybody wants to count my money, take 33 and multiply it by ninety thousand. Then add the other 17 houses that I'm building on vacant properties, and let me know what you come up with," Carl said angrily.

"Is that what you think this is all about, having a certain dollar amount, my nigga? The game is about leaving a legacy," Rome said. "It seems to me that you're trying to fuck it off."

"I'm not fucking off anything. I'm just looking into other business ventures. The shit I'm getting into, I'll be able to spend other people's money. *OPM*, nigga. Can you feel me on that?"

"Not really, because I don't know what it is you're getting into," Rome said. "I just hope you're making the right decision. The reason I asked you to come to H Town is because I need to talk to you about some serious shit that can't be talked about on the phone."

"I figured that much already. What's up?" Carl asked.

"You're not drawing any heat from the feds for that hit I put on that snitch-nigga, are you?"

"I know I'm probably a suspect, but I haven't been approached by anyone."

"That's good to hear. It had to be done. You know how we do it. If you're not rolling with us, you get rolled on."

"For sho'."

"I also wanted to talk to you about that missing money," Rome said.

"What about it?"

"Where's it at?"

"Nigga, I don't know where the motherfucking money is," Carl snapped.

"You know exactly where the money is," Rome said. "That bitch you fucking with got that bread. I know damn well you ain't gonna sit there and let a piece of pussy blind you like that. That bitch Beverly is either a thief or she a fed."

Carl sat there without saying anything. He had come to the same conclusion himself. He just didn't want to believe it. Now he wanted to kick himself in the ass. He never let anyone, especially a female, get next to him like this.

Rome walked over to him and patted him on the shoulder, trying to bring him out of his funk. "It may not be as bad as it seems, big homey. Obviously she has feelings for you, because if she didn't, those white folks would have buried your black ass. But I think she's a fed."

Rome walked to the bar to make drinks for both of them.

"I don't know if she is or not," Carl said. "But I'll handle her personally." He didn't want Rome to send killers after her.

"She's all yours." Rome smiled. He knew what Carl was thinking. "Now that we've taken care of our business, let me pull this Benz out the garage and hit these Houston streets and show these niggas how to come down!"

He punched Carl in the chest a few times.

CHAPTER TWENTY

U.S. District Court
Monday 08:00

"All rise for the honorable Judge Jon Hanson," announced the court bailiff.

"Your Honor, this court brings before you the United States versus Patrick Lewis on the charge of delivery of a controlled substance," said the district attorney Judith Hammer.

"Is the defense going to trial, or are they going to accept the plea offered by the DA's office?" asked the judge.

"Your Honor, the defense will reject the offer proposed by Ms. Hammer and enter a non-negotiable plea with the court," said Big Pat's defense attorney.

"Well, Mr. Lewis, I read the PSI on you before entering the courtroom this morning," the judge said. "Considering your lengthy criminal record and the amount of drugs you possessed, I felt the plea offered to you was more than reasonable. So instead of giving you 140 months, I'll lengthen the sentence to 200 months."

"Come on, Your Honor. Don't get vindictive because I advised my client to enter a non-negotiable plea," pleaded the defense attorney.

"Mr. Wilson, Mr. Lewis seems to be a pretty intelligent young man," the judge said. "I'm not punishing him for any mistake you made. I'm punishing him because he chose to be a career criminal. One more thing, Mr. Wilson: If you ever come into my courtroom and accuse me of being vindictive, I'll hold you in contempt. Are we clear on that?"

"Yes, Your Honor." The defense attorney walked out of the courtroom and went to console Pat's stunned family.

••••••

"Hey Carl!" Donna was happy to see him. She hugged him and invited him into her home.

"Is everyone here already?" Carl asked.

"They're in the den eating, watching a basketball game," Donna said as she escorted him to the den.

"Well look who just walked in," Charlene said mockingly. "If it ain't Mr. Austin Texas himself!"

Carl exchanged pleasantries with everyone. Lil Chris, Paul, Ghetto and Fast Black were there.

"I see those white folks got you scared!" said the always crunk Fast Black. "Look at you, losing weight and shit! You ain't been on the streets since that shit happened. How in the hell you gonna let somebody bar you from the streets you grew up in?"

"I'm not scared, and I haven't been barred from anywhere," Carl said as he and Fast Black had a stare down. "The feds are in my business, and I'm just trying to tie down some loose ends. That way I won't bring the heat on nobody."

"Y'all need to chill," said a worried Donna. "I'm not gonna have y'all in here tearing up my shit."

"Girl, they not gon' fight," Charlene said. "That's how these two dummies greet each other. You'll get used to these clowns."

"Nah, he ain't mad," Fast Black said cheesing. "If ol' Carl Fredrick gets mad, we'll put those boxing gloves on. He don't wanna see me in them gloves!"

"I didn't come over here to watch a basketball game," Carl said. "And I sure didn't come over to beat you up, Fast Black."

"Well state ya claim, gangsta!" Black said.

"Austin is officially on the map, because of all the concerts me and Paul are promoting. Now I want to put the icing on the cake," Carl said. He had everyone's attention.

"What you done schemed up on this time, Carl?" Charlene asked.

He laughed. "This is not a scheme. This is gonna be the biggest black event this city has ever seen."

Black rolled his eyes. "Man, get to the point."

"If you let me finish, I'll tell you, bitch-ass nigga." Carl had to exert his leadership on Fast Black. "We're gonna host Austin's first annual *Player's Ball.* I've already contacted everybody who's anybody. J Prince, Scarface, Jigga, Snoop, Erykah Badu and a bunch of other cats. This shit's gonna be big. I'm talking a red carpet event. Cedric the Entertainer has already agreed to host it for me."

Everyone at Donna's house was stunned silent. When they all thought Carl was fading, he popped up with a high-wire event.

"We're gonna have the *Player's Picnic* and everything," he said, "just like they had it in *The Mack.* Except we're gonna have players and gangstas from all over the nation." He was animated now.

"Carl, you one of the baddest niggas I've ever had the opportunity to meet," Paul said as the two embraced.

That compliment meant more to Carl than any other. Paul was there from the beginning, and they had been bumping heads for the past couple of months.

"Let all the niggas on the streets know they're invited," Carl said. "It's a thousand dollars a ticket. They better have their fake business cards ready, so they can do some networking," he joked.

Everyone laughed.

"Where's all this shit gonna take place?" asked Ghetto.

"The picnic will be at my house in Manor," Carl said. "And the ball will be at Club Link, since it's located on 6th Street. Make sure to tell all the women to wear their two-piece bathing suits. If they can't get in a two-piece, they ain't invited."

"You ain't got no swimming pool at your house," said Fast Black.

"Just tell them to wear their bathing suits."

"When is it going to take place?" asked Charlene.

"July 30th and 31st," Carl said. "Are there any more questions?"

Nobody spoke.

"Now that we're done with that, do you think you could bring me a plate of that fried fish, Donna?"

"Watch how you handle my lady," said a smiling Lil Chris.

"I didn't think you could talk anymore," Carl said. "You haven't said a word since I been here."

"I can't learn nothing talking," Chris said.

He and Carl embraced.

• • • • • •

Federal Building
Monday 08:00

"What has the investigation turned up, Scottsdale?" Deputy Alexander asked.

"Nothing much, sir."

"Fredrick and Atkins have shut down operations?"

"No drug activity," Scottsdale said. "They don't even go to their little club on 12th Street anymore. They go to work and then go home."

"All these hours and manpower for nothing," Alexander grumbled. "We missed our shot, Scottsdale."

"We might stumble upon something, sir. He might get convicted on the pending charges."

"Are you crazy? Fredrick is building an impenetrable wall around himself as we speak. I drove through East Austin the other day. Fredrick has houses being built everywhere, and he's letting everyone know they're his houses. Do you really think a federal judge is going to convict that boy? If so, he'll only get a slap on the wrist. Fredrick has support coming from strong voices in the community. If we would've caught him with his hand in the cookie jar, he wouldn't have a leg to stand on." Deputy Alexander looked exhausted.

"Fredrick just asked for permission to fly to Detroit," Scottsdale said, "so he can attend a Lakers/Pistons game. And the judge granted the request. Fredrick's going to game five."

"Why wouldn't he? He hasn't been convicted of anything."

"Do you want surveillance to follow him to Detroit?"

"Are you crazy or just not listening?" Alexander asked. "He isn't going to step outside the line again! I'm not gonna let an agent go watch the NBA Finals at the bureau's expense. I'm filing paperwork to bring closure to the investigation. Get in touch with Agent Richards, and let her know the investigation has been suspended. But I expect her to be available to testify at the trial."

"Done," Scottsdale said before leaving the office.

• • • • • •

"Hello. You've reached the Joyner residence," Asha's father said as he answered the phone.

"May I speak with Beverly?" Carl asked.

"She's not in at the moment. Can I take your name and number and have her get back with you?"

"Yes. My name is Carl. I'm a friend of hers. I'm calling from Texas. She knows how to reach me."

"Just a friend, huh? The way my daughter has been carrying on about you, I'd say you two being friends is an understatement."

"It's nice to know that Beverly has mentioned me to her father."

"Son, all that me and Beverly have is each other. We share everything. She's also told me that you're engulfed in a legal battle of some sort."

Carl had to laugh at that. He couldn't believe Beverly told her father so much personal information about him. "She didn't miss a beat, did she? Yes, federal authorities were led to believe I was into drug trafficking and some other illegal endeavors."

"Well, I hope you pull through this unscathed, son."

"Thank you."

"Look what the cat just drug in. My beautiful daughter!"

"Who's on the phone, Dad?" Asha asked in the background.

"I'm talking to your boyfriend, Carl. It was nice talking to you, Mr. Fredrick."

"It was a pleasure meeting you."

Asha's father handed her the phone.

"Hey, baby!" said an excited Beverly.

"How have you been?" Carl asked. He was happy to hear her voice. "And what have you been doing since leaving Austin?"

"I'm doing fine. I've been talking with my dad and catching up with old friends since I've been home."

"I know you've been talking to your dad," he said sarcastically.

"Why do you say that?"

"He just let me know that he knows all my business. I'm not tripping, though. I am who I am."

"I love who Carl Fredrick is. If you want me to come back to Austin, I will."

"Spend some time with your family. Everything is flowing smooth around here. My lawyer has built a support base for the money. The only thing that might stick is the assault."

"That's good to hear, baby. What else is going on? Have you found another woman?"

Carl laughed. "Another woman? Hell, I can't even keep up with the one I got!"

They both laughed.

"Besides," he said, "I don't have time. I'm working fulltime on my building projects."

"That's good. I don't like sharing."

Carl laughed this time. "The reason I called was because I have two tickets for the NBA Finals, game five, the Lakes versus the Pistons."

"I know who's playing in the NBA Finals, Carl!"

"Excuse me! Would you like to join me?"

"Of course I want to go."

"That's great. Catch an afternoon flight to Detroit in two days, June 15th. Then catch a cab to the downtown Hilton. I've already reserved a suite for us. If I'm not there, a key will be waiting for you at the front desk."

"I'll be there."

"I'll see you in two days," Carl said before hanging up.

Asha stared at the phone for a second. When she turned around, her father was standing there. "Well, what do you think of him, Dad?" She was smiling from ear to ear.

"I only talked to him on the phone for a few minutes. He seems like a pretty upfront person, though."

"He's very upfront."

"He seems to have your heart, and that's all that matters to me."

"Thank you, Daddy. I love you." Asha and her father embraced.

"I love you too, sweetheart."

"That's good to hear, because I have one more thing to tell you."

"What's that, Asha?"

"I'm pregnant!"

CHAPTER TWENTY-ONE

Detroit, Michigan

"Hello. How can I help you?" asked the hotel clerk.

"My name is Beverly Joyner. I'm supposed to pick up a room key that was left for me by Carl Fredrick."

"Yes. I do have a key for you."

"Thank you. Is Carl here?"

"No, he left about an hour ago."

"That's great," Beverly said. "It will give me time to freshen up. I haven't seen him in almost three weeks."

"What are you waiting for, girlfriend?" the noticeably gay clerk asked. "Gon' up to your room and jump in that Jacuzzi!"

"Could you do me a favor, please?" asked Beverly.

"Sure. What do you need?"

"When Carl comes in, don't tell him I'm here. I want to surprise him."

"You got it."

"Thank you." Beverly turned and headed for the elevators.

When she opened the door to the room, she was astonished by what she saw. There were bags of women's clothing everywhere. Chanel, Lagerfeld, Donna Karan, Gucci. If it was designer, it was in the room. When she thought her admiration for Carl was at an all-time high, he always did something to make it soar higher. Sometimes Beverly wondered if the charm would go away once he got her where he wanted her.

In the meantime she was willing to take that chance. She was so gone and in love with her educated gangsta.

She sat on the edge of the bed, and her mind went somewhere else.

This baby is constantly growing inside me. I've picked up eight to ten pounds in the first couple of weeks of pregnancy. What if he notices? I guess I'll have to tell him at that point. Let me hop in the shower and pamper myself before he gets back.

The room was a suite, with the bedroom and living area separated. When she opened the door to the bedroom, she was in for another surprise.

"I can't believe this!" she screamed, putting her hands to her mouth. *Rose petals? He's going all out for me. Damn. I don't deserve all of this. Too much deception.*

She walked to the bed and picked up and smelled a handful of rose petals. "I love you Carl Fredrick," she said before entering the bathroom. Her emotions spilled over again when she walked inside. There was a large bouquet of white, short stemmed roses with a large card that read:

"For a very special lady that I've only known for a short time. A woman that has captivated my every interest. These last three weeks without you have been the longest of my life. I can't wait to embrace you. I'll be there soon. Love, Carl."

"I love you too, Carl." Tears were streaming down her face. She'd never been happier in her life.

Beverly set the Jacuzzi temperature as hot as she could stand it and put in a little bubble bath. She stepped out of her clothes and got in. All of the surprises and excitement had really drained her. She dozed off to sleep almost immediately with thoughts of spending the rest of her life with the father of her child.

• • • • • •

"Look out, Cassius. Has my lady friend arrived yet?" Carl asked the hotel clerk.

"Yes, she's here. She made it in about forty-five minutes ago. Sister-girl has it going on, too!" added a smiling Cassius. "When you go up, act like you're surprised. She asked me to tell you she hasn't arrived yet."

"I gotcha," Carl said as he headed for the elevators.

When he entered the suite, he smiled. Clothes were scattered everywhere. He knew Beverly had been enjoying herself as she tried on the clothes he bought her. He walked into the bedroom and then into the bathroom and found her asleep in the Jacuzzi. His heart quickened at the sight of her. It was like he had never seen her naked before.

He picked up a sponge and started to sponge her breasts. A low moan escaped Beverly's lips, and he began to sponge her whole body. She opened her eyes and reached up and pulled him close to her. She kissed him deeply, until both of them were out of breath.

"You act like you haven't seen me in months," Carl said.

"It seems like years. Now are you just going to stand there or take off your clothes and join me?"

Carl stripped down to his birthday suit and joined his woman in the Jacuzzi. "We need more hot water," he said as he turned the jets back on.

"I missed you."

"I know," he boasted.

Beverly pinched him on the leg. "You're always so sure of yourself."

"Don't you want a confident man?"

"Of course I do. But you take everything for granted."

Carl was silent for a moment before speaking again. "When you told me you were leaving Austin, I was devastated. And you're right, at that point I had taken our relationship for granted."

"I'm sorry, Carl."

"There's nothing to be sorry about. I needed to be taken down a notch. I know that I wasn't about to lose you. I've never felt for anyone the way I feel for you."

Beverly turned and began kissing him. He pushed her up, so they could get out of the Jacuzzi. Once they toweled off, they headed for the bed of roses. They made love slowly, like they were trying to find each other again. Their hands interlocked, and they climaxed at the same time. But they didn't stop. They made love for the next two hours.

• • • • • •

Later they got dressed for the basketball game. Beverly chose to wear a pair of blue jeans that laced up in the front and sat low on her hips. She was going to wear a short skirt, but Carl told her they had floor seats, and she decided against it. She didn't want the cameramen putting her goodies on national television. She wore a peach, loose-fitting blouse that exposed the outline of her breasts. She also had on peach-colored heels that matched her blouse. She wore no makeup, just lip gloss that illuminated her smooth, chocolate skin.

Carl was immaculate too. Gucci from head to toe. He had his dress shirt open slightly, exposing his undershirt. The undershirt matched his cream colored loafers.

"You look like a movie star!" he said to Beverly. He embraced her from behind, kissing her softly on the neck.

"Thanks to my fashion designer boyfriend."

"I can't accept all the credit, baby. All I did was go in the stores and give the attendants your dimensions, and they bombarded me with clothes."

He reached into his front pocket and came out with a velvet jewelry box. He handed it to her.

"What's in the box?" Beverly asked, now having trouble breathing.

"You'll never know if you don't open it," he said as he kissed her on the neck again.

She opened the jewelry box and turned to Carl and kissed him. "These earrings are beautiful! I love you!"

"Put them on, so we can head to the game." He wiped tears from her eyes and kissed her softly on the lips.

When they made it down to the lobby, Cassius spotted them.

"Girlfriend, you look absolutely beautiful!"

"Would you mind taking a picture of us?" Carl asked, handing him his cellphone.

"I wouldn't mind at all! Y'all are going to be turning heads all over Detroit tonight!" Cassius was smiling and taking pictures at the same time.

They left the hotel and headed for a waiting limo.

"You're really going all out," Beverly said as they stepped to their ride.

"It's the NBA Finals, and it's Motown. Plus every time I step out of town, I'm going to show niggas how we do it Texas style."

Carl looked very handsome and confident.

•••••

They had a wonderful time at the game. Carl learned a lot about his woman. Beverly was a true basketball fan. She rooted for Kobe and the Lakers. She was sociable and beautiful. She was very intelligent. She was the kind of woman Carl had been looking for, for so many years – not so much for their compatibility, but because of her independence, intellect and her willingness to be flexible in her style of life. Beverly had all of those intangibles.

"You've been pretty quiet tonight, Carl." Beverly was glowing from her night out on the town with her beau.

"I'm just enjoying the time with you."

She looked at him and asked, "Do you think you could work your magic and get Kobe to take a picture with us after the game?"

"I don't know. The Lakers are getting their asses spanked. He might not be up to it, but I'll try."

"Okay, baby." Beverly squeezed his hand.

Carl waved to get the attention of one of the bodyguards behind the Lakers' bench. He walked to where Carl and Beverly were seated and asked, "How can I help you?"

Carl almost laughed. The 350 pound black man talked like a white boy.

"Me and my fiancé flew in from Texas to support the Lakers. She begged me to ask if Kobe would take a picture with us after the game."

Carl reached to shake the man's hand. He transferred five one hundred dollar bills so smoothly, Beverly didn't even notice.

"I'll ask."

The bodyguard walked over to the bench and whispered into Kobe's ear. Kobe and the bodyguard turned to look at Carl and Beverly. She was waving, with a big smile on her face. Kobe gave them a thumbs up, with a bright smile of his own.

"You did it again, baby!" said an excited Beverly.

Carl felt good watching Beverly enjoy herself. The final seconds ticked off the clock, and it was total mayhem inside the Palace of Auburn Hills. Kobe approached them on the side of the court, and the bodyguard took Carl's phone and started snapping pictures.

"Thank you, Kobe," Beverly said.

"It's my pleasure to do it for true Lakers fans," replied Kobe.

He and Carl shook hands and embraced.

"I have a big event going down in Austin at the end of the month," Carl told him. "Everybody who's anybody is gonna be there. We'd love to have you, if you can make it." He slipped him one of his business cards.

"I'll check it out," Kobe said before he walked off.

"Let's get out of here," Carl said to Beverly. "I have VIP reservations at Club Nipsy's, or would you rather go to a restaurant a friend of mine referred me to?"

"I'd rather go to the restaurant, so I can have you all to myself," Beverly said seductively.

As they rode in the limo, en route to Landry's, they barely said anything to each other, although Beverly was curled up in Carl's tight embrace. They were both wrapped up in their own personal thoughts. Beverly was wondering how their relationship would turn out when the feds made her testify against Carl in court.

He was thinking about Beverly's behavior. She didn't seem like herself, but he couldn't put his finger on it. Before long the limo driver announced they had reached their destination.

They entered the restaurant and were seated according to their reservation.

"What's wrong, Bev? You seem to be somewhere else." Carl was worried.

"I'm right here with you. I'm emotionally drained. This is a day that I'll never forget." She looked into his dark eyes with the deepest admiration.

"I've enjoyed myself too. It felt good to get away from Austin. I felt like the city was starting to strangle me."

"What's your lawyer saying, baby?"

"He promised I wouldn't see any jail time."

"That's great news!"

"Yeah. But I don't want to spoil our evening talking about my legal trouble. Let's order something to drink, while we look over the menu."

"That sounds like an excellent idea. Nothing too expensive, though."

"How about Chablis?"

"I don't want to drink tonight, but you can get a glass for yourself."

That comment added to the weird vibes he was getting from Beverly. Since when did she not like to drink?

They engaged in small talk and shared little kisses while they waited for their dinner to be served. They were really into each other. The waiter walked up with a serving tray. It had a sterling silver lid on it. They both agreed on something light because of the late hour. The waiter lifted the lid, and Beverly was in for the shock of her life. She was expecting sautéed marlin. Instead it was a diamond ring with a platinum band. She'd never seen a diamond so big. She was speechless, with her hands cupped over her mouth.

"Beverly, will you marry–"

She cut Carl off in mid sentence and said, "Don't do this."

"Beverly, I–"

"Please, don't."

She saw that he was determined. She felt like she had no alternative. She got up and dashed out of the restaurant, crying the whole time. The waiter was just as surprised as Carl was. So were the other patrons that witnessed the proposal.

Carl stared after her in shock. All he could do was rub his hands over his face in bewilderment. After a few minutes, he got up and walked to the entrance. He asked the valet if he had seen his date.

"Yes, sir. She got into a cab."

Carl went back inside the restaurant to pay his bill, but the owner wouldn't accept it.

"This evening is on the house. You have my deepest sympathies, Mr. Fredrick."

Carl had the limo take him back to the hotel, to see if Beverly had gone there. He knew in his heart that she hadn't, and he was right. There was no sign of her. He took his time gathering his things, and then he checked out of the room.

CHAPTER TWENTY-TWO

Paul, Charlene, Ghetto and a lady friend of his were enjoying a night out on the town. They were chilling at Baby A's Bar & Grill. They were all drinking and shooting the shit. Charlene spotted someone who was watching them.

"Baby, don't turn around, but I think I see Tracy McDonald's brother, and he's staring over here," she told Paul.

"Kevin?" Paul asked.

"Yeah. I think that's his name. The one with the purple Escalade."

"That's his motherfucking ass."

"I saw that Escalade when we were leaving Sweet Soul earlier," Ghetto said. "It was parked at the gas station across the street."

"That's not a coincidence," Charlene said with distress in her voice. "Him being parked across the street from our restaurant and now showing up at Baby A's..."

"Calm down, baby," Paul said as he stood up and locked eyes with Kevin, the brother of the deceased federal informant. "Let me go see what this ho-ass nigga got on his mind."

Kevin smiled and walked out of the bar. He got in his truck and left.

"That bitch-ass nigga left," Paul said as he returned to the others.

"He thinks you and Carl had something to do with his brother getting killed," Charlene said. She was scared.

"He has something on his mind," Ghetto agreed. "But he won't pull a move in a public place."

They remained at Baby A's for another hour, drinking and enjoying themselves.

"Let's get out of here," Paul said. "It's getting late."

"Is it past your bedtime, old nigga?" joked Ghetto. Everybody laughed. "I'll leave the tip, and you can take care of the bill."

"I'm tired of footing the bill. I'm not fucking your ugly ass!"

Everyone laughed at Paul's comment.

As they left the restaurant, Paul stopped to pay the bill. Everyone else headed for the parking lot. When they got outside, a black, convertible Mustang pulled up. The passenger came up with a gun and pointed it at Charlene. Ghetto saw what was happening before the girls did.

"Get down!" he screamed, running towards the women.

The gunfire was deafening. There must have been fifteen shots fired. Ghetto tackled Charlene and his lady friend.

"What the fuck?" Paul yelled as he ran out of the restaurant. He found Ghetto lying on top of his wife and the girl he brought with him. "Charlene! *Charlene*!"

"I'm hit in the leg," she said. "But I'm alright. I think Ghetto is hit too!"

The other girl wasn't shot. Paul pulled Ghetto off his wife and laid him gently on his back. People were pouring out of the restaurant to see what happened.

"*Somebody call the fucking ambulance*!" Paul screamed while attending to Ghetto.

Ghetto tried to tell Paul something.

"Just be quiet and wait for the ambulance," Paul said.

"Get this pistol off me. You know I'm on parole," Ghetto said before passing out.

"Lil' mama, come here," Paul said to Ghetto's date. "Take this pistol and put it in my car."

"Okay."

The ambulance arrived, and the paramedics started working on Ghetto and Charlene. Paul tried to call Carl but couldn't reach him. He left a message on his voicemail to let him know what happened.

●●●●●●

"What's up, Lil Chris?" Carl asked when he stepped off the elevator at the hospital.

"It's fucked up, my nigga. Ghetto got hit three times in the back. The doctor don't think he'll make it through the day. Charlene got hit in the hip. She's in surgery getting screws put in her shit." Chris was calm under pressure.

"Who done it?"

"Paul said it was Kevin McDonald."

"Yeah? Where's Paul?"

"He's in the waiting room with Charlene's family."

"Why aren't you in there with Donna?"

"I had to get some fresh air. We been cramped up in that waiting room all night."

"What you mean *cramped up*?"

"You'll see. Your mom and Ghetto's mom are in there."

Carl and Lil Chris walked back to the waiting area together, and it was chaotic. People were asleep in chairs. There were babies crying. Young men ran up to Carl asking what he was going to do about this. Carl saw his mom and aunt sitting in a corner by themselves. He made his way to them.

"How y'all holding up?"

His Aunt Mary's eyes were bloodshot from crying all night. She got up and hugged him.

"Carl, I hope my baby makes it. Me and your mother have been praying all night," Ghetto's mother said.

"He'll make it," Carl said, trying to console her. "One thing he's not is a quitter."

"I been calling you all night, boy," Jo Ann said. "Where in the hell have you been?"

"Sorry. I got here as soon as I could."

"With everybody talking about it was a hit, I started to drive to your house to check on you," his mom said. "But I wasn't about to leave my sister by herself."

"Don't worry about me," Carl said. "Nobody will come to my house."

"I think Paul wants to talk to you. Make sure you talk some sense into him. I know he's upset that his wife got shot, but the last thing y'all need is more trouble with the law," Jo Ann said.

Paul and Carl walked away so they could talk in private.

"Where the hell you been?" Paul had murder oozing out of his pores.

Carl looked at his best friend. He wanted to make sure he said the right thing. They didn't need to be arguing with each other. "Let's go outside and talk. There's too many people in our business in here."

When they got outside, Paul said, "I been trying to get in touch with you since last night. I left messages on your phone. What's up with that?"

"Nigga, don't try to check me," Carl said. "I'm a grown motherfucking man. I'm not gon' stand here and argue with you. I know you mad, and so am I. Just calm down, my nigga."

"I don't see how you're so fucking calm! My wife is in there having surgery, and we don't know if Ghetto's gonna make it."

"Need I remind you the feds are in our business?"

"I don't give a fuck about no feds, nigga! That nigga Kevin is gonna cry blood, and I'm talking about soon!" Spittle flew from Paul's mouth as he spoke.

Carl knew this conversation was going nowhere. He let it fade until Paul was able to think rationally. "I feel ya pain, my nigga. I really do."

He patted Paul on the back and told him, "I'll catch you later," as he walked back to his car in the parking lot. There was nothing he could do at the hospital.

• • • • • •

Federal Building

Scottsdale barged into Deputy Alexander's office. "Sir, I just received news of a shooting. Paul Atkins' wife was involved."

"Haven't you ever heard of knocking?"

"I apologize, sir. But did you hear what I said?"

"I heard you. What I want to know is why this shooting has lit a fire under your ass?"

"Because I know Fredrick and Atkins are going to jump on this. Tracy McDonald's brother is reportedly behind the shooting."

Deputy Alexander stared at his understudy. "So you're still working the informants?"

"Of course I am. I'll be doing that until Fredrick goes to court. We might be able to add something else to his file."

Alexander was proud of the way Scottsdale was taking the initiative on this case.

"You know this case is closed," he reminded him. "I can't reopen the investigation."

"I know, sir, but I don't want these guys to get away."

"You can't win them all, Scottsdale. But you can continue with the probe if you like. You might want to send someone over to the hospital to see what they can find out about the shooting."

"Good idea. I'll do that and have a light detail put on Fredrick and Atkins."

Deputy Alexander nodded his approval.

• • • • • •

On Friday night the line to get into Mid-Town Live was around the corner. A string of luxury cars pulled into the parking lot, and all eyes were on them. Carl, Paul and the rest of their entourage were dressed to impress, from their hats down to their gator shoes. All of them had on their most expensive jewelry. They were flexing hard.

They got out of their cars and stood in a circle to talk.

"We're not looking for any trouble tonight," Carl said. "But if it comes our way, we gonna smash the gas."

"Nigga, you ain't gotta give us no instructions. We already know what time it is," said the always crunk Fast Black.

Paul didn't say anything. He had a deadly look in his eyes that worried Carl. This could turn into a disastrous night. They walked to the front of the club and asserted their VIP status. They got a few catcalls from several women.

"Can we get in VIP with y'all?" a nice-looking yellow-bone asked.

"Hell naw, bitch!" answered Fast Black. "Holler at us on the way out the door, when it's time to go fuck something."

"Fuck you, ho-ass nigga!" screamed the girl.

Carl and the boys laughed. They approached the entrance of the club. Carl pulled the bouncer aside and slipped him a c-note. "Is Kevin McDonald up in here tonight?"

"He's here," replied the bouncer.

"How many niggas are with him?"

"It's four of them."

"They got any pistols on them?"

"Just Kevin."

"I appreciate that, big homey."

"I heard what happened," the bouncer said, looking worried. "Everybody saying Kevin was behind the shooting of Paul's wife. Y'all not gon' trip out up in here, are y'all?"

"We ain't looking for no problems," Carl said.

He went back and laced everyone up on what he learned from the bouncer. He told Paul, "Stay close to that nigga once we walk up on him, just in case he makes a move for his pistol. Fast Black, you and the boys keep his niggas at bay."

They made their way through the crowded club to the VIP section. Just like outside in the parking lot, they were the center of attention. A lot of the club-goers wore worried looks. The streets talked, and everyone knew what was going on.

As soon as they stepped into the VIP, Paul and Kevin locked eyes. Kevin looked calm, but underneath he was sweating bullets. He couldn't believe Paul and Carl would try to confront him in a club. Kevin and his boys were standing at the bar. Kevin was hugged up with a woman. When she peeped the play, she got the hell away from him.

"I'll talk to you later, Kevin."

Carl and his crew walked right up to him.

"What brings you boys up in Mid-Town tonight?" Kevin asked. "Don't y'all got a club to run?"

The tension must have reached the DJ booth, because the music stopped playing. Everyone was locked in on the scene.

"We had to shut down for security reasons," Carl said with a sinister smile on his face. "Somebody riding around shooting people."

"I heard about that shit," Kevin said.

"Bitch-ass nigga! You think it's a game?" Carl snapped. "We didn't come up in here to play with you. We came up in here to warn you. We didn't kill ya snitch-ass brother. I know you think it was us, because he snitched on Big Pat–"

"I don't know what the fuck you talking about Carl," Kevin said.

"Yeah, yeah, yeah. If Ghetto dies, you outta there, and ya family too," Carl said while pointing his finger in Kevin's face.

Kevin reached for his pistol. Paul's reaction was quicker than a thief in the night. He grabbed Kevin's hands and pushed him up against the bar. Paul then planted a vicious head butt to Kevin's nose. He twisted his wrist, until Kevin released his grip on the weapon. Carl reached down and picked it up. Paul landed an elbow to the side of Kevin's head and knocked him out cold. When he fell, Paul kicked him in the mouth and knocked out a few of his gold and diamond-encrusted teeth. He then took the heel of his gator shoe and commenced to stomping Kevin's face mercilessly.

The beating was so brutal, women started turning away, and some of the niggas did too. Kevin's boys couldn't do anything if they wanted to, because Carl had the pistol.

"Man, he's gonna–"

Before Kevin's friend could finish his sentence, Fast Black slept him with a two-piece to the chin. He then turned and grabbed Paul.

"*What the hell is going on in my club*?" Ms. Caldwell, the owner of the establishment, shrieked.

"Kevin here reached for a pistol, because we were having a small disagreement," Carl told her. "But he was a lil' slow. Paul took the pistol and beat the shit out of him."

He took the clip out of Kevin's gun, emptied the chamber and handed it to Ms. Caldwell.

"Did you have to beat him up like that in my club?" Ms. Caldwell asked Paul. "*Somebody call the police and an ambulance*!" she yelled to one of her bodyguards. "Carl, I can't believe you, Paul and the rest of these thugs came in here and tore up my place!"

"Bitch, fuck you!" shouted Fast Black. "If your so-called security wouldn't let niggas up in the club with pistols, this shit wouldn't have happened."

A few women were tending to Kevin. The only thing Ms. Caldwell could say was, "Mid-Town is closed for the rest of the night! Carl, you and Paul stay right there. You're gonna tell the police what happened in here tonight!" she demanded.

Carl looked at Paul. He knew that when the Austin PD hit the scene, Paul was going to jail.

CHAPTER TWENTY-THREE

It was three-thirty in the morning by the time Carl left the club. The police took Paul to jail for aggravated assault, despite the fact that witnesses told them Kevin had a gun. Carl went to the hospital to tell Charlene what happened and to check on Ghetto.

"Something has happened, Charlene," he said when he stepped into her room.

"I already know Paul is in jail. What possessed y'all to take your asses to Mid-Town?"

"His mind was already made up," Carl told her.

"One of y'all could've been killed!" She started crying.

All Carl could do was hold his best friends wife. There was nothing he could say to fix the problems they had on their hands.

• • • • • •

"Hello?" Carl answered his cellphone.

"What's going on down there in Austin?" Rome asked.

"Nothing much. I'm chilling up here at the hospital, checking on my cousin Ghetto."

"What was behind that shit that jumped off at Mid-Town last night?"

"Damn, nigga. You got eyes everywhere."

"That's besides the point." Rome was agitated. "When you do a nigga, you do him. Never give a motherfucker a chance to come back and do you."

"I'm not worried about Kevin. He's a ho."

"I can't tell he's a ho. He tried to fuck off Paul and his wife."

"Look–"

"Look nothing, nigga! When a nigga loses his brother, it makes him do things he wouldn't usually do," Rome said.

"Are you through?"

Rome didn't answer.

"I'm thinking about calling off the Player's Ball," Carl said.

"Nigga, you done lost your mind! That's all motherfuckers is talking about from coast to coast is the damn Player's Ball. This is your time to shine, nigga. Write yourself in history. You got the floor. Don't fuck it off."

"Alright. You right, homey. I'll see you at the ball," Carl said to his friend.

●●●●●●

Asha and her dad were sitting at the house sipping on lemonade while she replayed what had happened in Detroit.

"He asked you to marry him, and you walked out?" Her father didn't believe what he was hearing.

"Don't say it like that, Dad. You make it seem as if–"

"I make it seem like what? What do you expect from me when you come to me with your problems?"

"Dad–"

"Wait, let me finish, Asha. This guy has his feelings tied up in this relationship, and obviously you do too, because you're walking around with his baby in your stomach. When do you plan on coming clean with him about what's going on?"

"After I testify at his court hearing."

"That's a terrible idea."

"But I don't know what else to do."

"Let me solve one of your problems for you, sweetheart. You have no obligation to the FBI anymore. The moment you took that money and cocaine, your career in law enforcement was over. You have to jump on one side of the fence now, baby. As much as I hate it, I think you have to go Carl's way. You need to come clean *before* he goes to trial."

Asha tried to talk, but her father gave her the eye to let her know that he wasn't finished.

"Carl has to know that you're on his side before you take the stand," he said. "Not just him, but his family and friends, if you plan on being with him."

Asha was sitting on the couch rubbing her stomach. "I guess you're right, Dad. I'll get in touch with him now."

••••••

"Hello?" Carl sounded emotionless when he answered his phone.

"Hi, Carl."

"What's up?" he asked with a lack of interest in his voice.

"Why haven't you returned my calls?" Beverly asked.

"Things have been pretty hectic since I got back from Detroit."

"That's not a good excuse."

"It is what it is."

"I know you're upset about what I did. There was a reason for my actions."

"What was your reason for running out on me?"

"I'll tell you in due time."

"*In due fucking time*?! What the fuck does that mean?" His voice was getting louder and louder. "Look, Beverly, I'm through entertaining this bullshit. I have too much on my plate to be sitting on this phone playing childish games with you."

"I love you, Carl. And I hope to see you soon." Beverly disconnected and started to cry.

Carl was more confused now than he was before the call.

••••••

Beverly and her father drove from Macon, Georgia to Austin. It was against his better judgment, but he wasn't about to let his daughter drive that far with four million dollars in the trunk of her car. It was time for him to meet the man his daughter was so in love with. He wanted to make his own assessment of everything. When they reached Austin, they checked into a Holiday Inn.

Beverly decided to break the news to Carl's mother first, so she stopped by her house.

"Hey, Beverly," Jo Ann said when she opened the door.

"How are you doing, Ms. Fredrick?"

"I'm doing fine. Come on in." Jo Ann's attention went directly to Beverly's protruding stomach. "Can I get you anything?"

"No, thank you."

"Okay. So what brought you by?"

"I think you may want to sit down, Ms. Fredrick."

"Has something happened to my son?" Jo Ann asked nervously.

"No, Ma'am."

"How many months along are you?"

"Four or five. I'm not sure. I haven't been to the doctor yet."

"You need to try and get there. I'm not trying to disrespect you, but are you pregnant by Carl?"

"Yes, Ma'am."

A smile came to Jo Ann's face. This would be her first grandchild. "What did my son say when you told him about the baby?"

"I haven't told him yet, Ms. Fredrick."

"I don't understand. Why would you tell me before you broke the news to him? I'm sure he'd be happy. In fact, I know he would. My son is crazy about you." Jo Ann wore a look of confusion.

"I didn't come here to tell you about the pregnancy."

After a brief pause, Jo Ann said, "I'm listening, Beverly."

"I'm a federal agent, Ms. Fredrick."

"*What*?"

"I'm a federal agent. I was sent to gather information about your son's illegal activities."

"I need a drink," Jo Ann said as she walked to the bar and poured a strong shot of Crown Royal. No Coke, no ice. "Now let me get this straight. You're a federal agent, you're pregnant, and you're the reason my son's businesses got raided?" She was visibly upset now.

"Everything is true except the last part," Beverly said, matching her intensity. "Carl's actions put the FBI in his business."

Jo Ann made herself another drink. "Are you the one who took the money and other stuff out of his house?"

"Yes. If I hadn't, Carl's life would have been over."

"Where's the money?" Jo Ann asked.

"In the trunk of my car, sitting in your driveway."

"Come on, let's go," Jo Ann said. "We're going to break this news to Carl. Go park that car in my garage. We'll ride in my car."

••••••

"You alright?" Carl asked Paul when he picked him up from jail.

"Hell naw I ain't alright! These ho's took three days to charge me. Then they hit me with an attempted murder charge. That fool pulled a gun on me in front of a club full of people. I was just defending myself!"

"I'm not the one you need to be explaining it to. I tried to tell you at the hospital to slow your roll, but your mind was already made up."

"Fuck that nigga! That bitch-made nigga shot my wife and Ghetto."

"So we had to get right back at him, huh?"

"You damn right, nigga!"

"Then what are you doing all this motherfucking crying for, if you feel like your actions were justified?"

They rode in silence for a few minutes before Carl broke the tension. "Call my lawyer Mr. Ganne this afternoon and have him go talk with the parole board personally. He might be able to keep a blue warrant off your ass."

"Take me to the hospital to see my wife, nigga." Paul still had venom in his voice.

Carl's patience was running thin with his friend's attitude. They'd known each other for over twenty-five years and never had a physical altercation. Carl didn't want to have one now, so he didn't try to check Paul while his blood pressure was high.

"I'll take you to the hospital in a few minutes. My mama left three messages on my voicemail. She asked me to meet her at the restaurant. She said it was an emergency."

"Cool," Paul said. His anger was starting to subside.

••••••

Paul and Carl walked into the office at the restaurant. Jo Ann was sitting behind his desk with a big glass of liquor in her hand. Beverly was using the restroom when they entered.

"What's in that glass, Mama?" Carl asked with a look of concern.

"Hennessy," she answered.

"Something's wrong. You haven't had a drink in ten years."

"You damn skippy something's wrong!"

At that moment, Beverly stepped out of the bathroom.

"What are you doing in Austin?" Carl asked her, but his attention went to her belly.

"I told you I needed to talk."

"What's so important that you had to fly to Austin to tell me?"

"I drove."

"Well, what's up?"

The office went silent. Beverly turned her back to everyone in the room.

"You might need to fix yourself a drink," Jo Ann told her son.

"I don't think so, Mom." Carl walked over to Beverly. He placed his hands on her shoulders and turned her around. Tears were rolling down her face. He kissed her on the forehead and hugged her tightly.

With her face buried in his chest, Beverly said, "I'm a federal agent."

Anger registered on Paul's face, and Jo Ann took a sip of her drink.

"How many months are you?" Carl asked.

Before she could answer, Paul exploded. "This bitch just told you she's the law, and the only thing you ask her is how far along she is?"

Carl turned towards Paul and said, "If you call her one more bitch, we gon' rearrange the furniture in here."

"You got me fucked up," Paul said, moving towards him.

Both women jumped between them before they could come to blows.

"What the hell is going on between you two?" Jo Ann said. "Y'all are 33 years old – in here acting like some damn sixth graders. Y'all made me spill my drink!"

Beverly tried to explain to Paul what was going on, but Carl cut her off. "You don't owe that nigga no explanation!"

"Yes I do, Carl. He's your best friend, and he's involved," Beverly said softly. "So would both of you just calm down. Please!" she begged.

She sat down and told her story from the beginning. She left nothing out. Carl sat on the edge of his desk with a smirk on his face. Paul had a blank expression, as if he was weighing something in his head. Jo Ann watched both men, to make sure they didn't start fighting.

Beverly walked over and stood in front of Paul. She put her hands on his face and told him, "We all have to make sacrifices in our lives. And I made one. I chose Carl over my career in law enforcement. I love him, and I intend to be with him. Paul, I hope you're okay with that. I know how Carl feels about you and your family and how much he respects you."

Paul hugged Beverly and kissed her on the cheek to show her that he understood. Tears were streaming down Jo Ann's face. She was emotional and feeling the effects from the alcohol.

"There's one thing you forgot to tell us," Carl said smiling.

Beverly put her hands in the air and said, "What did I forget, Carl?"

"What's your damn name?"

Everyone doubled-over in laughter, even Jo Ann.

Beverly walked over to Carl and kissed him passionately. "My name is Asha Richards."

Carl smiled and stared down at her swollen belly.

CHAPTER TWENTY-FOUR

Asha and her father pulled into the circular drive at Carl's house.

"This is a beautiful home!" said an astonished James Richards. "I love the location. It's right outside the city limits, sitting out here by itself."

"It's real peaceful out here, Dad. We've taken long walks around his property."

"Let's go inside, so I can meet this man of yours, sweetheart."

Carl answered the door in leisure attire; Nike shirt, shorts and house shoes. He and Asha shared a short but very passionate kiss. James smiled as he watched them.

Carl extended his hand in welcome to Mr. Richards. He invited them inside.

"How's it going, sir? It's a pleasure to meet you. Asha's told me so much about you."

"Hopefully it was all good," James said.

"Hopefully it was all true!" Carl replied.

They all laughed. James laughed so hard, tears welled in his eyes.

Jo Ann walked in from the kitchen. She had on an apron. "What's so funny?"

James and Asha turned towards her. James was a handsome man and very experienced when it came to women, but he was awestruck by Jo Ann's beauty.

"You must be Carl's mother."

"That would be me. I suppose you're Bever – I'm sorry. I meant to say you must be Asha's father," Jo Ann said seriously.

"James Richards," he said as he extended his hand. "You're even more beautiful than Asha said."

"Thank you." Jo Ann blushed. It had been awhile since she'd been complimented by a man this handsome. "Son, dinner will be ready in about an hour."

"That's cool."

"Can I help you with anything?" Asha asked.

"Nope. All we're waiting for is the food to get done," Jo Ann said. She took off her apron and took a seat on the couch.

"I thought we'd have dinner and something to drink, so we can all get better acquainted," Carl said.

"That's a good idea, baby," replied Asha.

And that's what they did. Carl told Asha and her father everything he thought they should know at this time. James liked Carl. They had both traveled down some of the same avenues, when James was a much younger man.

After dinner Carl gave them a tour of his home and property, while walking hand in hand with Asha.

"Carl, what did you do out here?" Asha asked excitedly when they walked out onto his terrace.

"I just added a couple of amenities to better accommodate my guests for the Player's Picnic."

"It looks like you're gonna try to show out," replied Asha. Some of his swag was already rubbing off on her.

They went back inside and had more drinks. An hour or so later, everyone retired for the night. Carl insisted that Asha and her father stay at his home.

• • • • • •

Federal Building

"Is Deputy Alexander in his office this morning?" Asha asked his secretary.

"Do you have an appointment, Ms...?" the secretary asked coldly.

"It's Agent Richards, and don't play with me, you old bat!" snapped Asha.

The secretary was shocked into silence.

"Do I have to pick up the phone and call him myself?" Asha asked. "Better yet..." She made a B-line to his office and entered without knocking.

"What the hell are you doing barging into my office?" Deputy Alexander said.

"Sir, she just insulted me and came in here on her own!" his secretary said.

"I came to give you my letter of resignation," Asha told him.

"Gloria, leave us alone for a moment," Deputy Alexander said, and his secretary backed out of the room.

Alexander figured sooner or later Asha was going to quit. But what bothered him was her protruding belly. "What's your reason for wanting to leave the bureau?" he asked.

"I'm just not cut out for this type of work. I thought I was, but I'm not."

"When did you come to that realization, before or after you compromised this operation?" Alexander was eerily calm.

"What are you talking about?"

"Don't play with me, Richards. The writing's all over the wall," he said pointing at her stomach. "Fredrick pulled you to his side with his charm."

"I don't know what you're talking about."

"Okay, then who are you pregnant by?"

Asha took a deep breath. She sat in the chair in front of his desk. Her defenses were breaking down. "You win, sir. I'm carrying Fredrick's child. But he's not the monster you guys made him out to be. He does things for kids. He's a successful businessman, and he absolutely knows how to treat a lady."

Deputy Alexander waited for her to get it all out before he rebutted her argument. "First off, young lady, if I were you, I'd never make that revelation again about you and Fredrick's relationship. If I were anyone else, you'd have federal charges brought against you for obstruction of justice.

"And second, I don't want to hear anything about his good deeds. He's a piece of shit! There are thousands of successful black men out there who don't traffic narcotics and kill people for a living."

He reached into his desk drawer and pulled out the morgue pictures of Tracy McDonald. "This is the work of your boyfriend."

Asha turned away from the gruesome photos. Half of Tracy's face was blown off.

"You just fell for the flash and the glamour," Alexander said, bringing his voice down to a lower octave. "Agent Richards, I've been with the bureau longer than you've been on this earth. And honestly, it pains me to bust these young, black men who choose to step on the wrong side of the law. But I have a duty to uphold. As long as everything is done by the book, I can live with busting their asses."

Asha was crying.

"But you may have found a good one in Fredrick," the deputy said. "I wish you the best of luck. Now leave your letter of resignation and get the hell out of my office."

When Asha left the room, she was crying uncontrollably.

Gloria walked up and grabbed her by the arm. "May I speak with you for a second?"

Asha nodded. The secretary led her to a lounge area.

"Deputy Alexander gets attached to his work and the people who work with him," Gloria said. "He's the most honorable man I know. I was a fourteen year old prostitute in Oakland when he brought down the pimp I was turning tricks for. He arrested everyone at the house I was in except me. He could look at me and could tell I was young.

"I bypassed jail, and he took me straight to social services. The next day he and his late wife were there to file paperwork to gain temporary custody of me. I was at his home the next day and every day after that until I graduated from high school. He helped me enroll in a trade school, and I've been his secretary ever since. Wherever he's stationed, I'm stationed. Now get yourself together and straighten out that man you chose over the bureau."

Gloria smiled, and Asha felt a little better.

• • • • • •

Carl went to the hospital to check on Ghetto and Charlene. To his surprise, the waiting room was empty, except for his aunt Mary.

"Hey," Carl said as he walked up to her.

"Hey, boy," responded his aunt. "I haven't seen you up here in the last couple of days."

"I've been real busy. Why are you out here? Did they make you leave his room?"

"I'm tired of looking at all those tubes in my baby," she said. She eyed her nephew. "What do you mean you been real busy? What could be more important than your first cousin laying up in a hospital bed, fighting for his life?"

Carl could hear the resentment in her voice.

"I didn't come here to argue with you, Auntie. I came to check on Ghetto and Charlene."

"Don't ever call him *Ghetto* in front of me. Do you understand?"

Carl didn't answer.

"Charlene checked out of the hospital this morning," she said. "Can't you tell how empty it is in here? Paul and your other friends didn't have the decency to even speak to me before they left."

Carl stayed quiet, so she could get her anger out.

"The reason my son is in there all shot up is because of some punk you and Paul had killed. That's right. I got the whole scoop while sitting in this waiting room. Now that man's brother is trying to kill y'all."

Carl kissed her on the cheek and said, "I'm sorry, Aunt Mary. I really am."

He left her and walked into Ghetto's room.

Ghetto was still hooked to several machines, with tubes running through his mouth and nose. Carl hated to see his cousin so vulnerable. He felt like it was his fault, to a certain extent, just like his aunt said. He sat next to the bed and made a couple of calls. A few minutes later, he was still on the phone, staring out of the window. When he turned around, Ghetto was staring at him. Carl smiled.

"Can you hear me, kinfolk?"

Ghetto couldn't talk, but he nodded his head.

"You had everybody scared to death," Carl said as he walked over and squeezed Ghetto's hand. "But I knew you weren't gonna die, because real niggas don't die young." Tears ran down Carl's face for the first time since his father's funeral. "I'm gonna let your mom and doctor know you're awake," he said.

Carl said a silent prayer to the man above before walking to the waiting area.

"Aunt Mary, you need to go look at your son. He's awake." Ghetto's mom screamed and ran to his room.

• • • • • •

Carl and Asha planned to meet at the restaurant after they finished running errands that morning. Carl arrived first and had a table prepared for three. When Asha arrived, she walked up to him and they embraced and shared a soft kiss.

"How did your morning go?" he asked. He knew that she went to talk to her supervisor.

"He was furious, baby," Beverly said. "I told him everything. He said I undermined a federal investigation, and I endangered the lives of other agents – not to mention blowing their covers." Asha was feeling distraught, especially after the chat with her boss' secretary.

"Do you think they're gonna bring charges against you?" Carl asked as he reached across the table and grabbed her hand.

"I don't think so. My supervisor told me not to tell anyone else in the bureau what happened between us. And then he kicked me out of his office."

"With that said, it seems like he's gonna let you make it."

"That's what I felt too."

"Your father should have been here by now," Carl said. "Do you think he got lost?"

Asha smiled and said, "He never gets lost. He's probably sightseeing or something."

"Well, speak of the devil," Carl said, nodding towards the entrance. He waved James over to their table.

"This restaurant you have here is truly upscale, as far as looks go anyway," James said as he shook Carl's hand. "I want to see what the food tastes like. I'm starving." He bent to kiss his daughter before taking a seat.

"You're in luck Mr. Richards–"

"Call me James. That Mr. Richards stuff is for the office."

"Well, you're in luck, James," Carl bragged. "We have one of the best chefs in the south."

James noticed his daughter was quiet. "How you doing, sweetheart?"

Asha repeated the story she told Carl. Everyone sat quiet for a moment before James broke the silence.

"There's no need to be nervous now. You should have anticipated the consequences before you decided to sacrifice your career for Mr. Austin, Texas over here," James said in his no-nonsense tone. "Look, I'm usually not judgmental," he told Carl, "but when my only child is involved, I have to be."

"I understand, and I respect what you have to say," Carl said.

"I don't have a problem with you and my daughter being together, as long as you can tell me that all of your illegal endeavors are a thing of the past." James looked Carl in the eyes.

"Everything is gonna be on the up-and-up from this moment forward," said a solemn Carl.

"If that's the case, then y'all have my blessing to do whatever two consenting adults want to do." James was all smiles now.

"I love you, Daddy!" said Asha.

"I love you too, baby. And I'm hungry. So let's cut the emotional stuff and get something to eat!"

They all laughed at that.

CHAPTER TWENTY-FIVE

4TH of July Weekend

Things were starting to shape up in Austin, even though the federal case was still hanging over Carl's head. Ghetto was still recovering from his bullet wounds. Carl got his money back from Asha, and she moved in with him. Everyone who knew Carl could see that he was happy.

The Player's Picnic and the Player's Ball were right around the corner. Carl's name was ringing all over Texas. Gangstas were talking about him in circles across the nation. Carl knew that if the Player's Ball went over smoothly, Austin would finally be on the map, as far as Negroes were concerned anyway.

Carl threw a little get-together at his house. He wanted to make sure everyone was on the same page and knew what their duties were.

"Carl, you've done a lot of work out here, since the last time I came," Charlene said, looking at the rear of his house from the terrace. "A swimming pool and a Jacuzzi, a sand volleyball court, a covered basketball court and a concession stand..."

Everyone stepped out on the terrace to see what Charlene was talking about.

"You did the fool out here, nigga!" said Fast Black.

"You know I have to show up," said a calm and focused Carl. "This is our chance to show our naked asses. That's why I'm going all out."

Carl had everyone's attention. He went on to give everyone their specific assignments for the upcoming events. After they were all laced up, they went back in the house to chill. They ate and watched TV and talked about the ball. Everyone was excited.

Rome was there so he could go back and fill the H Town niggas in on everything. Carl pulled him to the side and introduced him to Asha.

"Rome, this is my fiancé."

"Hello."

"Asha, this is a good friend of mine and business associate. His name is Jerome, but we all call him Rome. You remember him from the Lil Wayne concert?"

She nodded. "It's good to see you again," she told Rome.

"Rome is the one who told me that you were either an FBI agent or a thief," said Carl.

That remark made Asha a little uncomfortable.

Rome said, "It's a good thing our boy Carl is a ladies' man, or everybody in this room would be sitting in federal prison."

That helped put Asha at ease. She and Carl laughed softly.

• • • • • •

On Monday Carl and Asha went to see a doctor about her pregnancy.

"How could you make a doctor's appointment without telling me first?" she asked as he drove.

He didn't respond, just kept his eyes on the road.

"A woman isn't comfortable with just anybody looking between their legs," she told him.

"We can cancel the appointment, if you want to make your own," he said.

"I don't know any doctor's in Austin."

"My point exactly. So why you doing all this motherfucking whining?"

Asha was caught off guard by his sudden aggravation. It was quiet for a moment.

"Why are you cursing?" she asked him.

He didn't answer.

"Just because I want to know a little about the doctor..."

"Do you think I would take you to just *any* doctor? Dr. Tobias Franklin is one of the best obstetricians in Austin. And he's a very close friend of mind."

"If you would've told me that in the beginning, I wouldn't have been whining," she snapped.

They rode the rest of the way in silence.

When they got to the doctor's office, they were escorted to an examination room. Dr. Franklin entered shortly after. Carl greeted his high school friend with a heavy embrace.

"It sure is good to see you, Carl," said the smiling doctor. "How long has it been, four or five years?"

"At least that long," replied Carl.

"Is this the beautiful lady you told me about?"

"Yes," Carl said happily.

"How far along do you think you are?" he asked Asha.

"Honestly, doctor, I don't know," she said.

"Well, let's have a look..."

Asha looked at Carl and wanted to apologize for the way she acted on the way to the appointment. She was instantly comfortable with Dr. Franklin.

"Just by the feel," he said, "I'd say you're at least twenty weeks along. You might be closer to twenty-four. How much did you weigh before the pregnancy?"

"About a hundred and eighty-five pounds." She was embarrassed about her weight, even though it was mostly muscle.

"Step on the scale for me, please."

The readout showed Asha now weighed two hundred and ten pounds. She was even more embarrassed as she looked at Carl.

"Looks like we have to put you on a diet," the doctor said.

"Is everything alright with the baby?" she asked.

"From the external exam, everything looks fine. After I perform a few tests, I'll be able to answer all of your questions and pinpoint a due date." Dr Franklin reassured Asha with a smile. "I'll be back in a sec."

As the doctor walked out, Carl went over and kissed Asha and rubbed her belly. She didn't say anything. She enjoyed his show of affection.

"I'll go to the waiting room while the doc finishes up his exams," Carl said.

Two hours later the doctor and Asha came walking into the reception area. They were laughing and talking like they'd known each other for years.

"Come on, Carl. Let's go in my office."

As soon as the door was closed, Dr. Franklin disclosed all of the information they were looking for.

"The babies are healthy, and Asha is healthy as well. I'm putting her on a diet that I expect you to hold her to, Carl. And I'm giving her some vitamins–"

"You said *babies*, doc?" Carl said, cutting him off.

"Yes, you're having twins. A boy and a girl."

Carl and Asha were both stunned by the revelation. Dr. Franklin kept shuffling through his papers. Every time he told a couple they were having twins, it was a surprise. Most of the time the shock came because they started to worry about financial problems. He knew that wasn't the case here. Carl was strapped with cash from his many business ventures.

After giving them the vitamins and other instructions, the doctor walked them back to the reception area.

"I hope to see you at the Player's Ball," Carl told him. "It's gonna be a very special night."

"Me and the wife just might stop by," said Dr. Franklin.

••••••

Carl and Asha spent the rest of the day together after they left the doctor's office. They went to the mall and did some shopping. She always enjoyed the time they were alone together, but she didn't like the funk Carl had been in since she came back to Austin.

They made it home later that evening. Asha went to the bedroom to get comfortable. She put on one of Carl's tee-shirts. He was sitting on the couch watching ESPN when she came back to the den.

When she walked in front of him, Carl smiled. He knew she was trying to seduce him with all that ass. Asha went to the kitchen and boiled some shrimp and made buttered cabbage. When she was through cooking, she brought the food to the den. She returned to the kitchen and came back with two big cups of Kool-Aid.

"What's in the cup?" Carl asked.

"Ghetto-Aid!"

They both started laughing.

Asha went to the bedroom and returned with three big photo albums and a large comforter. She spread out the comforter on the floor and turned the television off. She used the remote to turn on the CD player instead. She put an old school Keith Sweat CD on repeat.

Carl took the pillows off the couch and joined her on the floor.

"I wanted to show you some pictures of my mother," Asha said. She fed him the shrimp by hand while they looked at the photos. "That's my mom standing in front of a house she just sold."

Beverly's emotions were already building up. Carl saw the change in her mood as soon as she started talking about her mother. He slid in closer and put his arm around her.

"Your mom was a very beautiful lady. I see where you got your good looks from. She was tall, too."

Asha flipped through the album until she came to a picture of her and her parents.

"Your dad needs his ass whipped for those lil' ass shorts," Carl said and they both laughed.

"My dad had it going on!" Asha said.

It took an hour for them to go through all of the pictures. Carl took the dishes to the kitchen. When he came back, Asha stood up and pulled off Carl's gym shorts and his boxers. He took off his own shirt. Asha was in complete control. She pulled him to the floor. Carl helped her out of the tee-shirt, and they began to kiss passionately. She bit his neck, slowly making her way to his torso. The whole time she had his piece in her hand massaging it, caressing it.

Her soft, sensual kisses made it to his erection, and she took him into her mouth. Carl lay on his side and groaned softly. He pulled her hair back so he could watch her taking care of her business.

"Damn, Asha," he said in a hoarse voice. He pulled her hair softly.

She looked into his eyes with his dick still in her mouth. Her eyes were dripping with ecstasy, and that drove him over the top. He climaxed in her mouth. Asha took it out and continued to yoke it. More cum hit her in the face.

Carl groaned loudly, and his toes curled up. Asha took him into her mouth again and sucked until he got back hard. Once that was accomplished, she got up to go to the restroom and clean herself up.

She told him, "You better be in the bedroom when I get through, and you better be ready to fuck me." She still had that look in her eyes.

Moments later she walked into the bedroom and Carl was ready. They kissed passionately. She pushed Carl on his back and straddled him. She squatted down and guided his piece inside her. Her pussy was tight, wet and warm. Carl stretched her walls, and Asha started making a high-pitched shrieking noise.

"*I love you*!" she said and kept repeating it over and over.

Carl shot a load inside her, and she climaxed for the umpteenth time. She laid her head on his chest, and her hand returned to his piece. They were both speechless after the intense love-making session, but they weren't through.

Asha got on all fours when his dick grew hard in her hand. Carl got behind her and started hitting it from the back. Asha moaned and shrieked the whole time. Carl knew she was enjoying it, because her juices were all over his dick. He exploded inside her again.

They stretched out on the bed drenched in sweat. Asha had her back to him. Carl pulled the hair away from her neck and softly kissed her there.

"Will you marry me, Carl Fredrick?" Asha asked.

Carl kissed her again and put his hand on her belly. Moments later Asha was sound asleep.

She awoke to find herself alone in bed. She touched where Carl had fallen asleep next to her, but he wasn't there. Just thinking about their lovemaking got her wet all over again.

She looked at the clock on the dresser and saw that it was 7:30 am.

Let me get out of this bed, she said to herself.

She grabbed fresh, silk panties and went to take a shower. As soon as she stepped into the restroom, she saw a note stuck to the vanity mirror. It was written in Carl's neat handwriting. She took the note off the mirror and read it.

Dear Asha,

The answer to your question is absolutely yes! I'll marry you. This is the first time in my adult life that I've felt complete. I feel blessed that our lil "situation" turned out like it did. I don't know what I would have done if the tables would have turned the other way.

Another thing. You didn't have to propose to me. I was going to pop the question again. My love for you only grew when I found out you were a federal agent. There's not too many people who would have made that sacrifice. I know I'm not the best man in the world, but obviously you see something good in me.

Yours Truly

Carl

P.S. I need to give that fire pussy of yours a nickname!!

Asha cried after she read the note. All her fears about crowding Carl were quelled. She jumped in the shower. She couldn't wait to call a few people and tell them the good news.

CHAPTER TWENTY-SIX

Carl went to the Sweet Soul to do some paperwork and take inventory. When Asha returned his four million dollars, he stopped booking concerts. He also took his rental properties off the market. He couldn't stop construction on the houses that were being built, but that was okay. That was more money anyway.

After he finished at his restaurant, he drove to Given's Rec Center. He hadn't hooped in a while. He told all his homies to meet him there, so he could lace them up on the ball. After they played six pick-up games, everyone went out to the parking lot. Lil Chris was there with Fast Black, Paul, Dre, Hogg and his cousin Dee from the Sam Houston Boys.

"Everybody needs to be suited and booted for the Player's Ball," Carl told them. "We gonna show the nation that us Austin niggas are for real. Most of the niggas coming got money, and they from the streets just like us."

"What the fuck is you getting at?" Fast Black said. He always wanted to make his presence known.

"What I'm saying, ho-ass nigga, is when we leave the floor and go to VIP, don't put the trick dice down. These niggas is woke up, and I don't want no shit," said a very serious Carl.

"If I can't cheat, I ain't gon' gamble," Hogg said.

"Well, don't do no gambling, gangsta," Carl said. "Everyone will meet at the White Swan before we head downtown, so we can show some love to those who won't be attending."

They all started dapping it up.

"It's time to show out!" said Fast Black.

••••••

Asha walked into the kitchen and smiled. Carl had washed all the dishes they used last night. She sat down in front of the TV and tuned in to one of the morning shows. Then she called her dad, who had returned to Georgia. She knew that when he left, he was feeling kind of uneasy, despite what he said.

She told her dad about the doctor's visit. She told him how she and Carl had been having dinner together every night to work through their problems. She even told him about the note Carl left her this morning – minus the P.S. part. She and her father talked on the phone for thirty minutes. Afterwards, Asha knew he felt better about her situation, and he was excited about the twins.

She called Gwen when she got off the phone with her father. Gwen was still in Georgia. She decided to stay and spend a little time with her family. Asha gave her ten thousand for her troubles and said she would ask Carl to give her more money later.

"Bitch! What took you so long to return my call? I was worried sick about you," Gwen said.

"Hello. How are you, Gwendolyn?" Asha said sarcastically.

"Girl, I ain't playing. If I hadn't talked with your dad the other night, I was about to catch a bus to Austin to check on you."

"Everything's fine. Me and Carl are very much in love."

"I know that nigga was glad to get that money back."

"Anybody would be glad to get four million dollars back."

"I still think we should've kept it," said a laughing Gwen.

"He knew I took that money."

"So what? You're the law, bitch. He wasn't gon' fuck with you."

"It doesn't matter. I'm happy, and I have what I wanted. Can't you be happy for me?" asked Asha.

"Have you been to the doctor?"

Asha told her about the visit with Dr. Franklin.

"And guess what," said an excited Asha.

"What?"

"We're having twins!"

"Are you serious?" Gwen was excited now.

"A boy for him, and a girl for me."

"You always been the lucky one," Gwen said, pretending to be jealous. "I'm supposed to be in Austin with you, Asha. But I'm stuck in Macon."

"You're the one who wanted to spend time with your family."

"I know, but the honeymoon is over, girl. My mama and my sister are getting on my last nerve!"

"I'll ask Carl if you can come down and stay with us until you find a job and apartment."

"For real?"

"I'll ask him tonight. You know I can't leave you stuck out. You're my dog."

They talked on the phone for another hour. Asha told her how Carl's mother went off when Asha told her she was a fed. They both thought that was hilarious.

When she got off the phone, Asha felt great, even though she threw away her job in law enforcement. She knew she could always start a new career. She was smart and so was the love of her life.

•••••••

Carl made it back to the house mid-afternoon to find Asha sitting on the couch watching soap operas. He plopped down beside her, and they greeted each other with a peck on the lips. Then Asha kissed his neck.

"Ugh! You taste like sweat," she said with a sour face.

"I just got finished playing basketball."

"Go take a shower," she said, pointing to the restroom.

Carl took a shower and came back and sat next to her. She kissed his neck again and smiled. He smiled back and grabbed the remote and changed the TV to ESPN.

"You saw me watching TV."

He smiled at her but didn't change it back.

"That's alright," Asha said. "I need to talk to you anyway."

"What's on your mind?"

"My friend wants to come back to Austin."

"Why you telling me?"

"We planned to make Austin our home, but after all the stuff that happened with you, our plans changed. She helped me drive back to Georgia, and now she's stuck."

"You said all that and still haven't told me shit," said a smiling Carl.

"Can Gwen come stay with us until she finds a job and a place to stay?"

"No," Carl said and returned his attention to the TV.

She grabbed him by the arm to get his attention. "You're not even gonna think about it?"

"There's nothing to think about. There's only room for one hen in this coup, and that's you."

Asha stared at him in disbelief.

"She can stay for a day or two," Carl said. "Y'all can go out and find her an apartment, and I'll pay the rent until she gets a job. That will square everything up, for the shit she did for me. You already gave her ten thousand dollars."

"Fair enough," Asha said smiling. "Let me call Gwen and tell her the good news."

"Before you do that, I was wondering if you want to go to a jazz club with me tonight."

"You know I do!"

• • • • • •

On the Fourth of July, Paul and Charlene had a get-together at their home. When Carl and Asha arrived, there were cars everywhere. Carl had to park a block and a half away.

When they got to the house, people were standing in different groups, drinking and socializing. The weed smoke was thick in the air. Carl acknowledged everyone as they approached the house. He didn't bother going through the front door. He knew the majority of the party would be in the backyard where the barbecue pit was. The smoke from the pit was floating over the house like a heavy fog. And it smelled good back there, too.

Old school Johnny Taylor was blaring from Paul's entertainment center. As soon as Carl and Asha walked into the yard, Paul spotted them.

"My nigga!" He lifted a bottle of MGD. He had tongs in his other hand as he tended to the BBQ. He had an apron on over his Eddie Bauer get up. He looked like the host for one of those cooking shows, if it wasn't for the loud music and the marijuana smoke.

Paul sat his beer and tongs down, and he and Carl embraced like two bears. Carl could see that his friend was already lit. Paul stepped to Asha and placed a sloppy kiss on her check.

“I didn’t think y’all were gonna make it. We been partying since nine o’clock this morning,” said an intoxicated Paul.

“Uncle Carl! Uncle Carl! What’s up!” asked Paul’s oldest son. He rushed to his play-uncle with a big smile on his face.

“I been chillin’. What about you?” Carl asked as he bent down so they could be at eye level.

“I been hurting them boys on the football field,” the boy said excitedly.

“He ain’t bullshitting, either,” said a proud Paul. “It seems like every Friday they have to pack somebody off the field!”

“You best believe when football season starts in September, I’ll be there,” Carl said.

“I’m gonna hold you to that, Unc.”

“I’m gonna chill out here with the fellas,” Carl told Asha. “Charlene and the rest of the ladies are in the house gossiping about something.”

“Say no more,” Asha said. She walked through the glass patio door to find the women preparing side dishes to go with the barbecue.

“Girl, bring your pregnant ass over here and meet some of my friends,” Charlene said when Asha walked through the door. They hugged, and Charlene introduced her to her friends. “This is Carl’s wifey,” she said, and the hating started immediately.

“So we finally get to meet the federal agent,” Charlene’s cousin Trinisha said.

“*Ex-federal agent*,” Asha said, correcting her sharply.

“I hope you don’t think you’re too pretty to help us with this food,” Charlene said. She bumped Asha playfully.

“Let me wash my hands,” she said, heading for the sink.

The girls kicked it, being nasty and mannish for an hour before Charlene called the kids in the house to eat. Asha took Carl a plate, and they found a shady spot in the backyard under a big maple tree.

“That plate must be for both of us,” Carl said.

“It’s too much?” Asha asked.

“Not if we’re sharing.”

They sat on the grass and ate together. Towards the end of the meal, Carl licked barbecue sauce off the side of Asha’s mouth.

"Boy, stop."

"You had barbecue sauce on your lips."

He kissed her, sliding his tongue down her throat this time. She responded and didn't care who was watching. They sat there staring into each other's eyes, with Carl rubbing on her belly.

After they left Paul's house, they went to the shores of Town Lake and watched the fireworks show. It was almost midnight when they headed home.

Carl massaged Asha's feet and rubbed her belly and sides with warm cocoa butter. They fell asleep in each other's arms in the den. The French doors were open, with his new pit bulls there to stand guard. Asha never felt so loved.

CHAPTER TWENTY-SEVEN

In less than a twelve hour span, Carl and Paul's plans for the next day changed drastically. The Player's Picnic was cancelled.

Carl started receiving texts at 3 am, informing him that some shit had jumped off at a club on 6th Street. Later, some of Carl's friends staying at a downtown hotel contacted him to let him know an all-out brawl had erupted in the lobby. The incident happened at the same place Carl and Paul had housed their most exclusive guests and their entourages.

At 6:30 in the morning, Carl sat on the side of the bed with his head down, elbows on his knees.

Asha rolled over and saw him and asked, "What's wrong, baby?"

Carl stood and slipped on his boxers and a tee shirt. "Some niggas acted an ass last night at a club downtown." He was visibly upset.

"Who acted a fool, and what did they do?"

"I don't know exactly who it was at this point, but some of my guests were involved in a riot at the club, and it followed them back to their hotel. Three people were stabbed and several more injured."

"Oh my God!" Asha said. She put her hands over her mouth. "Did you know any of the people who were hurt?"

"I knew one of the girls who got sliced in the face with a bottle. I'm pretty sure I know everyone who was involved. I'm not tripping on that, though. Niggas gon' be niggas. I'm fucked up because it took me months of planning to put this shit together and only a few minutes for some stupid motherfuckers to put a black eye in the game."

Asha walked into his arms trying to calm him. She took one of his hands and placed it on her protruding belly.

"Paul told me not to put them Chi-town and New York niggas in the same hotel," Carl said. "I didn't listen, and them niggas went haywire."

He headed for the kitchen with Asha right on his heels. She understood why he was so upset. Even though he didn't participate in the foolishness, he'd be blamed because he was the organizer.

"What you plan on doing now?" Asha asked as she sat down at the breakfast nook.

"The picnic is a no-go," Carl said. "I'll be sending out messages to all my guests to let them know they're gonna have to cut the size of their entourages for the ball."

"They're not gonna like that, baby."

"I don't care. They can take their asses back to where they're from." Carl wasn't angry anymore, but his words were matter-of-fact.

He sat a glass of orange juice and some buttered raisin bread in front of Asha.

"Thank you, baby." She stayed hungry, ever since her doctor put her on a strict diet.

••••••

Carl was a very calculating person. Most successful criminals and businessmen are. He knew that his baller guests were expecting a good time today, and he had to come through for them. It took him two hours to come up with an alternate plan to replace the picnic. He had to get some help from Charlene and her cousin Trinisha.

Carl invited the men and a couple of street-savvy celebs to his house for a high-stakes poker game. Most of them arrived at 4 pm. Shortly thereafter, Paul and Charlene showed up.

"Let's ride, Asha," Charlene said, fanning the air.

"Ride where?" Asha didn't feel like getting dressed. She had her lounge-around-the-house clothes on.

"Girl, go grab that big-ass bag of yours that you call a purse and come on. We're going shopping. Then we're going to the Driscoll Hotel, where them niggas got kicked out this morning. We're gonna have us a girl's night. I'm not gonna let that money Paul and Carl spent on those rooms go to waste. Besides, you don't need to be up in here while these heathens are smoking this killa and those nasty-ass cigars."

"Go ahead and go," Carl said to Asha. He had a big stogie clenched between his teeth. "Be sure to text me the room number. I'll have these chumps broke in a couple of hours."

Laughter erupted around the poker table.

Asha changed into a warm-up suit and grabbed her overnight bag. She kissed Carl on the cheek, and she and Charlene were off. That part of Charlene's plan worked to perfection.

In the next few hours, Carl dropped over 60 grand on the table. He pulled up and watched the action from the sideline while nursing a drink. Lil Funk from H-town, Black Sydney from Brooklyn and West, one of Carl's local hustlers were the only ones left in the game. They had no less than 150 racks in front of them.

Carl chopped it up with Quan, a baller he knew from Chi-town.

"Why'd you cancel the picnic? I was looking forward to that basketball tourney and getting at some of them bad bitches I knew were gonna be there."

"After the shit that happened last night, I had to regroup," Carl said. "I wasn't about to let them ho-ass niggas come out here and tear up my shit and put my family and friends in danger. All them niggas is affiliated. I don't know who's who."

"What you mean by that? Everybody in this room is affiliated." It was clear that Quan took offense to Carl's comment.

"You heard what I said, nigga. I don't want all those bitch-made niggas around my family!" Carl's temper went from zero to a hundred in a heartbeat. "Them niggas up in the club acting like they teenagers. Is it something I said you don't like, nigga?"

"Hey, hey! Y'all niggas over there tripping," Black Sydney yelled from the poker table. "We partners up in here. Playas. Y'all niggas chill. Now, back to y'all," he said, returning his attention to the poker game. "Check or bet, nigga."

Quan threw up his hands in mock surrender. “I was wrong. They tripped out last night. I see where you’re coming from.”

Quan and Carl dapped it up.

At 9 pm sharp the doorbell rang. Carl went to answer it. Moments later he ushered 13 of the finest women a man could dream of into his den.

Black Sydney’s mouth went agape at the sight of the beautiful, scantily dressed women. “I fold.” He threw his cards in the middle of the table, and the rest of the players followed suit.

“Please don’t tell me this is a robbery,” Lil Funk said. He was dead serious.

All of the girls laughed. The leader of their crew was in the front. She was light-skinned with freckles on her face. She was short in stature and thick in all the right places. Her hair was naturally red and long. She wore a white pleated skirt that was very short, displaying all of her godly assets. Her breasts were bulging against the fabric of her halter top, and her six-pack looked sculpted. She was a dime piece. The rest of the women were just as voluptuous and scantily dressed.

“We’re not here to rob you gentlemen. We heard about the picnic being cancelled, so we decided to stop by and brighten the mood,” Sandy said. She was the one with freckles. She stepped to the poker table and picked up a rack that was in front of Black Sydney. “I love men with money.” She glared into Sydney’s eyes, fanning herself with the stack of money.

“If you can fuck anywhere close to the way you look, you can have that money, lil’ mama,” he told her.

The rest of the fellows were in total agreement.

“Would you guys like to indulge in some carnal mischief or resume your poker game?” Trinisha asked stepping to the forefront. She was dressed for the part. She had on blue, laced boy shorts that were jammed up her ass and pussy. She had a matching lace bra, but it was in her hand, exposing her perky, little breasts.

“I didn’t know you got down like that, Trinisha,” Lil Chris said. “I been wanting to fuck your lil’ sexy ass for the longest.”

Trinisha smiled at the remark. “Let’s go into Carl’s man cave and get comfy,” she said walking that way. All of the guys were locked in on her hooker walk. That little ass was perfectly round.

Everyone flopped down on the couches with women draped over them. Some of the women sat on the floor, sitting Indian-style, putting their product on display.

"If everybody is comfortable, I'll be leaving," Carl said. "I'm entrusting my home to you niggas, because I fuck with y'all."

"Are you sure you don't want to stay?" Sandy asked. "You won't be disappointed."

"Thank you, but I'm good," Carl said. He and Paul tipped their heads to everyone and headed out.

"Fire up some of that dro, so a bitch can get loose," one of the prostitutes said.

The blunts went into circulation.

"This is what we're gonna do, people..." Sandy stood in the middle of the room with a handful of business cards. "Can I use your hat, Mr...."

"Black Sydney," he said, filling it in for her because she didn't know his name. "Mr. N.Y.C., known throughout all five boroughs," he boasted.

Sydney stood 6-6 and weighed close to 350 pounds. He had coal black skin that was smooth and a booming voice that matched his stature.

"Can I borrow your hat, Mr. Sydney?" Sandy stood between his legs, staring into eyes that had seen just as much as hers, if not more.

He handed over the black, velvet fedora, exposing his shiny, bald head.

Sandy turned back to the audience and saw that the games had already started. One of the guys was finger-fucking one of the girls, with his tongue stuck down her throat.

"I'm gonna put our business cards in this hat," Sandy said. "Everyone is gonna pull a card and continue to pass the hat around. You'll be pleasured by whichever girl's card you pull out."

"I'm fucking your lil' fine ass," Sydney said, pulling Sandy into his lap. "Give that hat to them and come on." He led her down the hallway to one of the bedrooms.

"Sydney doesn't want to play by the rules," Sandy said over her shoulder. "You go ahead without me." She pretended to pout.

"Ashley, come with me. It's gonna take two of us to tame this one."

Ashley was the only white woman in the group. They went to the room to embark on a ménage à trois.

Lil Chris also had a threesome going. He was lying on his back watching Trinisha and another girl gobble up his dick. "I need to be flicking y'all up right now," he said.

Trinisha came up for air. "For five racks, you can do whatever you want, Chris."

"Grab my phone over there and start filming," he said to the other escort.

Trinisha began to perform for the camera, and the show was on. She sucked Chris' dick with no hands. Minutes later, he exploded with a volcanic cum shot on her lips and face. She slowly yoked his piece and started licking and sucking his sensitive mushroom again.

"*Damn*!" was all he could manage. This was a toe-curling experience.

She kept sucking, ignoring his protests. She slurped on his dick and fondled his balls until he was hard again. She was definitely putting on a show for the camera. She could care less about her reputation. She knew she would have more clientele after the video surfaced. She also knew that she could charge more once everyone saw her skill set.

Trinisha got on all fours in the middle of the bed. She looked over her shoulder and watched Chris put on a condom. She smiled and bit down on her bottom lip.

"If I knew you had it like that, you could've been up in this pussy a long time ago," she told him. "Get in this bed and take care of your business." She had a nasty, lustful look in her eyes.

Lil Chris pulled her to the edge of the bed, spread her red ass cheeks and started fucking her with long, hard strokes. The pussy had a good grip and was wet. He slapped against her pussy with each stroke. She moaned and shrieked with every thrust but never took her eyes off him. She enjoyed watching him work. She got weak after she came. She lay on her stomach with her ass still in the air. Chris got in bed with her and got back to work. He pulled her hair as he exploded again.

"*You got it good, nigga*!" Trinisha moaned.

●●●●●●

Sandy lie in the middle of the bed getting her pussy ate by Ashley. Sydney stripped out of his clothes, put on a condom and stepped behind Ashley. He rubbed the tip of his dick against her pretty, little pussy. He wanted her moist before he entered her. When he thought she was ready, he went in.

"*Shit*!" Ashley screamed. She ran away from the dick, until she was lying entirely on Sandy. She looked back at Sydney with a terrified look in her eyes. "I can't take all that. It's too much!"

Sydney couldn't believe what he was hearing. *What kind of prostitute can't take a dick?* he thought to himself.

Sandy kissed Ashley on the lips and said, "Go pleasure one of the other guys. I'll take care of Sydney."

Ashley walked out of the room happy that she didn't have to get fucked with a twelve-inch cock.

Sandy got on her knees in the bed and initiated a passionate kiss with Sydney.

"I'm gonna enjoy you pushing all that dick up in me. I hope you can go all night." She lie on her back and opened her legs wide to accommodate his frame.

Then Sydney did the unexpected. He dropped down and started eating her pussy. He treated her nest like it was a delicate flower. He pulled back her folds and softly licked her pearl tongue. He blew his hot breath on her ever-so-often, which drove Sandy over the edge. She couldn't stop the convulsions. Her orgasms came back to back.

"*Sydney! Ooh, Sydney*!" she moaned. Her essence was smeared all over his lips.

Sandy was a steel-hearted bitch who was always about her money. She couldn't remember the last time she climaxed while working. Sydney came up, and they shared a soft kiss. She stared into his eyes again, soul searching. She reached between her legs to make sure he had a condom on, and then she opened her canal with her fingers, so he could have an easy entry.

He pushed in slowly, not wanting to hurt her.

"*Damn*!" she said in a hoarse voice.

He didn't have half his dick in her, but her box was already filled. She stuck her tongue in his mouth, exploring. She bit his bottom lip. His short-strokes drove her crazy.

"*I'm cumming again, baby*!" Her nails dug deep in his back, and she let out a loud shriek after another orgasm rocked her body. "Put my legs on your shoulders, and fuck me, Sydney!"

"Are you sure?"

"*Fuck me*!" she growled. She knew she was about to be punished, but she wanted to make sure her client was completely satisfied.

He put her legs on his shoulders and started acting bad in the pussy. Her moans and shrieks got louder with every stroke. Her screams excited Sydney, and it wasn't long before he emptied his powerful load. He was immediately drained. He lowered her legs but continued to stroke her. She scratched him on his back again. If it hurt, he didn't show it.

He pulled out and lie down next to her.

"Your dick is magical, Sydney," she said, breathing hard.

"You a soldier," he said. "Can't too many women take my dick the way you did."

"I am a soldier, a working woman, have been for years. You took me to the brink. It was good, though. I'm glad you prepared me first by eating my pussy. You got my juices flowing."

He pulled her close to him. She backed into him in the spoon position.

He told her, "I want you to come back to New York with me."

"What?"

"You heard what I said, woman." He kissed her softly on the neck.

"We just met two hours ago, and you're talking about taking me home with you?" She rolled over to face him. "I'm a prostitute, Sydney, and I have been since I was fifteen." She couldn't believe the words were spilling out of her mouth. She hardly knew this man, but he put her at ease.

"You can come to Brooklyn and start over."

"Shut up, Sydney. This is just pillow talk after some good sex."

"I'm serious."

"Everyone in Austin knows me and what I do for a living. If you're serious, put me on your arm, and take me to the Player's Ball tomorrow night."

"Deal. Make sure your dress is sky blue, so it will go with the trim on my tux. Yeah. All eyes gon' be on us. And when we leave there, we gon' fly to Vegas and get married. You'll be Mrs. New York."

Sandy was taken aback by what he was saying. But she had always been an opportunist. She was definitely going to talk to Carl about Sydney. She liked this nigga's forwardness and his swag. Instead of shooting him down, she decided she'd ride it out and see where things went...

CHAPTER TWENTY-EIGHT THE PLAYER'S BALL

There was electricity in the air. Everything was going as planned. It seemed like the whole city was gathered on one city block. There were six limousines and a host of other luxury cars parked in front of the White Swan night club on 12th and Chicon. Carl chose the White Swan because it was a legendary night spot for blacks for the past three generations. This was also the area Carl hustled in. He wanted people who were not attending the ball to at least feel like they were a part of it.

There were cars parked everywhere with their trunks popped, repping their hoods with neon lights. All kinds of rap music blared from their speakers. The street playas were in full attendance tonight, draped in their finest jewelry, with their bottom bitches on their arms. The women walked around, popping that ass to the music. Most of them were dressed so provocatively, the men thought they were at a strip club.

The police were everywhere, but weed smoke still permeated the air. The police weren't tripping. They knew something big was going on. As long as there wasn't any fighting or shooting, they didn't care.

Carl and his entourage stood curbside in front of their limos taking it all in.

"There must be ten thousand people out here tonight!" Charlene said excitedly.

"Girl, I haven't seen this many black people gathered in one spot in my life," Asha said.

"Y'all might as well get used to seeing it like this," Carl said in a serious tone. "From this day forward, ATX will officially be on the map. Niggas from everywhere are gonna be flocking to this motherfucker."

Young players and women alike walked up and asked to take pictures with Paul and Carl. Everyone respected them. They were revered in the streets. They must have taken a hundred pictures before Carl got the call he was waiting for.

"Most of the celebrities and all the other important people have made it to the club," said one of his bouncers.

"We're on our way," Carl said.

"There's TV crews everywhere," the bouncer said.

"What did you expect? This is Austin's first annual Player's Ball," Carl said before disconnecting.

He informed everyone that it was time to head to the club and make their grand entrance. Carl and Paul dapped it up with a couple more people before getting into their limo.

When they arrived on 6th Street, people were everywhere. They started hollering when the limos pulled up. Everyone was surprised by the turn out – everyone except Carl. This was what he had planned. He anticipated the hype.

Women exited the first two limos. They were local business owners, and some of them were just boppers. They were all dressed seductively. Some wore transparent evening gowns. It was dark, but most of the girls wore shades, like they were celebrities.

The next limo was occupied by Lil Chris, Fast Black, Donna and Gwen. Their dress code was to the floor, with immaculate jewelry selections. The next limo to pull up had Paul, Carl and their ladies. The women screamed Carl and Paul's names and made sexual comments. It didn't matter that they had two beautiful women draped on their arms.

Carl wore a white tuxedo with powder blue accessories and blue gators on his feet. The only jewelry he wore was a diamond earring on the left side and a pinky ring full of ice. Asha and Jo Ann were dressed almost identically, with white evening gowns that plunged deeply into their cleavage. They both were powder blue stiletto pumps. The only difference between the women was their hairstyles and their jewelry.

Despite the pain Charlene still had, she refused to walk with a cane on this night. She looked stunning in a light blue gown with a slit that ran up to her hip, exposing her ebony, well-shaped legs. She wore a diamond broach around her neck along with her wedding ring.

The other limos were occupied by close associates of Carl and Paul. They got out and waved at the spectators as reporters swarmed Carl and bombarded him with questions.

"What is the purpose of this *Player's Ball*?" asked one reporter.

"Do you plan on taking a plea agreement on the federal chargers?" another one asked.

"Are you the notorious drug dealer you've been made out to be?"

"I have guests to entertain," Carl said with a big smile on his face. "I won't be taking questions tonight. However, I will allow *you* to come inside and check things out," he said to a black, female reporter.

He turned and walked into the club with Asha and his mother on his arms. He received a standing ovation when they got inside.

Instead of Cedric the Entertainer, Carl decided to go with a local comedian and closer friend of his named Don Dada.

"Damn! I thought Beyoncé had entered the building, the way you motherfuckers reacted when Carl walked in," said the sarcastic comic. "Why don't you boys come up here and address the crowd?"

Carl told Paul to handle it. When Paul reached the stage, he and Don Dada embraced. The comedian handed Paul the mic.

"Hello everyone," Paul said. "I'd like to welcome y'all to my city and thank you for attending Austin's first annual Player's Ball!"

"You think we were gonna miss the opportunity to come down here and kick it with two of the realest niggas in the south?" Jay Z called from the front row.

Loud barks came from the crowd.

"We got love for you boys up top too," said a smiling Paul. "I want y'all to know that we got a local news lady in here tonight covering this event, so let's be on our best behavior, or close to it."

Everyone laughed at that.

"I'm not going to stand here and acknowledge everybody up in here tonight," Paul said. "Everybody pretty much knows everybody, as far as the celebs go anyway. But I do wanna give shout outs to my friends who are flying under the radar. First off, I gotta acknowledge Carl Fredrick and his mother Jo Ann. And I gotta mention my beautiful wife and kids. Thank y'all for putting up with so much of my B.S.!

"I gotta give a shout out to the Sam Houston Boys, 12th Street Dre, Fast Black, the legendary Johnny 'J.B.' Beard and Bennie Mays. Over here you have Miss Mara of Mara Fashions," Paul said, looking around the room.

"Now let me give Texas a shout out, starting with H Town's finest. Over here you got Reginald 'Black' Elly and his boy Steve. We got some of Third Ward's finest: T-Money, Dwight, Big E, Big Walt, Big Pam, and before I forget, June-Boy's up in the house too. I see a lot of other people I know, but we have to keep the show moving forward. So if you mad because I didn't mention you, my bad. I can't call everybody's name!"

The crowd laughed at that.

"This isn't going to be a Player's Ball where you pick a pimp or player of the year," Paul said. "Not this first one, anyway. The people we're gonna honor or acknowledge tonight are people who've done a lot of civic duty in the community. Another reason for the ball is to do some networking. If someone comes up and wants to rap about business, acknowledge them. Enlighten them. Give them some game."

Everyone nodded in agreement.

"Now I'm gonna turn the show back over to the host," Paul said. "Mr. Don Dada!"

The comic returned to the stage. "I need to know is there anyone in here under the age of 18 tonight. If so, raise your hand."

No one raised their hand.

"That's great, because some of this shit is gonna be X-rated!" exclaimed Don Dada. "Paul knows every motherfucker in the United States! You hired me to host the show, nigga! Don't bring yo long-winded ass back up here no more, Paul!"

The audience erupted in laughter.

"I know y'all ready to get this motherfucker under way, so it's my pleasure to invite Uncle Charlie to the stage!"

The crowd applauded and several couples rushed to the dance floor as Charlie Wilson took the stage. During his performance, Carl made rounds to everyone's table. The celebs and commoners were already starting to interact. There was a high, positive energy in the club. By the time Carl made it back to his seat, Frankie Beverly and Maze were about to perform. Carl escorted Asha to the floor, and they danced through a whole set of songs.

In between performers, Don Dada told more jokes and acknowledged the black business owners who were the movers and shakers in their community. Carl's favorite rapper, Scarface, took the stage to end the night. He told everyone "The world is a ghetto," and surprised them by bringing the original Geto Boys up to perform with him.

At the end of his set, Scarface stepped off the stage and handed the microphone to Carl. Carl held Asha at arms' length and looked deeply into her eyes.

"Asha Nicole Richards, will you be my wife?" Carl reached into his coat pocket and retrieved a ring. It seemed like everyone in the club was holding their breath.

A smile came to Asha's face, followed by tears. She said, "Yes!" and the whole club applauded for over a minute. Almost every woman there had tears in her eyes. Carl and Asha kissed passionately.

"I love you," he said.

"I love you too!"

After that, the Player's Ball was officially over. Carl and Paul made their last rounds to thank everyone for attending. By the time they got out of the club and made it home, it was six in the morning. Carl and Asha stripped down naked and went to sleep.

••••••

They didn't wake up until two in the afternoon. Before they got out of bed, they made love for an hour or better. They took a shower put on tee shirts and shorts. They planned to lounge around the house all day. Carl had several dozen emails and messages on his phone. Everyone wanted to commend him on the Player's Ball. He returned every message.

Asha went to the kitchen and made ham and cheese sandwiches. They ate with very little conversation between them. They respected each other's peace of mind. At six-thirty that evening, Carl received a phone call that soured his mood.

"How's it going, Mr. Austin, Texas?" his attorney Robert Ganne asked.

"I was doing great until you called," retorted Carl.

"You act like you don't want to talk to the man who looks out for your best interests."

"It's not that, man. It's just here of late, every time you call it's never good."

"Now whose fault is that?" the lawyer asked sarcastically.

"What do you want?" Carl asked angrily.

"Calm down. I'm just reminding you that your trial starts in four days."

"Do you have everything under control?"

"I've covered all the bases. The only real concern is the assault charge. The judge we're going in front of is a hard case."

Carl didn't comment on that.

"I don't think we have too much to worry about," Mr. Ganne continued. "Your character witness list would soften anybody. I've called all of your witnesses into my office and had a one-on-one with them. They're ready."

"That's great," Carl said. "Is there anything else?"

"Yeah, there is. I suppose that's your federal agent girlfriend you're hugged up with on the front page of the Statesman..." The attorney laughed and hung up.

"What did the lawyer say, baby?" Asha asked when Carl got off the phone. "Is everything alright?"

"Everything's cool. He just reminded me that my trial starts in a few days."

A dark shadow fell over the room.

"How are you feeling?" she asked.

"I'm fine," he said, squeezing her thigh. "Everything will be just fine."

CHAPTER TWENTY-NINE

United States Federal Court

Carl arrived at the courthouse at 8:30 am the day of his trial. He exited a rental car with his mother, Paul and Charlene. They were all dressed conservatively. All of his friends wanted to come and give support, but at the advice of his attorney, Carl told them not to come.

He wasn't surprised to see more reporters at the courthouse. He saw the black news lady that he allowed into the Player's Ball. They made eye contact, and she winked at him. The rest of the reporters bombarded him with questions. Carl raised his hand to let them know that he wouldn't be responding to them. He and his entourage pushed into the courthouse.

When they entered the courtroom, they found Robert Ganne going through paperwork that was neatly stacked at the defense table.

"What's up?" Carl asked as he took a seat next to him.

"Getting prepared," Ganne said without looking up from his papers.

"You sound nervous."

"Why would I be nervous? I'm not the one who's facing prison time."

Carl gave him a look.

"This isn't traffic court," Ganne said. "This prosecutor is trying to send you up the river for as long as she possibly can."

Carl was speechless. A million images flashed through his mind's eye. He didn't want to lose his freedom – not even for one day.

"Relax," his lawyer said. "I'm gonna do my damndest to keep you out of prison. You're a very intelligent man with a lot going for yourself. I'd hate to see you throw it away behind something as demeaning as the drug trade."

You'd be broke, if it wasn't for drug dealers, Carl thought.

At nine a.m. the bailiff stood and told everyone to rise for the entrance of the honorable judge James Bisset. The judge came in and took control immediately.

"The case before this court is the *United States of America versus Carl Fredrick*," he said in a thunderous voice. "Will the prosecution be offering a plea-agreement, before we begin to call witnesses?"

Robert Ganne stood up and said, "The defense will not be accepting any plea deals. We're ready to move forward with the proceedings."

Without Judge Bisset's eyes leaving Ganne, he told the prosecutor, "I suppose you should call your first witness, Mrs. Willis."

"We call FBI Deputy Director Lawrence Alexander to the stand," the prosecutor said.

Alexander strutted down the aisle to the witness stand. Carl laughed to himself. Asha's description of him was dead-on. The judge swore him in, and the questions began.

"How are you doing today, Deputy Alexander?" asked the prosecutor.

"I'm doing fine," Alexander answered.

"I'm sure you're aware of why you've been called to the witness stand this morning."

"Of course."

"Could you inform the court of the illegal activities of Mr. Carl Fred–"

"*Alleged illegal activities*!" Ganne said, cutting him off.

"Mr. Ganne, I'm not going to let you make a mockery out of the judicial system or my court with your outbursts. Is that understood?" asked the judge.

"Yes, Your Honor."

"Proceed, Deputy Alexander."

"The bureau received information through an informant that Mr. Fredrick was purchasing and distributing large amounts of cocaine in Austin and the surrounding cities," Alexander said. "The bureau launched an intense probe into Mr. Fredrick's alleged dealings."

"Does the bureau usually launch intensive probes on the mere word of an informant?" the prosecutor asked.

"No, but this case is different. We had Mr. Fredrick under investigation a couple of years back–"

"Objection!" Ganne said. "The first investigation has no relevance with the case before the court today."

"Sustained."

"Could you tell us what information you gathered during the investigation?" the prosecutor asked.

"We sent a female agent to infiltrate Mr. Fredrick. We also had several details monitoring his movements."

"Was the female agent able to uncover any information?"

"Not very much. She uncovered a large sum of money, but no drugs."

"What about the surveillance?"

"He was seen in constant contact with people on our watch list," Alexander said. "He spent a lot of time in high-crime areas."

"Your Honor, I have no more questions for this witness," the prosecutor said.

"He's all yours, Ganne," said the judge.

"Deputy Alexander, I only have a couple of questions for you," Ganne said as he approached the witness. "This informant you talked about earlier, did he purchase any cocaine from my client?"

"No, he did not."

"You said Mr. Franklin spent a lot of time in high crime areas. Could you clarify for the court what kind of activities Mr. Franklin was involved in, in those areas?"

"He renovates and builds new homes in East Austin."

"No more questions," Ganne said as he sat down.

"You may step down, Deputy Alexander," said the judge.

"The United States calls Agent Asha Richards to the stand," the prosecutor said.

Asha had on a black, pin-striped business suit, but she couldn't hide her protruding belly.

"Ms. Richards, how were you able to infiltrate Mr. Fredrick?"

"I dined at his restaurant a couple of times, and he noticed me."

"What happened after that?"

"We went on several dates and became very close."

"Did he ever take you around any of the people who were on your watch list, Agent Richards?"

"Yes, he did."

"What did you witness?"

"Nothing out of the ordinary. He drank with them and played chess with them. That's about it."

"What about his business partner, Paul Atkins? Did they ever mention any illegalities in your presence?"

"No."

"So let me get this straight," the prosecutor said, getting agitated, "you went out with Mr. Fredrick for the last seven months. You worked at his restaurant for the last four and a half months. On top of that, you moved in with him. But other than the money you told your supervisor about, you never heard or saw Mr. Fredrick indulge in anything illegal?"

"That's right."

The prosecutor shuffled through her paperwork furiously. Out in the gallery, Charlene and Jo Ann had smiles on their faces. The prosecutor let her anger subside before she resumed.

"On the morning of July 1st, you witnessed Mr. Fredrick assault one of your fellow agents. Is that correct?"

"Yes."

"Could you tell us what led to that incident?"

"I'm afraid I can't. I didn't hear what transpired between the two. I didn't get out of the car until I heard the slap."

The prosecutor shuffled through more papers. She glanced at the defense table and flashed a quick smile before continuing.

"Agent Richards – no, I'm sorry, Ms. Richards, did you find it peculiar that Mr. Fredrick was able to spend the kind of money he did on you?"

"I never noticed him spending a lot of money on me."

"Is that so? Let me see here... Mr. Fredrick bought you a $10,000 bracelet. He flew you all over the country. You had courtside seats at an NBA Finals game."

"The money he spent on me was well within his means."

The prosecutor took a sip of water and then looked around before she started her next line of questions. "How long has it been since you resigned from the bureau?"

"Objection! That's not relevant, Your Honor," Ganne said.

"Oh, but I think it is relevant," the prosecutor said. "I have reason to believe Ms. Richards' testimony might be tainted."

"Objection is overruled."

Ganne was furious.

"How long has it been since you resigned from the bureau?" the prosecutor asked again.

"About a month."

"Has your relationship with Mr. Fredrick continued since your resignation?"

Asha had to think for a second before she answered. She felt like the prosecutor was trying to trap her. "I thought it would be wise to keep a line of communication open with Mr. Fredrick."

"According to my reports, you've been living with Mr. Fredrick for the past two weeks. I would say that's more than keeping a line of communication open."

Carl glared at his lawyer. He wanted him to help Asha out with an objection. But Ganne didn't say anything.

"Is it fair to say that you and Mr. Fredrick are engaged in an intimate relationship?" the prosecutor asked.

"Objection! That's irrelevant, Your Honor," said Ganne.

"I beg to differ," the prosecutor said. "Ms. Richards soiled this whole investigation."

"Objection overruled."

"Yes, we're in a relationship," Asha admitted.

"I have one last question for you, Ms. Richards. Are you currently pregnant with the defendant's child?"

Without hesitating, Asha said, "Yes."

"No more questions, Your Honor."

"She's your witness, Mr. Ganne," the judge said.

"I have no questions for her, Your Honor."

"Do you have any other witnesses?" the judge asked the prosecutor.

"No, Your Honor."

"I must say these proceedings went along rather quickly," the judge said. "If you're ready, Ms. Willis, you can go ahead and start your summation."

"I don't think a summation is necessary. I don't believe you have a problem construing the facts."

"I've been on this bench for many years," the judge said, shaking his head in disagreement. "I believe this is the first time the prosecution has elected not to give a summation. Ganne, you can go ahead with your summation."

Ganne picked up some papers and asked the judge if he could approach the bench. "Your Honor, I'm going to forgo my summation as well."

"Twice in one day?" the judge said sarcastically.

"I would appreciate if the court would recess and take some time to look over this list of character witnesses and their statements," Mr. Ganne said. "I also have an auditor's report from the IRS."

Ganne cut his eyes at the prosecutor. Defeat was written all over her face.

"Ms. Willis, I have a copy of these documents for you as well," Ganne said as he dropped a stack of papers on her table.

The first thing in the packet was a police report from when Carl was robbed at gunpoint. Ganne also included witness statements from the restaurant that indicated Carl asked the FBI agent several times if he was following him because he planned to rob him.

"Just for the record, Your Honor, I have everyone on that list available to testify," Ganne said. "I thought it would save the court some time if you looked over these documents during lunch."

"I'll do just that," the judge said before banging his gavel and sending them on a one hour break.

●●●●●●

An hour later, court was back in session. The judge waited for all of the spectators to return to their seats before he proceeded.

"Well, I looked through the documents Mr. Ganne presented, and I've considered the evidence brought before the court today. I'm ready to make a judgment on the United States versus Carl Fredrick. On the first count of tax evasion, I hereby find the defendant *not guilty*. Ms. Willis, did you read these auditor's notes before you sought these charges against the defendant?"

"No, Your Honor."

"Well, you should have, because you've wasted this court's time and the taxpayers. Mr. Fredrick has paid taxes on monies equaling one million dollars that's not in his bank account.

"On the second count of conspiracy to distribute narcotics, I hereby find the defendant *not guilty*. There's not one shred of evidence tying this man to any illegal activities. On the third count of assault on a federal agent, I find the defendant *not guilty*."

The judge banged his gavel to dismiss court, and he hastily left the bench.

Carl and his lawyer shook hands. Carl then walked into the gallery to share the moment of joy with his family. It would be a happy day throughout Austin.

Carl and his entourage got onto an elevator. Before the doors closed, Deputy Alexander stepped in the doorway. Everyone became quiet.

"How are you today, Ms. Fredrick?" Alexander sad, tipping his head in Jo Ann's direction.

"I'm fine," she responded, eyeing the agent suspiciously.

"Mr. Fredrick, Mr. Atkins, you boys should consider yourselves blessed. You slipped through the seams this time. But if you continue to indulge, your luck is bound to run out. It's only a matter of time."

The deputy stepped off the elevator and went on his way.

CHAPTER THIRTY

When they left the courthouse, the whole crew went to Sam's Barbecue. While they ate, several people walked up to congratulate Carl on his win in court.

"Baby, where's Asha?" Jo Ann asked her son.

"I don't know. Let me call her."

When she answered her cell, Carl could tell she was upset and had been crying.

"Where are you?" he asked.

"On my way to the house."

"What's wrong?"

"I don't know. I'm just confused."

"I'll be there in an hour."

Jo Ann watched her son. She knew something was wrong but didn't say anything. After they got through eating, Carl made his way to the house.

Asha was curled up watching TV when he walked in. Her eyes were red. Carl lifted her head up and sat down, putting her head in his lap.

"What's all the crying about?"

"That prosecutor treated me like I was a lowlife or something."

"How did you expect her to treat you? They know you sabotaged the case against me."

"That's what has me so upset. I don't think I should have sacrificed my career for you."

Carl frowned at that. He shot off the sofa and headed towards their bedroom. Asha was right behind him.

"Don't walk away from me when I'm talking to you!"

He spun around quickly and grabbed her shoulders. "I don't want to hear this shit! If you're having second thoughts about fucking with me, then tear your ass!"

Tears ran down her face. "It's a little too late for that, don't you think?"

Carl started undressing. He changed from his suit into some khakis and a designer shirt. "I don't have time to go through this with you right now. I have a flight to catch to H Town. I have some business to take care of in the morning."

"I'm going with you!" demanded Asha.

He smiled and said, "One minute you're crying. The next minute you want to be with me. I think I fell in love with a crazy woman." He shook his head. "If you're going with me, you need to get ready, so we can head to the airport."

••••••

When they arrived in Houston, they checked into a Hilton. They then went to eat at Harvey's Place. The restaurant had a buzz, and Carl wanted to check it out.

The argument they had earlier seemed to have never happened. Carl felt guilty about putting his hands on her, though.

"I'm sorry about losing my temper earlier," he said, holding her hand.

"Is that what you did?" She smiled, letting him know all was forgiven. "I don't know what came over me. I was wrong for what I said."

"Don't worry about that. It's over with. Let's enjoy this night and every moment we spend together."

"I love you, Carl."

"I love you too." They engaged in a passionate kiss.

"Have you been thinking about a wedding date?" she asked.

"August 30th."

"Why August 30th?"

"Because it would have been my parents' 35th wedding anniversary. Are you okay with that?"

"Yes. I just want to be *Mrs. Fredrick*. Where do you want to have it?"

"My mother said it had to be at a church, preferably hers. She already set up the pre-marriage counseling with her pastor."

"When did your mother decide on all of this?"

"After the Player's Ball."

"I don't have a problem with it this time, because I want to be your wife so bad. But in the future, I'd really appreciate it if you'd have my input on things like this."

"Yes, darling," Carl said as he leaned in and kissed her again.

They ate and talked and laughed for a couple of hours before they went back to their hotel room. When they got there, they made slow, passionate love. Asha had gotten so big, Carl had to take it easy on her. She still got loose, though. She got on top and rode him until they both climaxed. They fell asleep in each other's embrace.

••••••

Carl woke up at 6:15 the next morning. He watched Asha sleep for awhile. She was beautiful. She looked like a black Barbie doll, with her long, black hair strewn across her face. He had a Gabriel Union look alike. He pulled her hair back and kissed her gently on the neck. She didn't budge. Carl found that amusing. He pulled the sheets back and slapped her on the ass, startling her.

"Boy, it's too early to be playing," she said with sleep in her voice. "What time is it?"

"It's 6:30," he said as he got out of bed.

"Why are you getting up this early?"

"I told you I came down here for business. Now get up, so we can shower and get out of here."

They showered together. Every time he saw her naked, he got hard. He couldn't help himself. Asha stood in front of him. She reached back and felt his hardness. She laughed at him. She then propped her foot on the tub so he could enter her. She lay her head back on his shoulder and moaned softly as the warm water rained down on them. It didn't take long before he was spent. He bit her on the neck as he exploded inside her.

She was nearly breathless. "*I love you, Carl.*"

••••••

They arrived at Rome's condo at 7:30. It was located in far north Houston. When Rome answered the door, the smell of breakfast flooded Carl and Asha's senses. He and Rome embraced, and Rome kissed Asha softly on the cheek.

"I didn't know you were bringing your wife," Rome said as he led them through the apartment to the kitchen.

"She wanted to tag along," Carl said.

When they got to the kitchen, there was food all over the table.

"There's enough here to feed an army," Asha said.

"I don't know how your hubby eats at home, but when he comes to H Town, he eats like a newly freed refugee!" Rome said.

Asha smiled at the comment. She took in her surroundings as she sat down to eat. She figured Rome was single. His condo was neat and well organized but missing that woman's touch. The furniture was very expensive. She could tell that much.

"It sure is a blessing for us to be sitting down eating this breakfast," said Rome. "We've been friends for a long time, and I was praying those white folks didn't lock you up."

"It's definitely a blessing to be here. So much shit flashed before my eyes when I was sitting in that courtroom. I ain't gon' lie, I was scared than a motherfucker," Carl said truthfully.

Asha sat quietly and listened to the two friends talk. There was no mistaking how much respect they had for each other.

"Did you have to get on the stand and testify?" Rome asked Asha.

Her mouth was stuffed with eggs and toast with jelly. It took her a couple of seconds to answer him. "Yes, I had to testify. That prosecutor dogged me out."

"I can imagine. Them feds had to be pretty upset with you."

Carl decided to change the course of the conversation. "What's so important about this building project that you couldn't discuss over the phone?"

"Too many fine details," Rome said. "Too much stuff that I didn't know about construction that you do know. On top of that, I wanted to know what you thought about the location."

"What are you trying to build, a skyscraper, nigga?"

"No, but close," Rome answered as he bit into a biscuit. "How about a four story strip mall that's going to cover about a half a mile of land?"

"Man!" Carl leaned back in his chair. "That's gonna take a lot of planning and a lot of money."

"I talked to a couple of builders and contractors. They said a project this big would run anywhere from fifteen to twenty million."

"At least that much."

"That's why I called you down here. If anyone knows how to cut corners and save a buck, it's you."

"It's hard to cut corners on a commercial project. Building inspectors are gonna be crawling up your ass. Everything has to be by the book when you build shit for the public."

"Do you think you and your crew can handle a job this big?"

"If I was to get involved in this project, I wouldn't use my crew. I'd contract out the work to some local builders right here in Houston."

"Do you wanna partner up with me on this?" Rome asked, looking Carl straight in the eyes.

"I don't know. I'm not sure I can sacrifice the time that's gonna be needed for this."

"I can't pull it off without you, Carl. I know other cats running around with the cash to get down, but I don't trust them."

"I know you're not gonna try to pay for this whole thing with your own money," Carl said seriously.

"You damn right I am."

"Wrong. You never use your money on something this big. You take loans and you take on investors. Never spread yourself thin."

"You think them white folks gon' give a nigga like me a loan for twenty million dollars?"

"I know they will," said a smiling Carl. "All we have to do is put up some collateral and sell our plans to the bank, and it's a done deal."

"I'll go for the loans, but I don't want no investors. Just you. This land has been in my family for over sixty years, back when this area was nothing but farmland. I couldn't stand to see the white folks with their hands all on it. So you in or what?"

"Hold your horses, nigga. I got a couple more questions."

Carl sat there rubbing his chin, looking at Asha who had finished eating. "You feel like moving to H Town?" he asked her.

"Wherever you go, we're going," she said, rubbing her belly.

"Let's go look at the property," Carl told Rome. "And you can tell me more about your plans. If everything sounds good, I'm in."

• • • • • •

When they got back to Austin, Carl and Asha had a get-together at their home. Everyone was there, Paul and Charlene, Chris and Donna and Fast Black and Gwen. They were eating homemade pizza and spaghetti when the doorbell rang. Carl was in shock when he answered it.

"Are you going to stand there and look at me, or are you going to invite me in?" Deputy Alexander asked.

Carl invited him in and led him to the den where everyone was socializing. Asha was talking to Paul when the federal agent entered the room. When she turned around to see why everyone got so quiet, she lost her control immediately.

"What the hell are you doing at my house?" Asha screamed.

Deputy Alexander raised his hands and said, "Believe me, I didn't want to come out here. But I thought it would be best if I delivered the news."

Carl walked over and wrapped his arms around Asha to calm her down.

"Can we talk in private?" Alexander asked.

"Whatever you have to say, you can say it in front of my friends and family," Asha said.

"Alright then. At 4:30 this afternoon an arrest warrant was delivered to my desk with your name on it."

"An arrest warrant for what?" Jo Ann asked.

"Obstruction of justice, endangerment and conspiracy."

Asha buried her face in Carl's chest and started crying.

"The prosecutor has already put together a plea agreement," Alexander said.

"What kind of plea agreement?" Carl asked angrily.

"The prosecutor said she'd drop two of the charges, if Asha pled out to obstruction of justice and accepted a 30 month sentence."

"*Thirty months*?!" Asha screamed. She was crying her heart out. "I can't go to jail!"

"I think you should talk this over with your attorney, before you make any rash decisions," the deputy said.

"How could you do this to me?" Asha was devastated.

"I didn't have anything to do with this," Alexander said. "The prosecutor is pushing this case."

"Has a bond been set?" Carl asked.

"It's been set at a million dollars."

"*A million dollars*?" Charlene said loudly. "She ain't killed nobody!"

"I take it you came out here to arrest her then," Carl said.

"No, I didn't. She can turn herself in, in the morning."

"I appreciate you coming out here to tell us this," Carl said. "And I appreciate you letting her turn herself in." He and Deputy Alexander shook hands.

"I wish you the best, Asha," the deputy said as he turned and walked out the door.

Everyone tried to console her.

Carl got on the phone and called his lawyer.

"Carl Fredrick. What can I do for you?" Ganne said.

"Sorry for disturbing you, but this is important. Asha's ex-supervisor from the feds just paid us a visit."

"What did he want?"

"He came to inform us that Asha has been charged with several crimes. Her bond is set at one million."

"Jesus, Mary and Joseph! Did he arrest her?"

"No. He gave us a chance to surrender in the morning."

"That's good. You and Asha need to meet me at my office tomorrow morning."

"Do you think the restaurant will be enough collateral to cover that bond?"

"It should be. I'll see you in the morning," Ganne said and was gone.

••••••

"Boss, what are you doing creeping around the office this late at night?" asked Agent Scottsdale.

"I could ask you the same thing, but I already know the answer," Alexander said. He walked past Scottsdale into his office.

His assistant was right on his heels. "What's in the bag, sir?"

Alexander laughed as he retrieved a cup from his desk. He pulled a bottle of brandy out of the bag. He opened his fridge and got two cubes of ice and then poured two fingers of liquor.

"Would you like a drink, Scottsdale?"

"You know I don't drink on the job, sir. And I've never seen you do it either."

"There's a first time for everything. And goddammit, I'm mad, Scottsdale."

His assistant continued to watch him with concern in his eyes.

"Someone under my supervision leaked information to the prosecutor about Asha," Alexander said.

"What makes you think that?"

"There wasn't enough information from Carl's trial to warrant all of those charges." He drank the liquor in his glass and poured another shot. "The prosecutor's trying to send this little girl to prison for two and a half years."

"She's not a little girl, and she broke the law, sir."

"She's never even had a traffic ticket before."

Scottsdale didn't say anything else. He was going to find the leak and get him or her transferred before his boss, the man he respected and learned so much from, did something that he might regret.

••••••

Asha's arrest and bond arraignment went smoothly. The court accepted the restaurant as collateral. Ganne told them to meet him at Sweet Soul later. He wanted to stick around and see if he could talk the prosecutor down some on the plea offer.

Carl was on the phone when the lawyer entered. He hung up immediately when he saw the look of disappointment on his attorney's face.

"What happened?" Carl asked as he walked around his desk.

"Nothing. The prosecutor won't budge. I asked if she would consider probation. I told her to show some sympathy for the kid Asha's about to have. She wasn't trying to hear it. She even threatened to take the plea agreement off the table and prosecute to the full extent of the law."

Asha shot Carl a nervous look.

"Did you tell the prosecutor that I would be willing to take a plea deal, if they let Asha go?" Carl asked.

"Yes, but she said you're an honest business man, as far as she's concerned."

"Dick sucking ass bitch," Carl said angrily. "How much will it take to get Asha probation?"

"I know you're trying to look after your girlfriend, but the federal government doesn't care about that. They got betrayed by one of their own. All they're looking for is retribution. They want to set an example."

Carl started pacing the floor. He stopped at the liquor cabinet to make himself a drink. Asha walked up and stopped him.

"Is there anyone else you can talk to?" Carl asked again.

"I've tried everything. The only other possible way is if you were to cooperate, give somebody up."

"You know that's not gonna happen."

"I need to call my father and fill him in on what's happening," Asha said.

"Before you do that, let Ganne try a couple more avenues first," Carl said.

"Carl, I know you'll do anything to help me," Asha said, "but these folks aren't gonna give me a slap on the wrist. These are the consequences I have to pay for falling in love with you. But it was worth it."

"Asha–"

"Baby," she said, cutting him off, "I'm going to take the thirty months. Mr. Ganne, tell the prosecutor I'll accept the deal, as long as she'll wait until I have the babies and give me a little time to help Carl get situated."

"I'm sure she'll go for that. If not, I'll go to the judge. You're doing the right thing, Asha. If you went to trial, we'd lose."

Carl was killing mad. He couldn't imagine being without Asha for two and a half years.

She left the room to call her father.

"Hey, Asha. How you doing, sweetheart?" her father asked.

She started crying.

"What's wrong?" her father asked.

"Daddy, I love you."

"Calm down and tell me what's wrong," James said as his cellphone connection started to break up. "Call me on my office line."

Carl came to the room and tried to comfort her as she dialed the other line.

"Now tell me what the hell is going on," James said.

"They brought federal charges against me yesterday."

"For what?"

"Obstruction of justice."

"I'll be on the next flight."

"There's no need. Everything's under control down here. I didn't mean to worry you, but I had to let you know."

"What's Carl doing about this?" Her father was getting angrier by the second.

"I'm sitting here with Carl and his attorney. There's nothing he can do."

"They're not going to send you to jail, are they?"

Asha's crying grew worse. "I've already agreed to take thirty months in prison."

"*Thirty months*? Have they lost their damn minds?"

"Daddy, don't do this. Please. I made a decision, and I got caught. It's time to pay for straddling the fence."

"Jesus. Jesus. *Jesus*!" James started to weep now. He couldn't help his daughter. He felt like a failure as a parent.

"It's gonna be alright, Dad. I promise. If anything changes, I'll call and let you know."

CHAPTER THIRTY-ONE

One month later

Carl had been spending a lot of time on the streets with his homies. He'd been neglecting his businesses. He was actually feeling a little reckless. On Saturday he found himself in the alley behind the White Swan. All of the young hustlers were back there pushing their packages. Carl and some of the old heads were smoking weed, observing the scene and shooting the shit. Carl even had a cup in his hand.

"You sho' been out of character lately," Fast Black said.

"I'm chillin'," Carl replied.

"I've seen you smoke killa every now and then. But here of late, you been smoking every day. On top of that, you been sipping that lean."

"I'm good."

Fast Black laughed. "You good, huh? Your motherfucking ass is stressing." Some of the old heads laughed at that. "I talked to Percy yesterday. He told me he's been trying to get in touch with you for two days, so you could give him the money for the house you're building on Poquita."

"I'll take care of it," Carl said.

"You ain't taking care of shit," Fast Black said rather calmly. He was one of few people who could check Carl. "You off your stick, nigga. Percy and the rest of them niggas you got working for you is trying to feed their families. They can't afford to chill like you, nigga. You need to get on point and take care of your business."

Carl didn't respond. His attention went to a group of young girls who were walking through the alley. They all had on short shorts and skimpy tops. The tallest of the bunch spoke to Carl.

"Hey, Carl."

"How you know me, lil' mama?" He had a smile on his face.

"Who don't know you?" She and her friends giggled. "Me and my mama stay in one of your rent houses on Clifford."

Fast Black wasn't turned-on by the young girls in the least bit, and neither would Carl be, if he wasn't so high.

"If you're Sharon's daughter, that means you too young to be out here on the streets," Carl said.

"I'm eighteen."

"Bitch, you *sixteen*!" snapped Fast Black. "It's all good though, Carl. Everybody up here running through these lil' hoes."

"I don't know about my friends, but I ain't fucked no nigga out here," Ebony said in a sassy tone.

Carl pulled her to the side. He wanted to see what level her mind was on. For her age, she was stacked in the ass department. There was no hiding that.

"Look at this, ho-ass nigga," Ebony said as she showed Fast Black her driver's license. "I just graduated in May. You hating because don't nobody want yo funky ass!"

Before Carl could get at her, Paul's truck pulled into the alley. Paul saw his friend with the girl and called him over.

"What's up, big homey?" Carl asked with a slurred voice.

"Charlene just called me from your house. She was out there visiting Asha, and her water broke."

"*What*?"

"You heard what I said, nigga. She fixing to have them babies."

"Where she at?"

"Charlene's taking her to Brackenridge."

"I'm on my way," Carl said walking off.

"Nigga, you don't need to be driving. You high. Get your ass in the truck. I'll take you."

Carl didn't argue. He walked to the passenger side and got in.

"Give me your keys," Paul said. When he got them, he said, "Look out Black."

"What's up?"

"When you leave from up here, take Carl's car to the house," Paul said, tossing the keys.

"That's a bet."

••••••

When they got to the hospital, Charlene waved them over as they approached the reception desk.

"Carl! Asha's having complications with the babies."

"What kind of complications?" he asked nervously.

"I'm not sure. But Dr. Franklin is in there with her right now."

When he got to the room, Carl pushed past everyone to get to Asha's bedside. He bent over and kissed her sweating forehead.

"Something's gone wrong, baby," Asha told him. She was scared. She had a distant look in her eyes.

"Just relax. You'll be okay. Dr. Franklin is the best."

Asha was relieved that Carl kept his composure. "I'm not due for another five weeks," she said.

"It's alright. Just stay calm. I read in a magazine that women carrying twins usually don't do the whole nine months," Carl said as he smoothed back her damp hair.

Dr. Franklin gestured for Carl to meet him outside the room.

"I'll be back in a second," he said.

"Don't leave me," Asha said, squeezing his hand.

"I'll only be a few seconds."

One of the nurses walked up and started asking Asha questions. That gave Carl a chance to step away. He and the doctor shook hands when they made it to the hallway.

"Shoot straight, doc," Carl said, glaring in to his friend's eyes.

"She's hemorrhaging real bad." Dr. Franklin rubbed his hands over his mouth and chin.

"What's causing it?"

"At this point, I can't tell you. But I do know that it's extremely dangerous for her and the babies. We have to deliver them ASAP. I gave her a shot to induce labor. All we're waiting for now is for her to dilate."

Carl didn't know what to say. He was scared. He saw his mother, auntie and Fast Black entering the lobby, but he didn't stay and talk to them. He went back to Asha's bedside.

She was taken to the delivery room thirty minutes later. They were still waiting for her to dilate, but she never did. She was hemorrhaging worse. Carl felt her grip on his hand getting weaker. Dr. Franklin stood on the other side of the bed monitoring the machines. He saw that Asha's heartbeat was weakening.

"Carl, she's going to need an emergent C-section, and I mean right now."

"Do what you have to do, doc," Carl said frantically.

With that, the doctors and nurses moved into place. They prepped Asha for surgery and transferred her to the surgery unit. By then she was unconscious. Carl continued to rub her face. Fifteen minutes into surgery, her heart monitor flat-lined.

"What the fuck is going on?" Carl said hysterically. "She's not breathing!"

Without looking up from what he was doing, Dr. Franklin said, "The babies are almost here." He told one of the nurses to be ready to resuscitate the mother.

"Step back, Carl," the doctor said as he pulled the first crying baby out and handed it to a nurse. "It's a girl," he said and yelled out the time of birth.

He usually let the father cut the umbilical cord, but he didn't have time. He did the same for the next baby, which was a boy.

Dr. Franklin taped Asha's stomach and started trying to revive her.

"Ready!" said one of the nurses.

"Ready!"

They hit Asha with the shock pads.

Dr. Franklin looked on with a heavy heart. He had never lost a patient up to this point. He'd worked through complications, but nothing this serious. This patient meant a lot to him, because of his bond with Carl.

Carl stared at Asha's lifeless body, as if he was willing her to get up. Every time the emergency crew shocked her, he could feel it.

Three minutes after the babies were delivered, Asha regained a pulse. Carl lowered his head and thanked the Lord. Dr. Franklin moved her to the intensive care unit, so she could be monitored closely.

"Thank you, Tobias!" Carl said, hugging the doctor. He had tears running down his face.

"Don't thank me. Thank God."

"I've already done that," Carl said as he embraced him again.

"Go talk to your family, and let them know what's going on. Then swing by the nursery and take a peek at the twins." Dr. Franklin had to take a break. He was exhausted.

••••••

Eighteen hours after the delivery, Asha finally regained consciousness. She opened her eyes to find her best friend Gwen standing there.

In a hoarse voice, Asha asked, "Are my babies alright?"

"The twins are fine," answered Gwen. "Just worry about yourself right now."

"Where's Carl?"

Gwen pointed to a chair on the other side of the room. Carl was sound asleep.

"Wake him up for me," Asha said in a weak voice.

"Girl, let him sleep. He's been standing by your side for damn near 24 hours."

Asha was crying. "I wanna see my kids," she demanded.

To her surprise, her father walked through the door.

"What are you doing here, Daddy?"

"You thought I was going to miss the birth of my first grandbabies?" James walked up and kissed her on the forehead.

The talking in the room woke Carl. He stood and stretched his muscles and yawned. He walked over to the bed and kissed Asha on the lips.

"Boy, your breath stinks," she said in a weak voice.

They all laughed.

"Your breath ain't too nice either," Carl said.

"What do the twins look like?" Asha's eyes twinkled.

"They're beautiful. I'll let the nurse know you want to see them."

Carl walked briskly out of room. The mood in the room went from somber to happy.

James sat next to the bed with thoughts of his own. He wished his daughter had never laid eyes on Carl. He didn't care if he had all the money in the world. All he knew was that in two months his daughter was going to federal prison. To him, nothing was worth sacrificing your freedom.

Carl returned to the room five minutes later. A nurse was right behind him, pushing an incubator that carried the twins. Asha sat up in bed and stared at the tiny bundles of joy.

"When will I get to hold them?"

"Right now," the nurse said with a smile. "Which one do you want?"

Asha couldn't pick.

"Here's the boy," the nurse said. "He's underweight. He needs to gain a couple pounds before he'll be ready to leave the hospital."

Asha cried when she had her baby in her arms. "Can you tell me what happened to me?" she asked the nurse.

The nurse was caught off guard by the question. "I'm not sure, Ms. Richards. The doctors are running tests as we speak. They believe you may have had a small tumor in your lower abdomen or in your ovaries. But please don't quote me on that."

"I won't." Asha looked up at Carl and then down at her little boy. Now she wanted to hold both babies at the same time.

The next couple of days were uneventful. Everyone camped out at the hospital. On the fourth day, Asha and the twins were cleared to go home.

••••••

When the new parents made it home from the hospital, Asha went straight to the bedroom they designated for the nursery. It was just how she left it.

"You could've at least organized some of this stuff," she complained.

"For what? You would have changed everything around," replied Carl.

"You probably right. At least you put their beds together."

"Paul did it while I was at the hospital."

Asha stood on her tip-toes and kissed him. Carl Jr. started crying, so they went back to the den where they left him.

"He's probably hungry," Asha said.

"He needs something to eat, with his po' lil' ass," said a smiling Carl.

"Leave my baby alone," Asha responded playfully. "Where's my dad?" she asked as she fed her son.

"I don't know. Probably at his hotel room." Carl sat on the sofa, flipping through channels on the TV.

"Why is my dad staying at a hotel?"

"You need to ask him that," Carl said without looking up from the TV.

"I'm asking you."

"Because ya motherfucking daddy is blaming me for all the problems we're having," snapped Carl. "And I'm not gonna pacify his motherfucking ass, either."

"Hey, you need to cut out all that cursing. I heard you as soon as I got out of my car," Jo Ann said as she walked into the room.

Carl didn't acknowledge his mother's presence. Asha had pushed him past the boiling point. He wasn't going to let it go until he got everything off his chest.

"I'm a grown man. I don't have to kiss nobody's ass. I'm in love with you, not ya motherfucking daddy. If he don't like what's going on in our lives, fuck him!"

Carl slammed the remote and broke it then walked out of the room.

"Ms. Jo Ann, can you hold junior for me?" asked Asha.

Jo Ann took her grandson and gave a warning before Asha ran off after Carl.

"That boy has the weight of the world on his shoulders. He almost lost you while you were giving birth to those babies. And he knows he's responsible for you going to prison. So take all that into consideration..."

Asha took heed to the advice. She went to the bedroom and saw that Carl had taken his shirt off and was lying across the bed. She went to the bathroom to get some rubbing oil. She got on the bed and straddled his back and started massaging him with the oil. He was very tense.

"I'm sorry, baby," Asha said.

Carl didn't respond.

"You were right about what you said. You don't have to win favor with my father. But I want you to understand that I love and respect him the way you do your mother."

"Deeper." Carl was talking about her massage.

She started digging her thumbs into the muscles in his back.

"It's about me and you and the kids, baby," Asha said. "Only God comes before that."

"That's how I've felt from the first time I laid eyes on you," Carl said.

They talked a while longer before Asha stripped down to her underwear. Carl took off his pants, and they curled up in each other's arms.

CHAPTER THIRTY-TWO

"Sir, did you know that Agent Richards had her babies the other day?" asked Scottsdale.

"You mean *ex-Agent* Richards? Yeah, I heard," Deputy Alexander said without looking up from his computer.

"From what I hear, she almost got out of doing her prison time."

"Why do you say that?"

"She had complications and almost died during delivery."

"How are you gathering this information?" Alexander asked. "Are you still having her trailed?"

"You know better than that, sir. Richards' attorney requested a two month extension, so she could recoup from her near-death experience."

"Hmmm. Did the judge grant it?"

"The judge asked the prosecutor if she had a problem with it, and she stated fifty good reasons why it wasn't a good idea. The judge denied the request."

"That prosecutor is a real bitch. Did you ever find out where that leak came from, Scottsdale?"

"No," he lied. He already had Agent Collins transferred to another unit.

••••••

Carl woke up before Asha. He nudged her softly before she stirred awake.

"Why are you waking me up?" She was bone-tired.

"We have kids to look after now."

"Go look after them. I'm tired."

Carl laughed. He pulled her out of bed and directed her to the shower. They took their time and bathed each other. They got dressed and went to the kitchen. Asha looked out of the French doors and saw Gwen and the rest of her and Carl's friends sitting on the deck with presents strewn everywhere. Her hands went to her mouth, and she turned to Carl. She jumped into his arms and started kissing him.

"I definitely appreciate the affection," he said, "but this wasn't my idea. It was hers." He pointed at Gwen.

Gwen entered the house at that moment. "I guess you thought since the twins came a little early, we were going to cancel the baby shower," Gwen said with her hands on her hips.

Asha and her best friend embraced.

"I love you," Asha said, beginning to cry. She had been very emotional over the last couple of months.

"Girl, stop crying," said a sassy Charlene. "This is a happy occasion. We already been through the drama."

Asha turned and hugged her. "You're right." She smiled through her tears.

"Open up them presents," said Charlene.

"Before we do that, do you think I could have a word with you and Carl?" Dr. Franklin asked.

The three of them walked to the swimming pool. "Is there something wrong with me, doctor?" Asha asked nervously.

"No, no. You're perfectly healthy. I apologize for scaring you. I know you two would like to know the cause of the complications we had during your delivery."

"Yes," Carl said.

"At first we thought you may have had a tumor," the doctor told Asha. "But when we took a better look, we found that you had a ruptured blood vessel in your uterus. That's what caused the hemorrhaging."

"So I'm good now?" Asha asked.

"Yes. The blood vessel will heal on its own."

"I can have more kids?" she asked, full of enthusiasm.

"Yes," Dr. Franklin answered smiling.

Asha turned and kissed Carl. They walked over and told the others the good news.

••••••

The following weeks passed quickly. Carl worked on his building projects while Asha took care of the twins. She and Carl dreaded the day she had to turn herself in to federal authorities. In his 33 years of living, Carl had never faced a responsibility as hard as taking care of newborns. He knew that his mother was going to help him, but he was still intimidated.

One morning he and Asha took a walk around the property.

"I'm gonna miss you and the kids," she said sadly.

"We'll miss you too. I'll be there for you all the way," Carl said.

"Yeah?"

"You said that like you don't believe me."

"How often do you plan to come visit me?"

"I'll fly out with the kids every few weeks."

They walked for a second. Asha knew Carl was going to be her rock. He was the most responsible man she had ever been with.

"Just go down to New Mexico and do your time," he said. "Stay out of trouble, and don't let them dykes turn you out," he said jokingly.

Asha snatched her hand from his and said, "What the fuck you mean, don't let nobody turn me out?"

Carl was caught off guard by her anger.

"What you mean you hope I don't get turned out?" she asked again, now standing squarely in front of him.

"Don't let them dykes suck your pussy," he said, still smiling.

Without warning, Asha spun sideways and kicked him in the stomach. In the next motion, she fired a kick to his head, but he blocked it. He stepped back in a defensive stance.

"You lost your mind!" he said.

She charged him. She missed with the knee to the groin, but the attempt angered the shit out of Carl. He pushed her back and knocked her off balance. But Asha wouldn't quit. She rushed him again, this time with flurries of kicks and punches. Carl defended them all with ease, the ones that would do damage, anyway. He grabbed her and wrestled her to the ground and held her in a full body lock. He didn't release her until she stopped trying to fight back.

He was amazed by the way she could fight, but was angry that she attacked him.

"Do you still think a bitch will be able to turn me out?" She was breathing hard.

"I was just playing with your stupid ass!" Carl shouted.

"I don't appreciate you playing with my sexuality."

He saw that her anger was subsiding. He walked to her with his guards down and wiped a smudge of dirt from her face. She looked into his eyes.

"You got me all dirty, out here playing with you," he said. "Where did you learn to fight like that?" he asked as they headed back to the house.

"I took karate classes when I was a kid. And I trained at the bureau. Where'd you learn how to wrestle? I can't believe I couldn't get out of that hold."

"I had the best instructor in Austin."

"Oh yeah? What style did he teach you?"

"Backyard karate!"

"What?" Asha said laughing.

"Self-taught karate," Carl said, "by the honorable Bennie Mays."

They were both laughing now.

When they made it inside, Jo Ann was feeding the twins. She saw how dirty they were and looked at them suspiciously. Asha stopped and kissed the babies, and then she and Carl headed for their bedroom.

• • • • • •

Carl and Asha had a small wedding at Wesley Falls United Methodist, which was his mother's church. Reverend Freddie B. Dix oversaw the ceremony. Carl's closest friends were in attendance, along with a few family members. Asha's father, her aunt, her cousin Raymond and Gwen were there. Paul was Carl's best man. Gwen was the maid of honor.

Their attire was traditional. The men wore black and white tuxedos. Asha wore a long, white wedding dress with a veil. All of the bridesmaids wore beige.

The ceremony was beautiful. After they exchanged vows, and Carl kissed the bride, his cousin Gregory sang a rendition of Ginuwine's *Changes*. It couldn't have been performed better. The whole church was in awe of Gregory's voice.

The reception was held at the Red Lion Hotel. Everyone danced and partied. The only time Carl and Asha weren't together was when she danced with her father. Carl approached Asha's father and made amends. He demanded that James stay at their house while he was in town. The two men in Asha's life shook hands and hugged.

••••••

Asha had to fly out the next morning to turn herself in to the feds. Her emotions were starting to get the best of her. She had been crying most of the evening. Carl consoled her the best he could. He tried to get her to relax. He talked her into smoking a joint of dro with him. He knew she got high, because she started laughing and playing around. He also knew this would be their last night at home together for two and a half years. He wanted to make love to his wife.

He stood over the bed and pulled her to her feet. He slipped the strings of her nightgown off her shoulders. The nightgown fell to the floor. Carl looked at her body admiringly. Despite the fact that she had just had twins, she was still fine. Her breasts were swollen. Her stomach was a little big, but Carl didn't care about that.

Asha pulled his boxers off, and he was standing at full attention. She started caressing his piece and biting his bottom lip. They kissed with a deep, almost violent passion. Carl picked her up and laid her across the bed. Her legs fell open, and Carl's face went between them. He peeled her pussy lips back. He wanted to taste her moisture. She let out a loud moan as he stroked her clit with his tongue. He sucked and licked until she started to convulse. Her juices were smeared on his lips.

He made his way back up, and they kissed again. She sucked her juices off his face and explored his mouth with her tongue. She was on fire. He entered her, and she dug her fingers into his back. It was the first time they made love since the twins were born.

"*Ooh shit*!" was all she could manage to say.

Carl didn't say anything. He kept pumping away until he exploded inside her. He started to slow down, but Asha was still throwing the pussy at him.

"*Don't stop, baby. This is our last night together. Please don't stop*," she said, breathing hard.

She crawled from under him and turned onto her stomach. He got behind her and watched her play with her pussy. His dick got right back hard. He started fucking her doggy-style.

She clenched the sheets and said, "*Yes! Fuck this pussy*!"

Carl took long, hard strokes. He was trying to knock the bottom out of the pussy. Moments later he exploded again. They were both breathing hard, sweating profusely. Carl lay down beside Asha, and they stared into each other's eyes.

She reached down and stroked his dick and said, "I guess our marriage is consummated."

They both laughed.

••••••

They woke up early the next morning. Jo Ann had a big breakfast prepared. Carl grabbed his phone and started snapping pictures. The doorbell rang, and he went to answer it. When he returned to the kitchen, he was followed by Fast Black and Gwen.

"What are y'all doing here this early?" Asha asked.

"I don't know about her, but I was told there was gonna be a big breakfast cooked over here," Fast Black said on his way to get a plate.

"Boy, you don't have no manners, do you?" Jo Ann said.

"I didn't know you was back there, Mama," Fast Black said.

The whole clique showed up next. Asha knew what was going on then. It was a going away party. She started to cry.

"You didn't think we were gonna show up and see you off?" Charlene asked as she walked up and hugged Asha. "You're a part of this family."

"We'd all be in the feds, if it wasn't for you," Fast Black said between bites of eggs.

"Y'all don't know how much this means to me," Asha said. She was still emotional. "I don't know what to say."

They all sat and ate and talked.

Carl and Asha left for the airport at nine o'clock. They boarded a plane to New Mexico. Once they got settled in, they began to talk.

"There's nothing to worry about. I'll be there for you one hundred percent," Carl said, squeezing her knee.

"I know, baby."

"Not just me," he said. "Everyone sitting at that breakfast table is here for you. Money, pictures, books, magazines. Everything you're allowed to have, you'll have it. That five grand in your purse should hold you for a minute."

Asha watched Carl like a star-eyed child.

"You're not going to say anything?" he asked.

"Nope. I just want to look at my handsome husband."

"When I leave you this afternoon, I want you to be in good spirits," Carl said. "I can't tell you how it's going to be in there, because I've never been locked up. You're a soldier." He started to choke up. "I'm glad you made this sacrifice for me, Asha. I'll forever be in your debt."

A big smile came to her face. "Just be good to me."

They arrived at the prison in New Mexico at one o'clock. Carl put his hands on her cheeks and kissed her on the forehead then softly on the lips.

"I love you, Asha."

"I'll always love you, Carl."

She turned and followed the officer out of the room.

EPILOGUE

Carl threw himself into his work at Club Link and his real estate properties. He and Paul went to basketball games together and other events. But for the most part, they were doing their own thing now. The word on the street was they were beefing. Everyone in the family laughed when they heard that.

Charlene continued to work at the hospital. She also helped Carl and his mother with the twins whenever she had time.

Lil Chris was still young and ambitious. Although Carl didn't want him hustling, he gave him the front money to buy five kilos, and he turned him on to Rome. Paul told him to make sure he flew under the radar and kept those hoes and niggas out of his business. And despite their ten year age difference, Chris and Donna were inseparable.

Fast Black was simply Fast Black; obnoxious, rude and always ready to get in somebody's ass. He never was that much of a hustler. Carl and Paul kept him fed, and that wasn't going to change. He regulated the streets for them. Now that they weren't hustling, they had to find something else for him to do. More than likely, they'd use him as a carpenter's assistant at the building site.

Carl rented an apartment in Houston. Rome's strip mall project consumed all of his time. Jo Ann was against it, but Carl demanded that she and the twins move to Houston until the project was finished. He couldn't stand to be away from his kids. Carl came home dirt-tired every day, but he always found the energy to play with and feed the twins every night.

True to his word, he flew out to see Asha every three weeks. He'd only take the kids with him every couple of months. It seemed to Carl that Asha was more stressed each time he saw her. He didn't mention it. He just tried to brighten her mood.

Charlene, Donna and Gwen all flew out to see her on a regular basis. Her father flew in from Macon every couple of months. It tore James apart to see his pride and joy sitting behind bars. He started drinking heavily to deal with the pain.

••••••

"Ninety-five, ninety-six, ninety-seven..."

"Get up off that floor. Ain't no man gon' want no woman with a whole bunch of muscles," Asha's cellmate Sonya said.

"Shut up," Asha said and started doing push-ups.

"I said get up off that floor and take a wash-off, and get your black ass in the bed."

Asha did what Sonya told her. She didn't feel like arguing tonight. She was still upset that they put her in general population. Everyone knew she was an ex-fed before she hit the cell block. Her life was in danger, and she didn't even know it.

Asha had beat up two girls her second day on the compound. They thought she was just going to roll over. Her enemies planned to put a world of hurt on her. They were going to stab her. That's when Sonya stepped in and saved her.

Sonya had been on the compound for eleven years and was very respected. She talked to her brothers back in Detroit, and they told her that a nigga named Carl Fredrick was official, and that Asha had laid her freedom on the line for him.

Sonya talked to the girls from the other clique and asked them to step off. And they did. Asha knew that she'd be protected as long as Sonya was around, but nothing was for sure in prison. Sonya could get transferred at any time.

Asha got into her bunk thinking about Carl and the twins. Her sentence felt like an eternity, but compared to some of the other women there, Asha knew she didn't have it that bad. She just had to keep her head up and do her time, hour by hour, one day at a time.

ABOUT THE AUTHOR

Derek C. Watson Sr. is an inmate in the Texas Department of Corrections. Hailing from Austin, he is no stranger to the gritty lifestyle he writes about. He is highly respected by his peers and foes. Derek's passion for writing developed during his incarceration, and *Down for the City* is his first novel. He has accomplished many things while in prison, most notably earning a degree from Trinity Valley Community College.

CPSIA information can be obtained at www.ICGtesting.com
Printed in the USA
LVOW07s0758260616

494140LV00001B/17/P

9 780996 75052